FALSE IMPRESSION

Further Titles by Veronica Heley from Severn House

The Ellie Quicke Mysteries

MURDER AT THE ALTAR
MURDER BY SUICIDE
MURDER OF INNOCENCE
MURDER BY ACCIDENT
MURDER IN THE GARDEN
MURDER BY COMMITTEE
MURDER BY BICYCLE
MURDER OF IDENTITY
MURDER IN HOUSE
MURDER BY MISTAKE
MURDER MY NEIGHBOUR
MURDER IN MIND
MURDER WITH MERCY
MURDER IN TIME

The Bea Abbot Agency mystery series

FALSE CHARITY
FALSE PICTURE
FALSE STEP
FALSE PRETENCES
FALSE MONEY
FALSE REPORT
FALSE ALARM
FALSE DIAMOND
FALSE IMPRESSION

FALSE IMPRESSION

An Abbot Agency Mystery

Veronica Heley

severn
House

This first world edition published 2014
in Great Britain and 2015 in the USA by
SEVERN HOUSE PUBLISHERS LTD of
19 Cedar Road, Sutton, Surrey, England, SM2 5DA.
Trade paperback edition first published
in Great Britain and the USA 2015 by
SEVERN HOUSE PUBLISHERS LTD.

British Library Cataloguing in Publication Data

Heley, Veronica author.
  False impression. – (The Bea Abbot Agency mystery series)
  1. Abbot, Bea (Fictitious character)–Fiction.
  2. Murder–Investigation–Fiction.
  3. London (England)–Fiction.
  4. Detective and mystery stories.
  I. Title II. Series
  823.9'14-dc23

ISBN-13: 978-0-7278-8445-9 (cased)
ISBN-13: 978-1-84751-562-9 (trade paper)
ISBN-13: 978-1-78010-610-6 (e-book)

All Severn House titles are printed on acid-free paper.

Severn House Publishers support the Forest Stewardship Council™ [FSC™],
the leading international forest certification organisation. All our titles that
are printed on FSC certified paper carry the FSC logo.

Typeset by Palimpsest Book Production Ltd.,
Falkirk, Stirlingshire, Scotland.
Printed and bound in Great Britain by
TJ International, Padstow, Cornwall.

ONE

Bea Abbot ran a successful domestic agency from her house in an upmarket London suburb. She believed in helping people in trouble, but she did ask them to respect her working hours. Unfortunately, this murderer was no respecter either of her, or of her routine.

Tuesday, late afternoon

Bea Abbot had problems of her own before Leon Holland arrived to disrupt her working day.

He was a man of about her own age who had recently managed to insinuate himself into her life. She hesitated to call him a friend, because in her book 'friendship' required a certain degree of trust, while Leon Holland would make a clam look like an open book. He liked her to be available whenever he needed a partner for a business function or an evening at the theatre, and he frequently suggested she might enjoy a tumble in bed . . . an invitation which she had so far declined. What he did not do was confide in her about his business affairs.

To give him his due, he had never before interrupted her work to ask for help.

The door into her office was ajar as usual, so she heard the stir when he arrived at the agency. Her staff adored him, partly but not wholly because he usually brought them a box of cakes. She heard him enquire if Mrs Abbot were free for a cuppa, and then, without waiting for a reply, he knocked on her door and walked in.

He was carrying a tote bag, instead of a box of goodies.

Bea was on the phone to a customer. She was going to tell him to get lost when she saw that, despite wearing a social smile, Leon vibrated with tension. She told her client she'd ring back later and cut the call. Normally, she'd have offered him a cup of tea in her office, but . . .

'Trouble?'

He nodded.

She could feel her nerves tighten. He wouldn't come to her for help without good reason. She closed the file she'd been working on and went through to the main office to tell her manageress that she was taking a break. The agency occupied the basement of her house, so it only took a moment for her to unlock the communicating door to the stairs and lead the way up to her living quarters.

As she headed for the kitchen, she heard him dump his overcoat and travelling bag in the hall.

She took a tray of tea things into the big living room to find him lying back in an armchair with his eyes closed. That was unusual, too. Leon had an enviable capacity to work a twelve-hour day and go on to dinner or the theatre without showing any signs of tiredness.

He was a big, well-built man, who just missed being handsome. She noted that the laughter lines around his eyes seemed deeper than usual, and there was an upright cleft above his nose which she hadn't noticed before. As she set a cup of tea down on the table beside him he said, 'Should I feel guilty about interrupting your day's work?'

'Probably.' She'd never seen him look so tired. So defenceless. A moment later he sat up, smiling, sipping tea. As bright as a button, banishing fatigue.

She took a chair opposite. 'What's wrong? And don't say "nothing".'

'Ah.' He turned the cup round in his hands, looking down into it. 'You've used tea bags. I had an aunt who used to read fortunes in the tea leaves.'

'What happened if she saw disaster looming?'

'Ah. Yes. Precisely.'

So somewhere along the line he'd met with a setback big enough to make him break his routine and visit her on a working day. In *his* working day, too. Perhaps he'd tell her what it was, and perhaps he'd come because he needed space. A time out.

But why? Didn't he have a suite of rooms in the Holland family mansion not far out of London, with servants at his

beck and call? Didn't he own a flat in the Barbican for overnight stays, with a chauffeur-driven Rolls to waft him wherever
he wished to go?

He set down his cup, empty. She refilled it. Waited.

He looked at his watch. Checked the time by her clock on
the mantelpiece. His fingers drummed on the arm of his chair.
She prompted him. 'You've been away on business for a
few days. It went well?'

A nod. Earlier that year Holland Holdings (International)
had been split into two. Leon's much older elder brother,
Briscoe – who had hitherto owned and run the multi-company
organization as his private fiefdom – had retained control of
the overseas companies but had handed responsibility for the
British ones over to Leon.

Leon had had a successful business career in his own right
and had at that point been intending to take early retirement.
He'd stepped up to the challenge with some reluctance, but
had seemed to be coping well. He'd reorganized some of the
businesses; he'd appointed some new managers and confirmed
others in their posts. The markets had responded favourably,
and he had seemed comfortable in his new shoes.

Obviously, something had gone wrong. But what?

If he didn't want to talk, he wouldn't. She glanced at the
clock. She'd abandoned a client in the middle of a discussion
about staffing for a silver wedding party. She needed to get
back to her desk.

He said, 'What time did I arrive? Will the girls downstairs
remember? Will you?'

'You need an alibi?' She half laughed. Then saw he was
serious. 'For what?'

'I don't know.' His frown deepened. '"By the pricking of
my thumbs, something wicked this way comes." Tell me I'm
imagining things.'

'What things?'

He ignored that. Stood up. Yawned. Hands behind his back,
he went to look out of the tall sash windows at the front of
the house. Was he avoiding her question, and if so, why?

Her house was in a quiet, tree-lined street of cream-
painted Georgian terraced houses. A self-satisfied street of

well-maintained, expensive properties. The prospect was pleasing, though it didn't seem to please him . . . perhaps because dusk was blurring the picture? He drew the curtains without asking her permission to do so.

It was a something and a nothing, but it irritated her. True, it was getting dark. She got up to switch on the side lamps and considered drawing the curtains at the back of the big room as well. The house was built on a slope. At the front there was a small flight of stairs leading up to the portico at the front door and a steeper flight descending to the agency rooms below. At the back, French windows gave on to a cast-iron staircase going down to a walled garden.

Standing at the rear window Bea allowed herself to relax for a moment, taking comfort from the hints of spring in the garden outside. The bushes and trees that lined the walls were still leafless, but crocuses and miniature daffodils were beginning to bloom in the terracotta planters on the patio. In the mornings, small birds fought over the containers of nuts dangling from shrubs near the house, but as the sky darkened they had taken shelter for the night. Yes, it was getting dark. Time for an arrow prayer. *Tell me the right question to ask, Lord?* She pulled the curtains to.

He said, 'May I take you out this evening? Perhaps even cadge a bed afterwards? The flat at the top of the house is empty at the moment, isn't it?'

No, it wasn't. 'Well . . .'

He made a gesture of frustration. 'I forgot. You've been lumbered with my niece. How's that working out?'

Bea hesitated. Briscoe, Leon's older brother, had married late in life and sired a daughter, Dilys. He'd never paid much attention to the girl, and Bea could understand why. Dilys was a walking disaster with the self-confidence of a jellyfish. She couldn't make a cup of tea without dropping her teaspoon into the sugar. One of her father's business managers had 'married' her bigamously for her money, and then kept her cowed with verbal and physical abuse. Dilys had produced three children only to have her 'husband' and two of her children wiped out by his real wife. Dilys had survived after a fashion, but she was fragile, to say the least.

Dilys's Aunt Sybil, sister to Briscoe and Leon, three times married – or was it four? – who was more at home in the States than in the UK, had asked Bea to give the girl a bed and a job for a few weeks.

'Dilys,' Sybil had said, 'is driving Briscoe mad. She wants to cook for him. She enquires about his underwear and tries to supervise his diet. He's got his own team of housekeepers and nurses and dieticians and physios and the Lord alone knows what, and he doesn't want them upset by her.'

Bea was amused. 'I can imagine.'

Sybil sighed. 'The fact is, Dilys hasn't anything to do, but nothing I suggest is acceptable. I really need to go back to the States for a while on business. I offered to take Dilys and her daughter with me. Dilys says she doesn't want a holiday, so I'll take Bernice, who is always good company, which is more than I can say for her mother. I know it's an imposition to saddle you with the girl, but would you please look after her for a couple of weeks?'

With some reluctance Bea had consented, and had even agreed to let Dilys stay in the temporarily vacant flat at the top of her house. She'd regretted it ever since. Talk about a wet Wednesday . . .

'Well,' said Bea, 'she's not exactly—'

'I didn't see her down in the agency rooms.'

Bea tried to excuse the girl. 'She may have popped out to the shops. She often runs errands in the afternoons if we're not busy.'

He wasn't really interested. 'Never mind. May I take you out this evening?'

'I didn't expect you back till tomorrow, and I have a dinner date.'

He rounded on her. 'With your ex-husband? The portrait painter who sleeps in any bed but his own?'

She felt herself redden. 'Yes. Not that it's any business of yours. A gallery is mounting a show of his recent work, and I said I'd go along. He's giving me supper afterwards.'

Leon went to stand by the mantelpiece, looking at the pretty ormolu clock under the old-fashioned and slightly foxed gilt-framed mirror. 'So, you're busy and Dilys is occupying the

top flat. I don't want to take a chance on getting a black cab.
Do you have the number of a local minicab firm?'

'What about your own car? Is your chauffeur off sick?'

'I've been driving myself, but the car's in dock at the
moment.'

'Surely you have a courtesy car?' She clicked her fingers.
'Wait a minute. That's not the right question. The right question is: why do you need an alibi?'

He sent her a look she found difficult to read. When they'd
first met, she'd thought his eyes were brown, but when he was
stirred up, they flashed hazel with greenish lights. As they did
now.

She tried to put the pieces of the jigsaw together. 'Let me
see if I've got this right. Your brother has been ailing for some
time, and I must suppose he is finally ready to retire from
directing the affairs of the multi-billion overseas division of
Holland Holdings. The news has got out that he's moving on.
The jackals are on the prowl, seeking whom they can devour.
China and India are eyeing one another up. Meetings are being
held in boardrooms across the world, strategies are being
devised to snap up his overseas empire. Perhaps to divide it
into smaller parts? They are all wondering how much to offer
and what terms would be acceptable to the existing shareholders. Am I right?'

He continued to stare at the clock. Half past five of an
afternoon and all was very far from well.

She narrowed her eyes. 'Whose shares do they have to buy
to obtain control? Your brother's, of course.'

Would Leon want to buy his brother out? But to do so, he
would have to raise billions, if not trillions. She wasn't sure
he was cut out to be an international Captain of Industry.
The British companies which he'd taken over were prospering
under his chairmanship, but in Bea's estimation he lacked
the steely ambition necessary to want to rule the world.

Well, if he didn't want the job, then the corporation would
be up for grabs. She tried to think who else might have shares
in the overseas division of Holland Holdings. 'You have some
shares, don't you? And your sister, Sybil? Ah, wait a minute.
Sybil's taken Dilys's daughter to America for a while. I'm

sure you're in daily contact with her, but it seems a strange time for her to be away from the seat of power. Let me guess: has she given you her proxy?'

He neither confirmed, nor denied. Which probably meant she had.

She rubbed her forehead. 'Who else has shares? Possibly Adamsson, your chief accountant. Now who would he want to sell to?'

A shrug. 'He takes his holidays in France. I suppose he might be thinking that way.'

'Who else?'

'A man my brother was at school with. Somewhere back in the Dark Ages, when they were both starting up in business, they gave one another a certain number of shares. Lord Lethbury has offered me his shares at three times their value. He said that if I didn't buy, he'd sell to the highest bidder and make another fortune. He's a wealthy man and well padded against the recession, which is why my brother keeps pushing Lethbury's son at Dilys.'

'What!' Had Dilys mentioned that she was being pursued by a man? Perhaps she had. But not as if she were interested . . . though it was difficult to tell with Dilys, who drifted through the day, only touching the ground in spots. Wait a minute. Hadn't the girl had some flowers delivered for her? When Bea had asked who they were from, she'd blushed and said it wasn't anybody of importance.

But, she had blushed.

Bea was annoyed with herself for missing the signs. Dilys had been entrusted to her care, and she'd failed to spot that there was a man hanging around waiting for her to wake up. 'You mean to tell me that your brother is trying to marry her off again, so that he doesn't need to provide for her in future?'

'That's a possible reading of the situation, yes.'

'Aaargh!' Bea raised both arms to the heavens. 'How dare he! The girl is in no state to make decisions about her future. What's the boy like?'

'Orlando? All right, I suppose. But it won't work. I'm told he has a position of sorts at an advertising agency, arranging photo shoots. He wears pink jeans, and his hair is more ginger than blonde.'

'If he came to me for a job, what would I try to find for him?'

'Cocktail waiter. Or, more likely, toy boy.'

She spurted into laughter.

He shook his head. 'No, I do him wrong. He's honest enough, I believe, and supposed to be good at his job.'

'Does Dilys know she's supposed to be taking an interest in this young man?'

'Does she even know what day of the week it is?'

'Good point.' No, she didn't.

Why did Leon need an alibi?

Bea frowned. She had enjoyed being Leon's partner at various functions, even though sometimes she'd been bored by the politicking that went on behind the scenes. She liked being dined and wined by this attractive, amusing man. She relished being taken to watch the latest play or musical and occupying the best seats in the theatre as a matter of course. She'd liked his company, too. She'd not realized how much until now. She wasn't at all sure how he felt about her, but he'd come to mean a lot to her.

It was disconcerting to someone who prided herself on being independent, to realize how important a place this man had come to occupy in her life.

She wasn't stupid enough to fall in love with him. Of course not. She was, she told herself, merely concerned for a good friend who seemed to be in trouble. Nevertheless, she felt the need to move close to him as he stood by the mantelpiece. He was watching her in the mirror. He was taller than her by a few inches, even when she was wearing her highest heels. Her ash-blonde hair gleamed in the light of the side lamps. Neither of them looked their age, and his plentiful light-brown hair was only now beginning to show a few silver threads. As it happened, both were wearing grey, though his handmade suit was enlivened by a dark-brown tie, while she had a string of amber beads around the high neck of her fine wool dress.

He said, looking into her eyes in the mirror, 'Marry me?'

She took half a step back, attempted a laugh and shook her head. 'You must be feeling threatened, to propose.'

'I mean it.'

'Perhaps you do, but . . . bad timing.' She put her hand up to touch his cheek.

He took her hand in his and held it there. 'I need you, Mrs Abbot.'

'You need an alibi. Why?'

'I was late for an appointment which had been set up for me. My nerve failed me. I ducked out and flew to you for shelter.'

'You have nerves of platinum or titanium, or whatever the strongest metal is. Can't you tell me what's wrong?'

He turned away from her, to pace the room. 'A week ago my chauffeur left without notice. I drove the Rolls myself until it developed a fault and I put it into the garage for repair. Two days ago – Sunday afternoon – the courtesy car wouldn't start. I was due to go up to Birmingham by train, for some meetings early the following morning, so I decided to walk to the station. A van came out of nowhere, clipped my heel and roared off before I could pick myself out of the hedge.'

'And that makes you think your life is in danger?'

'Isn't it absurd?'

But, he needed an alibi. Why?

She drew in a sharp breath. 'It all comes down to the sale of your brother's corporation, doesn't it? Who'd go that far to influence you, or to wipe you out? Have you made a will? Who benefits if you die? Your brother, or Sybil . . . or . . . No, not Dilys, surely!'

He nodded. 'Once I got on the train I found some paper and roughed out a will. I got a couple of people in the carriage to witness my signature. I've been carrying the paper around with me until I can get to a solicitor. I've named you as the chief beneficiary.'

'What?' She put a hand to her head. 'No, you mustn't!'

'Because it puts you in the firing line?'

'No, I . . .' She gave a nervous laugh. 'You're not going to die. Besides, what would I do in big business circles?'

'Who else would I leave it to? My sister Sybil? She has

more than enough of this world's goods already. Dilys? No; how could she cope? If Dilys's daughter Bernice were twenty years older, I'd leave it to her, as I think she may well develop into a businesswoman, but she's only a child now.'

She sank into a chair. 'But to name me . . .? You're mad!'

'I have an appointment with a solicitor tomorrow morning. Until then, I need a chaperone.'

'You mean, a bodyguard?'

'Do you have one on your books?'

'Are you serious?'

'Very. I'm not going anywhere without protection.'

'What about your own staff?'

He shot her a hard look. Of course, it must have been someone at the Holland mansion who had scuppered his car in order that he might be run down on his way to the station. Which meant he couldn't trust anyone there.

Finger to lip, she went through her files in her mind. Lighted upon a name. 'I'll need to go down to the office. Will you come?'

She hastened down the stairs to the office with him at her heels. Her staff were preparing to shut down for the day. Bea reminded herself to ring back the customer whom she'd been talking to earlier. In the meantime . . . She flicked through her records. Someone had offered . . . some months ago . . . If the man were available? He might be working . . .

A deep voice answered the phone.

'Lucas? Good, you're not working today, then?'

Lucas was a big, good-natured, black taxi-driver who'd once helped Bea out of a tricky situation. He'd enjoyed the brush with danger and had said she could call on him any time and he'd be delighted to help.

Bea handed the phone over to Leon and made herself scarce. A wash and brush up was necessary. Also a fresh application of lipstick. She always felt better able to cope with her war paint on.

She returned to her office to find Leon had finished with the phone and was sitting in her chair at her desk. 'Lucas is going to look after me.'

'He's a good man, but not a professional bodyguard.'

'He knows where I can hide out for a few days. Get some breathing space. He says that if I go to a hotel, there'd be no one to account for my movements overnight.'

'Oh.' She hadn't been really sure that she should take Leon's fears seriously. Was Lucas overdoing it, playing at Baddies and Goodies? Was Leon?

'He's taking it seriously. I'm not sure that I can.' He went to look out of the window at the darkening garden. The sycamore tree at the bottom of the garden was still leafless, and through it you could see the spire of the church nearby. Did Leon pray when he was in trouble? She'd never asked him.

Bea did try to, but sometimes there was no time for anything but an arrow prayer. So here goes: *Dear Lord . . . keep him safe.*

He said, 'Tell me this is a bad dream.'

She had a sudden thought. 'You haven't touched your iPad or your smartphone since you arrived. Won't there be messages for you?'

'My smartphone is registering a number of calls from my brother's office and from my managers. I haven't responded to any of them. It occurred to me to wonder if my phone had been hacked or was being traced. I stopped off at a superstore and bought myself some pay as you go phones so that I could phone out but no one would know where I was. I tried phoning Adamsson on his mobile number. It was him I was supposed to meet today. His phone is out of commission. He lives with his elderly father, who doesn't like answering the phone. I tried there, too. Also no reply.'

'Tell me why you ducked out of the meeting.'

He grimaced. Tested the grille over the office window to make sure it was locked and drew the floor-length curtains, shutting out the dusk. 'The venue had been changed at the very last minute. I was sent the details by text. I didn't like the look of it.'

'Why not?'

'Aren't you due out somewhere? Lucas said he'd beep three times when he arrived. He said I wasn't to get in any old cab. He gave me his licence number. I'd better be ready for him, hadn't I?'

She couldn't bear it. She dived into his arms, tucked her head in the angle of his neck and shoulders and held him tight. She could feel his heartbeat against her.

His arms closed about her, and he put his head against hers. 'Do you realize that's the first time you've come to me for comfort? Perhaps I should invent a story about being in danger every day.'

It wasn't an invention. Something was wrong, and he *was* in danger. She was sure of that.

She could feel him breathe in and out. She could smell the fine linen he wore. He used a very light aftershave, but that was overlaid with a hint of tea.

There was a smile in his voice as he said, 'If you've left lipstick on my collar—'

'I use lip-gloss.'

'I'd wear the badge with pride. Perhaps not even send the shirt to the laundry for a couple of days. But I draw the line at mascara.'

'Waterproof.' She tried to draw away, but he caught her back.

He said, 'I ought not to have come here. They – whoever *they* are – if indeed it's not all a figment of my imagination – would guess I'd come here, and your staff would confirm it. You know nothing, right?'

'But I don't.'

'I wish I'd had you with me this afternoon. I saw something that caused me to turn tail and hare back to the cab, but I can't think what it was. I was only out of the cabbie's sight for, maybe, three or four minutes. Bea, you've got the right kind of brain for puzzles, but no . . . I shouldn't have come here. If I'm in danger then the last thing I should have done is put you in danger, too. If you're asked, say I annoyed you by arriving unexpectedly, that we argued and I went off in a huff. Say that you don't know where I've gone. That should keep you safe for a while at least.'

She shivered. He really was in danger? He seemed to think so, anyway. What could she do to help? 'Money. Do you have any? Can you use your credit cards?'

He drew in his breath sharply. 'I'm getting paranoid, aren't I? Surely . . .'

She rushed to her desk and unlocked the top drawer. 'Take my building society debit card. It's one I don't often use, because I ought to change the pin number and haven't. It was my late husband's birth date. Here . . . I'll write the number down for you and—'

'Got it.' Looking over her shoulder. 'Destroy that. I'll use my new pay as you go mobiles or public phone boxes to ring you, and we'll use that pin number as a code.'

Now it was her turn to aim for a lighter note. 'Talk about cloak and dagger!'

He caught her up in a bear hug, and then let her go. 'I must go. Remember, you've fallen out with me.' He set off for the stairs, and she followed. As they reached the hall, they heard a taxi tooting outside in the street.

He collected his overcoat and bag and opened the front door, saying, 'No, I'm not going to apologize!'

Did he think someone was watching? Was that why he'd drawn the curtains at the front?

Arms akimbo, she followed his lead. 'I'm in two minds to call the police—!'

'You invited me in!'

'Bastard!'

She could see Lucas leaning out of his taxi, wide-eyed. One or two passers-by looked interested, but she didn't observe anyone acting suspiciously. Leon dived into the taxi, and it drove off. She went back inside and slammed the door on the world.

TWO

'Was that Uncle Leon?'

Bea started. Dilys was standing halfway up the stairs which led to the upper floors. She was wearing an expensive pale-pink sweater over a black skirt. Pale pink was definitely not her colour: it made her look washed out. Dark hair, dark eyes large with distress. How much had she overheard?

'Indeed,' said Bea, as lightly as she could. For two seconds she wondered about taking Dilys into her confidence and decided against it. The girl was far too fragile. It would be best to pretend that nothing was the matter. 'He asked after you. Did you have to go to the shops for something?'

'No. I mean, yes. I mean . . .' She twisted her hands. 'You sounded awfully cross with him.'

Bea shrugged. 'It was nothing.'

'It didn't sound like nothing.'

'Men forget their manners sometimes. Did you get something in for supper?'

'No, I didn't.' Dilys sounded defiant. 'I can't be expected to be your housekeeper as well as work in the office.'

Bea suppressed a longing for her previous lodger, Maggie, who had been able to combine her own career with being their part-time housekeeper without any trouble. Maggie and her new husband had moved into a flat nearer his work a couple of weeks ago, and Bea missed her enormously.

Dilys was quite right: Bea ought not to expect her to be a Maggie-substitute. 'No, of course you can't do both, Dilys. Are you going out tonight?'

The girl rarely went out in the evenings. It had taken Bea some days to persuade her even to ring up an old friend and go to the pictures with her. Or him, if Leon were to be believed.

'I'm not sure.' Again, the hand twisting. 'You're going out, aren't you? It says so on the calendar in the kitchen.'

Bea clapped her hand to her head. 'So I am. Thanks for reminding me. I've got to make a phone call, and then I'll be off. Would you like to come with me? It's a private viewing of some pictures—'

'Oh, no. I wouldn't like that at all. Don't worry about me. I'll be quite all right by myself.' She stole away up the stairs, and a moment later Bea heard a door close on the top floor.

Bea glanced at her watch and wondered if her client might still be available. She didn't like to let her down, but time was marching on . . .

Why did Leon think he needed an alibi?

First things first: she must ring her client back. She went down the stairs to the silent office, mentally running through the list of people on her books who might be available for the job.

Wednesday morning

Bea had once heard someone say, 'No good deed goes unpunished.'

Personally, that was not the way she wanted to live. She was all in favour of giving deserving people a helping hand.

Define 'deserving'.

Bea set her teeth. She was not, repeat NOT going to shout at the girl. Shouting wouldn't help. Dilys was in tears already. Aaargh!

Bea aimed for a quiet, reasonable tone. 'But Dilys, you must have been warned about viruses? You worked in one of your father's offices before you got married, didn't you?'

The girl wailed, hands over her face, rocking to and fro. 'Yes, but . . . I didn't . . . It just . . .!'

Bea controlled herself. What she wanted to do was to kick the girl around her office, rather as if she was a football. Or put her in a large crate marked 'Return to Sender'.

Now *that* would make Bea feel better. Very much better. Except that the sender in this case was Dilys's Aunt Sybil, who had flown off to Los Angeles or Seattle or New York; some place, anyway, in which diamond-encrusted harpies transacted business with billions or even trillions of pounds as a matter of routine.

'I didn't think!' sobbed Dilys.

Which reminded Bea that she'd meant to ask Dilys about the trace of a man's aftershave which she'd recognized in the house that morning. It wasn't Leon's. Definitely not. The strange thing was that it rang a bell with Bea, though she couldn't think why. It had only been a trace . . . Perhaps she'd been mistaken. Anyway, it was not a mystery which she had to solve at that particular moment.

Because if she didn't sort out the problem with the virus in their computers, they could say goodbye to the agency's future. They had clients on their books expecting well-trained personnel to turn up on time and be prepared to cook, clean and shop for them. Not to mention au pairs and personal assistants, butlers and bottle-washers, chauffeurs and dog-walkers. With a smile.

Prioritize, Bea.

She pushed a box of tissues over her desk to the girl. 'Well, let's see what we can do to save the situation.'

A note of hope crept into Dilys's voice. 'It can't be so very bad, can it? I mean, all I did was to plug the smartphone into my computer to give it a charge, and then . . . oh! And Carrie screamed at me that I should have known better, and now they all hate me and . . . and . . .'

Carrie was the agency's super-efficient office manageress. She was middle-aged with a thickening body, but there was nothing wrong with her brains. Carrie had summoned Bea down to the agency just as she'd started to read the newspaper over breakfast. Usually, Bea was down before the agency staff arrived, but she hadn't slept well for worrying about Leon and had taken her time getting up.

Carrie's language had been colourful. Bea had known what to do, but the damage . . .!

Bea held on to her temper. 'Don't take on so, Dilys. We've stopped the others from booting up, and with any luck we can isolate the virus to those two computers. Meanwhile Carrie's getting our neighbourhood geek in to deal with them.'

Sniff, sniff. 'I wasn't to know, was I? I'd got down early because I know you don't like my being underfoot at breakfast time, and I thought I'd make a start and that you'd be pleased with me. Instead . . . I can't bear it!'

For some reason, the old tale of Bluebeard popped into Bea's mind. Didn't he hang up his wives by their long hair if they disobeyed him? Presumably, he killed them first? She really must check. How pleasing it would be to hang Dilys up by her hair, perhaps behind the door on the coat hook? Until she'd learned some common sense.

Bea said, in the kindest voice she could manage, 'It's not the end of the world, and—'

'I thought I was helping.'

'I quite understand. Now go and clean yourself up, and we'll see what can be done to put matters right. We've unplugged all our computers from the network and can connect with our customers via our smartphones. There won't be any web access, and we won't be able to print anything, but we can function after a fashion.'

Sniff, sniff. 'Yes, but they're all *looking* at me. And if they can't use their computers, they'll blame me for losing their jobs, and I can't face them, I really can't.'

Bea ground her teeth and then told herself not to do that, as her dentist had said it removed the enamel. 'They won't lose their jobs, Dilys. We may be inconvenienced for a while, but I wouldn't sack anyone just because we've got a virus.'

Dilys blew her nose. 'You mean, you won't sack me, either?'

Bea managed a smile. 'Of course not. Now, if you can't face the girls, I suggest you go upstairs and see what you can rustle up for lunch for us.'

'Oh. Yes, I suppose I could do that, only . . .'

Bea braced herself.

'. . . I really can't manage your microwave. It's so different from the one I used to have.'

Just in time, Bea stopped herself from rolling her eyes. 'There's a manual for it in the cupboard above. Why don't you have a look at that?'

When Dilys had dragged herself away, Bea clapped both hands to her head and gave a silent scream. Then she took a deep breath and went out into the main office to see how Carrie was coping. She was relieved to see that most of the girls were currently on their smartphones to clients.

Good. That would help a lot.

Down the stairs from the street came Keith; overweight, bushy hair and beard all over the place, carrying a laptop and a case full of unidentifiable bits and pieces, ready with a laugh and a shake of the head to rescue this office full of silly girls who didn't know enough to come in out of the rain when it poured . . . or to guard their smartphones with safety devices.

'Blessings on you, Keith.' Bea gave him a thumbs up and hurried into her office, where the phone was ringing. Her outside line.

'Is that Mrs Abbot? Holland House here. Mrs Evans speaking.' A sharp tone of voice, not young. This would be old man Holland's housekeeper? A formidable woman, according to Leon. Not someone Bea had ever been introduced to. Bea prepared for action stations. 'Mrs Abbot speaking.'

'Mr Holland is concerned that Mr Leon is failing to answer his phone. Have you seen him?'

So, the game was afoot. Leon had dropped out of sight, and they wanted to know where he was. Take care. 'Mm, well, yes. He did call in yesterday for a while but—'

'Really? What time was that?'

'Oh, I don't know. Lateish. I was rather busy, so . . .'

'How long did he stay?'

'I really didn't notice. I had a cup of tea with him, and then he went. I suppose he overslept, wherever he is. May I ask why you—?'

'He didn't come back here last night. Mr Holland sent him a voicemail message and wishes to be sure he has received it.'

Bea was vague. 'Doesn't he have a flat in the Barbican?'

'We sent someone over there to see. No, he's not there, either.'

Bea tried to sound amused. 'You mean, he's temporarily mislaid? I suppose you'd have heard if he'd had an accident? Have you tried the hospitals?'

'No, not yet.'

'Well, what about his mobile?'

'He's not picking up. Nor answering his emails.'

'How odd. Do you think he's been mugged?'

Silence. Heavy breathing. The woman didn't know how to deal with this, did she?

Bea said, 'Are you there? Look, I'm awfully busy. I expect he'll turn up. Bad pennies always do, don't they?'

'You think he's a bad penny?'

'Oh. No. Not really. No, of course not. Forgive me if I'm not being terribly helpful, but he was rather, well, you know, yesterday. Men don't always know when to stop, do they?'

'In what way?'

'I don't think I need to go into details, do I? Suffice it that I asked him to leave.'

More heavy breathing. 'So he left you about . . . what time?'

'Really, I can't . . . I suppose . . . It was getting dark. He called a taxi and left. Then I went back to work. Look, I don't understand why—'

'Did you happen to hear where he was going?'

'Of course not. I wasn't interested.'

'I thought you two had a special relationship.'

'I don't know that I'd call it that, exactly. I thought we could just be good friends.'

'Until he overstepped the mark?'

'Precisely.'

A pause. 'I think he's been under something of a strain recently. Things have not been going too well for him. He must have told you about that?'

Bea managed a light laugh. 'Goodness, we don't talk business. We are not on those terms. I believe he's worried about his brother's health. Isn't he going to retire or something?'

'I really couldn't say.' Permafrost.

'Ah well. Now, if you don't mind, I really must get on.'

'Would you let me know if he happens to contact you? It really is most urgent.'

'I don't think it likely,' said Bea, crossing fingers and toes. 'Not after, you know, he went far too far. I should have seen it coming, but . . . well, water under the bridge.'

She put the phone down and realized someone was watching her. Dilys, looking as if she were about to cry. Again. 'Uncle Leon's missing? Oh, no!' She collapsed into a chair, tears spurting.

Bea gritted her teeth. 'Come on, Dilys. No need for histrionics. I don't suppose for a minute that he's really missing.

He probably decided to stay in town last night instead of driving back home to the country. He'll bob up again, just you wait and see.'

'But he never doesn't answer his mobile, not ever! Something awful has happened to him, I can just feel it!'

Bea exhaled. 'Look, I had to speak pretty sharply to him last night, and he probably went looking for a woman to—'

Dilys shrieked, rocking to and fro. 'He wouldn't!'

'Of course he would. He's a man, isn't he? Pull yourself together, Dilys. Goodness me, what a carry on about nothing.'

It was never any good telling anyone to pull themselves together. Bea knew that, so why had she thought she should say it to Dilys? Bother the girl. Bea didn't *want* to dislike her, but was beginning to find her extremely irritating. Also, Bea was needed in the big office next door. She could hear Keith and Carrie's voices raised in argument.

Bea attempted a kind voice. 'Dilys, if you're so worried about your uncle, why don't you ring round the hospitals, see if he's there?'

'You're so heartless! How can you be so calm when he's gone missing? For all you know he might be lying dead in a field somewhere.'

'That's enough!' With an effort, Bea brought her voice down from a shout. 'I have to see what's happening next door. I agree, it would be better if you kept out of the way of the girls for the time being. So if it will put your mind at rest, why don't you do something useful and start ringing round the hospitals?'

Sniff, sniff. The girl nodded, blew her nose on a used hanky that squeaked, and got out her mobile. 'Where's a list of the hospitals? Have you got their numbers?'

'Phone book.' Bea fished it out from a drawer and placed it on her desk. 'Now, if you don't mind . . .'

Bea left the room, carefully shutting the door behind her. And leaned against it.

Dilys had taken her mobile out of her pocket to use. It wasn't a smartphone.

But, she said she'd plugged a smartphone into her computer first thing that morning, which had infected the system with a virus.

Dilys was not exactly the techie type.

Dilys's little daughter Bernice had a smartphone and used it as to the manner born. So did her Great Aunt Sybil. So did her Uncle Leon. So did Old Uncle Tom Cobley and all.

Everyone had a mobile of some sort nowadays, but they varied in size and capability. Bea had seen Dilys use her mobile before. It was an antique, a cellphone of dubious parentage. It might have a camera, but Bea would have been surprised to hear that Dilys knew how to use it.

So whose smartphone had Dilys plugged into the system early that morning?

And, returning to a niggle which had been at the back of her mind, whose aftershave had she smelled in the hall that morning?

It hadn't been Leon's, definitely. What other man had been in the house recently? Ah, she had it. It was Oliver's aftershave that she'd smelled. Of course!

Oliver was a clever lad of mixed parentage whom she'd taken off the streets and encouraged to fulfil his potential. He was now doing well at university, but she kept his room at the top of the house vacant, for use in holiday time. He was not expected back for a while, as he'd been invited to go on some survey or scientific exploration or other. He might be tinkering with the mathematics of space and gravity, or computing the results of another moon mission for all she knew. He did try to explain what he was doing now and then, but she didn't expect to understand it. If Oliver had returned unexpectedly, though, he'd have barged in with a hug and a demand to be fed.

She'd had a text from Oliver the previous day in which he'd rhapsodized about the local food in some far off place that she'd never heard of.

It hadn't been Oliver in the hall.

So who had been walking around the house either late last night, or early this morning? Dilys must have seen him, but she hadn't screamed blue murder as she would have done if he'd been a stranger. Which meant that Dilys knew him.

Problem. Had Dilys taken the man in because she liked him and wanted to see more of him? No. Because there was no reason why, in that case, she shouldn't have told Bea about it.

She might have been too shy to tell Bea?

Um. Well. At a stretch.

Dilys was a doormat, pushed around first by her family and then by her abusive bigamist 'husband'. Even now, if she made a mistake her reaction was to burst into tears.

So . . . let's suppose someone she knew came to the door after Bea had gone out last night and spun her a sob story about needing a bed . . .? And come on rather strong about it, ordering the girl *not* to tell Bea?

At some point this man had told Dilys to take his smartphone downstairs and plug it into a computer because it needed a charge. And the silly thing had done just that.

Next question: did whoever it was know that his smartphone had been infected with a virus? Had he deliberately put the agency out of action for the day? And if so, why?

A name leaped into Bea's head.

She dismissed it. Why would he . . .? Surely . . .! No. Ridiculous.

Carrie's face swam in front of her. 'Mrs Abbot, it's going to take all day. But Keith says . . .'

Bea listened and nodded. Keith was doing all he could.

Bea tore her mind away from Dilys to say, 'Let the girls work on their mobile phones and keep written notes of what they arrange. We'll reimburse everyone for what it costs them.'

Carrie smiled and nodded.

'And then,' said Bea, 'as they can't use the Internet or print anything off, they might make some routine calls, checking on our clients' satisfaction rate. Pick up any problems. That's always time well spent. And Carrie, why don't we ask Keith if he'll come in once a month to check for viruses and deal with any minor problems?'

'Put him on a retainer?'

'Just what I was thinking,' said Bea. 'He'd better have a look at my computer while he's at it. I'll leave Dilys in my office for the time being, and I'll be upstairs if anyone needs me.'

There was no point going off at half-cock. If there was a man in the house, then there was only one place he could be, and that was in the flat on the top floor, currently occupied by dismal Dilys.

First things first. Bea stood still in the hall and sniffed. No, the trace of aftershave was no longer there. She'd heard there were people whose olfactory nerves could distinguish between different scents even days afterwards. Her sense of smell was nowhere as good as that, but this particular scent had definitely been the one Oliver used. Mind you, lots of other men might use the same aftershave.

Perhaps the man had been in the kitchen? Dilys had got up and had an early breakfast before Bea had dragged herself out of bed. By the time Bea had tottered downstairs, Dilys had infected the office computers.

Kitchen. Bea looked around. Winston, their large, furry cat, was lying on the work surface, pretending to be asleep. Everything looked clean and neat and tidy, except for the cup of coffee which Bea had been about to drink when Carrie had called for help. There was her piece of toast – a bit chewed around the edges – and the empty dish into which she'd poured out a helping of muesli, laced with milk. Winston had clearly finished off the breakfast Bea had never had. Despite which, he now 'woke' up and demanded sustenance. Thinking hard, Bea dished him out a sachet of his favourite cat food.

She pulled open the dishwasher. She made a habit of running it last thing at night and had done so when she'd returned from the evening out with her ex-but-still-friendly husband. It had been a good evening. The gallery had done him proud. A fair number of art critics had turned up, and there'd been a good sprinkle of red dots marking pictures which had been sold during the course of the evening. Her ex had taken Bea round the corner for an Italian meal afterwards. Very pleasant. And she'd managed not to think about Leon. Much.

She'd been really tired afterwards and had refrained from asking her ex in for a nightcap, though he'd hinted he'd like one. She'd come in, checked that the alarm was on, staggered to the kitchen for a glass of water, been met by the cat. Fed him, put the dishwasher on, thought there was a funny smell around the trash bin, decided to investigate on the morrow, and went up to bed with Winston for comfort.

Fast forward to this morning.

It had become one of Dilys's jobs to empty the dishwasher first thing in the morning before she had her breakfast. She usually put things away in the wrong places, but it wasn't too difficult to find them again. So, the dishwasher should now be empty, except for the plates and cup Dilys had used for her own breakfast.

The dishwasher was empty, full stop. Which meant that Dilys must have eaten breakfast upstairs.

Trash bin. Yes, it was a bit whiffy. Pizza packaging for two.

Dilys was a picky eater, had hardly put on any weight since she'd been 'widowed'. Dilys didn't care for strong flavours. No anchovies, for instance. Yet the pizza packaging announced that someone had devoured an extra large pizza with ham and anchovies, together with a small sized ham and tomato. Oh, and under those two packets was another, empty, for garlic bread. Dilys didn't eat garlic because she was afraid it made her breath smell.

Bea marched up the stairs. On the first floor there was the master bedroom and en suite. Hers. Next door to that was the guest bedroom and en suite. Both empty, exactly as they should be.

On the top floor was the flat which she'd created for Maggie and Oliver, now both absent. It was a light and airy space containing two small bedrooms, a shower room and toilet, a kitchen, and a decent-sized living room.

Bea didn't think to mount the stairs quietly. Why should she? This was her house, and if she had an uninvited guest, she had every right to deal with him . . . or even her, come to think of it. This was a well-built house though the plumbing might sometimes be cranky. She could hear water running on the top floor. In the shower? Or in the kitchen? Was that the rumble of a washing machine?

The living room. Clean, neat and tidy. Except that the television was warm. Someone had been watching it within the last minute or so. Not Dilys, who was down in Bea's office in the basement.

Maggie's bedroom. Dilys had been sleeping there. The bed was neatly made, her clothes all put away.

Oliver's bedroom. The bed had been slept in, and the room stank of aftershave. A good quality leather handbag, of the type used by some men instead of a briefcase, lay on the floor. A laptop, open, on the side table. Some toiletries on the chest of drawers: Oliver's, presumably, which their 'guest' had been using. A pair of shoes under the bed, a leather jacket thrown over a chair. No sign of any guest.

The kitchen. Breakfast dishes for two, used. Coffee mugs, percolator. Also used. The washing machine was churning.

The bathroom. Draped in white, a screaming banshee confronted her, carving knife in hand.

There was only one thing to say, and Bea said it.

THREE

'For heaven's sake, Orlando!'

The apparition gaped.

Bea reached over, took the knife out of his hand and inspected it. 'If you've blunted one of my good carving knives, I'll have your guts for garters.'

Curly fair hair with a reddish tinge. A pixie's face with pointed chin and, yes, pointed ears. He had one bath towel around his torso and another draped, toga fashion, over one shoulder. 'But . . .!'

'Get some clothes on and explain yourself.'

'Oliver's clothes don't fit me.'

Thank goodness for small mercies. 'But his aftershave does? Where are your clothes, then?'

'In the wash. You can't expect me to wear things two days running, can you? Dilys said they wouldn't take long.' A light tenor voice, without much weight.

As he spoke, the washing machine sighed to a halt and beeped. Bea indicated that he lead the way into the kitchen. 'Feel free to use the drier. I'm surprised you didn't get Dilys to go out and buy some clothes for you.'

A shudder. 'Oh, I wouldn't do that. She has very poor taste.'

Bea returned the knife to the block, saying, 'Don't expect me to iron your shirt for you.'

'I can do that.'

Yes, she bet he could. He was as gay as all get out, and how old man Holland could ever have thought he'd be a possible husband for Dilys was a complete mystery. Mind you, Dilys probably hadn't even noticed that he wasn't exactly macho man.

He set the drier working, resettled the towel over his shoulder and looked Bea up and down. 'You're not quite what I expected.'

'Ditto,' said Bea.

'Dilys said you weren't bad looking for your age. Who does your hair?'

'What! Never you mind.'

Head on one side. 'I could give you the name of—'

'Don't try to avoid the issue. Why are you here?'

He showed the whites of his eyes. Ready to bolt? 'Dilys invited me.'

'Dilys hid you. And fed you. And plugged your infernal smartphone into our office computers, which has infected the system and brought the agency to a standstill.'

He grinned. 'Did it? How odd. It must have been that email I got from the Royal Academy. A bit strange, I thought at the time. I mean—'

'Did you infect our system deliberately?'

A hurt look. 'I wouldn't dream of it. Really. Not at all my style.'

'All right. I accept that. But it has caused us a lot of aggro and upset Dilys no end.'

'Well, she *is* easily upset.'

'So am I, though it takes me a different way. Back to basics. Why are you here?'

The whites of his eyes showed again. His breathing quickened. He looked away. He was going to lie. 'I had a call, I was needed on a job, a television series, in Spain. I have to get out there straight away, but I'd lost my keys, the keys to the flat I share with my friend, and he was out last night, an all-nighter, I remembered that too late, and I couldn't get in to get my passport and my clothes, and I couldn't think at first what to do, and then I remembered where Dilys was staying, and I called round to see her, and she invited me to stay for the night. I'll ring my friend and get him to let me in as soon as he's back and then I'll be out of your hair.'

What nonsense! 'Do you normally attack your hostess with a knife?'

'Well, no. I was not quite myself.'

Bea brushed past him and into Oliver's bedroom. She picked up the leather jacket and dived into the pockets. 'Keys.' She held them up for him to see.

'Those keys are not . . . They're from our family's place in the country.'

'Oh? There's an IT geek downstairs, attending to the problem you imported into our system via your smartphone. If I ask him to check on the last call you received, would it be from someone in your office about going to Spain?'

He looked away again. Resettled the towel over his shoulder. 'I really don't know how the Romans kept their togas in place. They didn't use safety pins, did they?'

Bea said, 'Let me guess. You were asked to attend a certain meeting. The venue was changed at the last minute. You got there in good time, and then what happened?'

He gaped like a goldfish.

Lost all colour.

Almost, he slid to the floor. At the last minute he clutched at the table. Bea pushed him into a chair and put the kettle on.

So Orlando and Leon had both been lured somewhere and . . . whatever it was that had happened had sent them both fleeing for cover.

She said, 'You need tea. Strong. With sugar.'

He recovered quickly enough and gasped out, 'Sorry! Stupid of me. You haven't seen the news this morning?'

She gave him a sharp look. 'You had the telly on to see . . .?'

He nodded. His colour was returning. The towel had fallen off his shoulder again. He was well built enough to satisfy the eye, but his skin was so fair that he would have to avoid the sun.

His hands shook as he accepted the mug of tea which Bea put in front of him. 'Are you going to call the police?'

The police? But . . . whatever it was that had happened, it involved Leon as well as this lad. 'Not till I find out exactly what's going on. Start at the beginning.'

He turned the mug round and round. 'Well, you'll probably find it hard to believe, but I've never really got on with my father.' He flicked a glance up at her, and she nodded, understanding exactly what he meant.

She made herself a cuppa and sat opposite him. 'Go on.'

'When I won prizes at school for art and design, my father never congratulated me, though my mother did say she'd wanted to go to art school herself, only she got married instead. They did let me go to art school, but afterwards they wanted me to go into the family business, and there was a terrible row when I said it just wasn't my scene. I found a job where I could be myself and a flat share, but still they thought that one day I'd "come round" to their way of life. I'm an only child, and they were both on at me to get married and produce grandchildren. They said I'd grow out of wanting to be with Charles – he's my soulmate.'

'And flatmate?'

He nodded. 'We were planning to make it legal, but when I told my father – this was about six months ago – he was livid. He had these plans, you see, for a dynastic marriage into the Holland family. To Dilys, now she's been widowed. I mean, don't get me wrong, she's a sweet little thing. Somewhat silly, but I suppose if I'd been that way inclined, I'd have gone along with it.'

'Your mother?'

'Died, two years back. I miss her.'

'Go on.'

'My father concocted this weird and wonderful plan. He'd set me up in a business of my own if I'd forget about Charles and see if I couldn't make a go of it with Dilys. I'm hardly making ends meet at the moment, London is *so* expensive, so I had to take him seriously, though I really couldn't see that it would ever work. So I asked how much and . . .'

He shuddered. 'It was a nice lump sum. Not by his standards, of course. He doesn't think the same way as other people about money. He thinks I wouldn't understand about playing the stock market, though I have dabbled a bit here and there, and not without success. But success on my terms is not what he considers success. If I think in terms of thousands, he thinks . . . thought . . . in millions. I bargained for a time limit. If Dilys refused me or made it clear she wouldn't marry me, I'd still get the money. He said he'd give me six months. It was a good offer, but . . .' He twisted in his seat. 'I had to promise to try really hard to like Dilys that way. And I did try. Even he had to admit that I tried. I squired her here and there, and sent her flowers and helped her choose a new wardrobe and arranged for her to have her hair done at a decent place. It didn't work. But then, I'd never really thought it would.'

Bea felt cold anger at the way the men had been manipulating the girl. 'Did it work for Dilys? Did she know about your bargain?'

A shrug. 'I don't think she knew, but it didn't work for her, either. A few weeks ago she broke down in tears and told me she knew that her father and mine were keen on the match, but that she didn't think she could go through with it. She was dead scared of what her father would say when he found out. Asked me what she ought to do about it. I was so relieved, I can't tell you. But I didn't want to own up, either. The deal was for six months. I had to keep to the letter of the law or my father might refuse to honour the agreement to set me up in business. So I said we'd go on pretending for a while and that I'd think of something.'

'You didn't tell her you were gay?'

'Sort of. Yes. I'm not sure she understood. You know what she's like. Too naive to be true.'

'So what went wrong?'

'I really don't know.' His brow corrugated, and he looked anguished. A small child caught in adult machinations. 'I think there was some sort of row between my father and old man Holland about money. My father said Mr Holland should contribute half of the money due to me, but Mr Holland wouldn't play ball. Yesterday morning I had a text from my father saying he wanted me to meet him with this man Adamsson, who's old man Holland's chief accountant. The six months are nearly up, and I thought they were working out the nitty gritty of how I was going to get my money. I was a little surprised that they hadn't waited till the very last day of the six months, but pleased. I can't tell you! At last! I took a couple of calming pills and drove out there to meet them.'

'Then you had a phone call . . .? Who from?'

'It was another text message. From my father. Funny, that. I'd never known him text before, he always said you can't teach an old dog new tricks, but there it was, in black and white. We were supposed to have met at the accountant's house way out in the sticks, and I could understand he wouldn't want us to meet at the office under old man Holland's nose, because he was so picky about anyone selling any of his precious shares, wanting to know who'd bought and sold them, always checking the percentages, according to my father who's known him since the Dark Ages. I think they were at school together, can you believe it?

'Anyway, you'd think the chief accountant to Holland Holdings would have a big detached house with a double garage, or a penthouse flat somewhere exclusive, but apparently he'd never moved out of the house his parents bought when they got married half a century ago, though his mother's dead now, and he lives there alone with his aged p. It's a small three-bedroom house in a terrace overlooking a park in Ealing. Not exactly what you'd expect. I have a little car for work – there's an underground garage at our flats – but while I was driving out there, I got this second text from my father saying the venue had been changed. We were to meet in a car park at the swimming pool about a mile further on. It's a council-run swimming pool, modern, in some sort of park.

'I got there a minute or two early. It wasn't difficult to find the place, but I couldn't see where we could meet and talk in private. The car park is a big one, divided into "bays" by hedges of evergreens which have grown up so much, you can't really see through them. I parked in the first bay nearest the road.

'It was early afternoon, before the schools came out. Pretty deserted. Hardly any other cars. There was a school bus parked on the other side of the swimming pool. A whole lot of kids were piling into that. The bus drove away as I walked along the bays, thinking it was a weird place to select for a meeting, because you couldn't exactly sit in the back of a car and talk business, could you? Then I saw my father sitting in a car in the last bay, alone. I tapped on the door of his car and spoke his name. He didn't move. Didn't answer. I pulled the door open, and he fell sideways towards me. Oh, God. Am I going to be sick?' He put both hands over his mouth and retched, but controlled himself.

Bea poured a glass of cold water and handed it to him. 'You mean he was dead?'

A nod. He took the glass and drank. Licked his lips. 'I touched his neck. He was still warm. But dead.'

'Was the heater on in the car?'

A wild look. 'How should I know? I thought he'd had a heart attack at first, and then I saw the blood on his shirt. His overcoat was open and . . . I touched him, got blood on the cuff of my jacket. There was no knife that I could see. Maybe it was a gun?'

'Really dead?'

He nodded. Closed his eyes. Sipped some more water. 'My stomach has always been delicate. I can't keep anything down when I'm upset.'

'You're doing fine,' said Bea, encouraging him. 'What happened next?'

'I didn't know what to do. I ran around the bay, yelling for help. There was one other car there. A woman was sitting in it by herself. I thought she'd just come out of the baths and was waiting to drive home. I went over to her, banged on her window. Her eyes were closed. Nice looking, fortyish. I wanted her to come with me over to my father, to help me to . . . I knew he was dead, really. Only, I wasn't thinking straight. I shouted. She didn't reply. I pulled her door open and touched her, and she . . . she didn't move.'

'What? She was dead, too? But how?'

He wailed, 'I don't know, I don't know! A knife, perhaps? They were both wearing dark clothing. I didn't see any bullet holes or . . . I don't know! I never liked him, I shouldn't say that, should I, but I never wished him dead. I keep seeing him!' He covered his own eyes with his hands.

Bea tried to think. 'You phoned the police?'

'My first thought was to get help. There was no one else around, but I had the strangest feeling, shivers down my back. I tried my pockets and realized I'd left my phone in the car, at the other end of the car park. I started to run back there . . . and that's when I spotted Leon walking towards me, looking around, just as I had done a few minutes before.'

'You recognized him? You know him well?'

'Not well. We don't have much to do with one another. He swims in different waters.'

Bea subdued a smile. Yes, he certainly did.

Orlando said, 'When I saw him, I realized how it would look, that he would assume I'd killed them, though why I should have done so, and who the woman was . . .' He lifted his hands in a helpless gesture. 'I suppose she was killed because she saw my father being attacked, but perhaps it was the other way round. I don't know. I don't know!

'I didn't reason it out, but ducked into the shrubs. My heart was beating so fast, I thought he'd hear it, but he stopped, he was looking at something, I don't know what. He got his phone out, but apparently there was no reply to his call. I prayed he'd go on down the bays, that he'd find the bodies and raise the alarm. I thought I could slip past him while he was looking the other way, but he legged it back the way he'd come. He'd arrived in a taxi which had taken its time turning round, and he shouted at the cab driver that he'd changed his mind and wanted to go on somewhere else. I don't think he saw me. No, I'm sure he didn't.'

No, he hadn't.

Orlando rubbed his eyes. 'I was terrified. I could see how it was going to look. I couldn't understand how . . . how anything! And what about the woman? I'd never seen her before in my life. I wondered if she'd quarrelled with my father and . . . but why? And why there? While I was dithering, a car drove into the first bay and parked next to me. A woman disembarked a load of kids, and they all went off to the pool. I stayed where I was till they'd gone, then I got into my car and drove away, forgetting till I was way out of there that my fingerprints would be on the car doors. I didn't dare go back. I couldn't think what to do, or where to go. I'd been set up, hadn't I? Leon, too, I shouldn't wonder. I drove out to Denham, had a couple of drinks, and threw up. Then I rang Charles at work.'

He sent her a sideways look. 'Actually, Charles and I, we haven't been getting on all that well. The arrangement about Dilys with my family had upset him. He said that if I'd really been serious about him, I wouldn't have agreed to it. So when

I rang him, told him what had happened, he wasn't . . . I mean, it probably was good advice, but—'

'He told you to ring the police?'

'I couldn't. But I couldn't think what else to do. I thought if I could get to Spain, or South America . . . only, what would I do for money? If only I could lay my hands on my money and my passport! I had tucked away a couple of thousand here and there, but once the hunt was on, wouldn't they freeze my accounts? Then I thought of Dilys, staying here. I thought she might get my money and my passport for me, if I gave her my keys to go in while Charles was at work. So I rang her, asked if she'd be by herself, and she said you were out. So I left the car near the end of the tube line and came in by Underground.'

'Did you tell Dilys what had happened?'

'Sort of. I left out about my relationship with Charles.'

Dilys was standing in the doorway. 'What was that about Charles? He's your boyfriend, isn't he? I'm not a complete idiot, you know. Did you really think I didn't know what was going on between you two? You really ought to make up your mind whether you want a girl or a boy.'

'Oh,' said Orlando, hand to heart. 'You gave me such a start. I didn't realize you were there.'

Dilys was frowning. 'I'm glad you've told Mrs Abbot what happened. I know you swore me to secrecy, but I couldn't sleep properly for worrying about it. I do realize you could be in trouble if the police knew you found the bodies, and I would like to help you, but honestly, I don't think running away is the right thing to do.'

She said to Bea, 'I phoned round all the hospitals and Uncle Leon hasn't been taken to any of them, so we ought to phone the police about him, too, don't you think?'

Bea thought this had gone on long enough. 'He phoned me just now. He's perfectly all right, spent the night with friends.'

'Oh, right. Then one of the girls downstairs cut herself on some paper, and I found the Emergency Kit and dealt with it, I don't think she needs to go to hospital, or anything. Keith said I'd done it beautifully. He's nice, isn't he? He asked if you wanted him to deal with Orlando's smartphone, only of course he thinks it's mine, and I said yes, please. And there's someone who keeps calling on your private landline, and Carrie keeps telling them he's got the wrong number but he keeps ringing back, and Carrie said I'd better tell you in case it's some stalker or other and you'll need to get the police on to it.'

Bea felt a cold shiver run down her back. 'What number does he think he's calling?'

'How should I know?' Dilys checked that the drier had finished its cycle, pulled Orlando's clothes out, and tossed them to him. 'Do you want me to iron your shirt?' And, without waiting for his reply, got out the steam iron and ironing board.

Bea got to her feet. 'Orlando, she's right. I'm going down to make a couple of phone calls now. I know someone in the police force who will give you a fair hearing, and I'll see if I can get hold of him. All right? Promise me you won't try to run away.'

He looked strained, almost grey. 'They'll crucify me.'

'This policeman will be hard on you for not reporting what you saw, but he doesn't go in for torture.'

Down the stairs she went, making a diversion into the kitchen to have a quick look at the morning paper, which she'd started to read over the breakfast she hadn't had. Yes, here it was.

'*Mystery deaths in a car park . . . two schoolchildren were horrified to discover the bodies of . . . identified as Lord Lethbury, 63, found sitting in his Mercedes, with a bullet wound . . . and Mrs Margrete Walford, 48, soon to be ex-wife of Sir Ben Walford, whose current bitter divorce case, with allegations of . . .*'

The landline rang, and Bea picked it up. Leon's voice. 'What number are you?'

Bea's dead husband's birthday had been on the twenty-ninth of November. She said, 'Twenty-nine eleven. You've seen the papers?'

'I have.' Grimly. 'I need to talk to the police. Any chance of your getting hold of that inspector you're friendly with. What's his name? Durrell?'

'I'll do my best. There's been a development this end, too. Orlando was lured to the car park with a similar text message.'

And at that moment, Bea nearly dropped the phone. 'Hold on a mo! I've just thought . . . You still haven't used your smartphone, have you? Can you bring it here? Do not, I repeat, not, try to use it.'

'It's been hacked?'

'Worse. Can you bring it straight over?'

'But . . .'

She crashed the phone down and raced out of the kitchen and down the stairs. 'Keith! Where's Keith?'

A babble of voices replied. Keith reared his tousled head from the desk at which he'd been working. 'Want me?'

'That smartphone, the one that caused all the trouble . . . tell me you haven't touched it yet?'

He held it up in his big, capable paw. 'Right as rain now. She's lost all the stuff on it, but that's a small price to pay.'

Bea clapped her hands to her face. 'Of course. Right. You weren't to know. Is there any possible way you could get back anything that was on it? A text message, in particular.'

'Shouldn't think so.' He was appallingly cheerful about it. But then, he didn't know he'd just destroyed Orlando's alibi. He said, 'The young girl said it was all right.'

The young girl? He meant *Dilys*?

'Yes, of course,' said Bea, feeling rather faint. There was something in the Bible about fools doing more damage than wicked men. If she could find the passage, she'd get Dilys to write it out by hand a hundred times. Not that that would do any good.

She said, 'Thank you, Keith. How much longer do you think it will be before we're back online?'

His brow furrowed with concentration. 'Give or take, the rest of the day. It's a fair whatsit, this one. Any chance of the young girl bringing me in a sandwich or two? She did offer.'

'She's busy at the moment. I'm sure she'll remember in a little while.'

Bea went into her office to sit down and think. Told herself to take some deep breaths. Drew the landline phone towards her and set about trying to contact DI Durrell, an old friend who appreciated her cooking and her keen wit. Or so he said. She was of the opinion that he thought more about his stomach than he ought, but she could rely on him to listen carefully and not jump to conclusions. He was climbing the career ladder slowly but surely, hampered – or assisted – by the fact that he was of mixed race. As he said, he got the best of both worlds but, despite laws to ban this and that, not everyone agreed. He was intelligent, appreciated graveyard humour and liked to drop in for a chat and some home cooking now and again. Even if he hadn't been assigned to the murders in the car park, he could probably be lured to visit her with the promise of some food. He had a fondness, she remembered, for a juicy bacon, lettuce and tomato butty as a snack between meals . . .

'Is that Detective Inspector Durrell? Bea Abbot here. Hi! Long time no see. Fancy an appetizer? Or a late lunch, tips on murders included.'

'You're serious?'

'I'm always serious about food. And murder.'

'Any murder in particular?'

'Plural. Murders. Nice, fresh meat. Oh dear, what bad taste. Forget I said that.'

Pause. 'A man and a woman? Hitting the headlines?'

'A current divorce case. A title. What more could the tabloids ask?'

'Not my case.'

'I guessed as much, but my informants – witnesses – want to talk to the right person. One of them, you've already met.'

'Witnesses? Two of them? What is your connection?'

'A friend. Leon Holland.'

'What? You mean your friend Leon, of Holland Holdings? What has he got to do with the price of bread?'

'Shall we say half past twelve for home-made soup, a BLT and some rather good ice cream? Coffee to follow.'

'You do know it's an offence to try to bribe a police officer?'

'When you've heard their stories, you can call up the cavalry.'

A long, long pause.

Bea said, 'Are you still there?'

'No. I'm not. We have not had this conversation. They must ring in, say they've some information about the case. They must give their statements to the right man . . . no, wait; I think it's a woman. I can't make lunch, but I accept your invitation to supper. Seven o'clock, shall we say?'

She caught on quickly. 'Yes, of course. For supper. I suppose they'll have given their statements and returned by then.'

'Speaking hypothetically, yes. You believe in their innocence?'

'Oh, yes.'

'I assume they have solicitors?'

'I'll see to that. If it's supper, I might have to change the menu.'

'Is my friend Maggie doing the cooking?'

'She and her husband have moved out to their own place, nearer his work. I'll see to it.'

'I'll bring some after-dinner mints, shall I?'

FOUR

Leon arrived as she put the phone down. Taking off his coat, he said, 'Lucas sends his regards. I slept in his spare room last night. Woke up to find an imp sitting on my chest, demanding I read it a story.'

Leon was on edge, a little too bright, his eyes everywhere. 'I wasn't sure what gender it was at first. I think it was female, though the story it wanted was all about trains. She knew it off by heart and corrected me if I missed a word.'

Bea wondered if he regretted never having children of his own. His partner for many years had not wanted children, but now she was dead he didn't seem to be looking for anyone who might help him to remedy the omission. He adored his little great-niece, currently on holiday in America with her great aunt . . . but was that enough?

She set that thought aside for the moment. 'I've news. My friendly detective inspector is not the one dealing with this case. He advises you to tell the police what you saw, and to do so straight away.'

He pulled a face. 'I didn't see anything that would help.'

'Did you work out what it was that caused you to turn tail yesterday?'

A nod. 'What was all that about my smartphone?'

'I'll tell you in a minute.' She'd heard Orlando coming down the stairs. He was dressed in his own clothes but looked nervous. Did he regret having promised not to bolt?

Leon nodded to him. 'Orlando.' And sent an enquiring glance towards Bea.

She nodded back. 'Dilys let him in, and he stayed here overnight. He must go in to see the police as well. Relax: he's your alibi.'

'Really?'

'Yes, really,' said Orlando, with a grimace. 'I've just realized, would you believe it, that I'm now Lord Lethbury. I don't think I'll use the title, or sit in the House of Lords. Not my scene.'

Bea tried to work it out. 'So your father wasn't just a life peer, and the title passes to you?'

'That's all I will be getting. There's a socking great country house, cold as charity, run by a distant cousin who moved in when my mother died. She's never liked me, and I've never liked her. She didn't like my father, either. I don't think she likes anyone, but she's kept the house going after a fashion. I hope he's left her something in his will, because she exists on her old-age pension and hasn't anywhere else to live, but I doubt if he gave her a thought. He was a wealthy man. I suppose the lawyers will have a field day, fighting over his estate. I won't be getting any of it. He told me he was leaving it all to the Tory party if I didn't alter my way of life. Not that I want it. Any of it.' He shuddered. 'Somebody walked over my grave. I still can't believe . . . I still keep seeing . . .'

Bea sighed. 'It's lunchtime. You two won't get a decent meal at the police station. You'll most likely have to wait around for hours till they can find time to take your statements. Let's eat here before you report for business. Dilys has made us some soup.'

She crossed her fingers, hoping Dilys had found the salt and not used too much of it. The girl was domesticated after a fashion, but at sea in someone else's kitchen.

Bea led the way into the kitchen, sniffed and relaxed. 'Dilys, that smells delicious.'

Dilys wiped moisture from her brow. 'It's a family favourite. Leek and potato with some parsnip added. I promised to take some down to Keith. He's going to have to work through his lunch hour, poor thing.'

Soup was poured, tasted, pronounced excellent. Plates were cleared. Dilys took soup and bread down to Keith, while Bea set about making some BLTs. The delicious scent of frying bacon filled the air, dragging Dilys up from the basement to fetch the next course for herself and Keith. Leon hardly touched his portions. His eyes switched from Orlando to Bea. Calculating this and that. Not saying why.

For afters they had blackberry and apple tart, rescued from the freezer and warmed through in the microwave. Dilys didn't appear for hers. Leon toyed with his.

Coffee. Bea cleared everything away and said, 'Right. Now we're fed and watered, we'll be better able to cope. My friendly policeman is not able to help us. Some woman has got the case. He says you've both got to volunteer statements about what you saw and did, and do it today. He reminded me it might be helpful for you to take a solicitor with you. I suggest that, before we contact a solicitor, we rehearse what you are going to say. Leave out anything irrelevant.'

Leon gave her a long, hard look, then nodded. 'You mean, don't mention anything but the facts. Agreed. But I think I have to start with my near fatal accident. The Rolls was in for repair. On Sunday afternoon the courtesy car I was using refused to start. I had arranged to go up to Birmingham by train, stay the night, and be fresh for my first appointment early on Monday morning. I didn't want to cancel, so I chose to walk from home to the station. I was nearly run over by a van that came out of nowhere.'

Bea said, 'I'll play devil's advocate. Who wants you dead?'

'I don't know. I'm involved in some complicated financial transactions, but . . . I can't see how anyone would gain if I were to be bumped off.' And that sounded like the truth.

'I expect you were imagining it,' said Bea, although she didn't think he was. 'Carry on.'

He fished his smartphone out of his pocket and put it on the table. 'On the Monday, while I was still in Birmingham, I received a text message on my smartphone, supposedly from Mr Adamsson, rearranging my appointment to meet with him for the following day, Tuesday, at his home. Mr Adamsson is the chief accountant for my brother's overseas corporation. I didn't query it because we had already made arrangements to meet when I returned from Birmingham, although not at his home and not on that day.'

Orlando was agitated. 'What, what? I had a text, too. To meet my father at Adamsson's house.' He frowned. 'I've been thinking, was it really my father who texted me to meet him? I've never known him text before. It didn't occur to me then, but now I'm wondering . . . Could someone else have texted me but made it look as if it came from his phone?'

'I've been thinking that, too,' said Leon. 'But if Adamsson didn't text me to meet him, then who did?' He stared into space.

Bea glanced at her watch. Time was marching on. 'I think you should leave all speculation to the police. Just say what you did. Leon, you got back from Birmingham, and . . .?'

'I arrived back in London at midday and asked a black cab to take me out to Ealing, to Mr Adamsson's house. On the way I had a second text from him to say the venue had been changed—'

'Same here,' said Orlando. 'Except that the text was supposedly from my father, and I drove myself there.'

'I was wary. Why had the venue been changed, and why to a swimming pool? It didn't make sense. Mr Adamsson is not the cloak and dagger sort. And where were we supposed to have this all-important meeting? In the cafe at the swimming baths? Was I being lured somewhere so that another hit and run driver might finish me off? When we got there, I told the taxi driver to hold on for a few minutes. I walked along the parking bays. I kept close to the verge, listening for an oncoming car. I saw Adamsson's car in the second bay. He's a small man, but he has a weakness for large, expensive cars which he changes every year. It's possibly his only weakness. His current car is a black SUV with a distinctive number plate. There was no one in it. I got out my phone, tried his mobile. No response. I felt something was wrong, so I hightailed it back to the cab.'

Bea said, 'Let's get this absolutely clear. How far did you get into the car park?'

'Two bays only.'

'That's right,' said Orlando. 'I saw him coming and dived into the bushes. He stopped and stared, tried to phone someone, then turned round and went back to his cab.'

'You were hiding in the bushes?' Leon was incredulous. 'Why?'

'Playing hide and seek, what else! No, I was in shock. I'd just found my father, dead. And another woman whom I'd never set eyes on before. I wondered if there was a gang of muggers in the vicinity, targeting anyone who parked there that day. I thought I might be next. I realized I'd been lured to the spot under false pretences, and at first I thought you might be someone coming to finish me off.'

'Just say what you did, Orlando,' said Bea.

Orlando heaved a sigh. 'I arrived, parked in the first bay and walked along till I saw my beloved papa sitting in the Mercedes, waiting for me. Or at least, that's what I thought till I tried to get his attention. I opened the car door, and touched his shoulder and he fell over, towards me. I nearly passed out from the shock.'

Orlando had gone rather white about the mouth, but managed to continue. 'I felt sick. So yes, Inspector Bea, I was lured there as well, and by the same methods. Texts on my phone. But unfortunately I can't prove it, as a virus seems to have wiped everything out. Texts, everything.'

Leon prodded his smartphone. 'Bea, you warned me not to use this, and I haven't. Can it really be true that someone has been sabotaging our phones?'

Bea said, 'What other explanation can there be? You've both received texts sending you to an unusual venue. Later, although he didn't realize it at the time, Orlando's phone was infected by a virus delivered via a seemingly ordinary email from a concern that he recognizes. He thought his phone needed a charge, so he asked Dilys to plug it into one of our computers this morning. She did, and infected our system. Our IT geek cleaned the virus off his phone but, in doing so, has removed all the texts and phone calls which took Orlando out to the car park. I'm thinking the virus was sent deliberately, to destroy the evidence which sent him there.'

Leon looked grim. 'And mine? You think that if I'd gone on using it, another message would have infected my phone and wiped out all the messages on it so that I couldn't prove why I'd gone to the car park?'

'Do you want to risk it? Take it to the police as it is.'

He raised his hands in frustration. 'They'll ask me: who really sent those messages? And I don't know.'

Orlando held his head in his hands. 'I thought it was my father at first. Now, I haven't the foggiest.'

Leon said, 'Adamsson himself? I don't think so.'

'And the content seemed to be OK?' asked Bea. 'No mistake was made in the wording or the signature?'

Both men shook their heads.

Bea was frowning. 'You'll have to let the police have both smartphones. See what they can make of them. Did you see anything else of interest at the car park, Orlando?'

Orlando had his fingers in his mouth. He took them out and slapped one hand with the other. 'I really must *not* bite my nails. You mean, after I found my revered papa dead? I don't think I'd have noticed if a little green man from Mars had dropped in for a chat. I wonder if I can get my doctor to give me a prescription for sleeping tablets over the phone?'

'And you definitely didn't recognize the woman in the other car?'

He shook his head. 'Ought I to have done?'

Bea pointed at Leon. 'You recognized her?'

Leon, too, shook his head. 'I didn't get that far into the car park. I saw her picture in the papers this morning, but to the best of my knowledge I've never met her.'

Bea's frown deepened. 'I think – I'm not sure – but I think we were on the same table at a charity drive a couple of weeks ago, the one at the Dorchester. Remember?'

'Really? No, I don't remember. I meet so many people.'

'Have you worked out why you left the car park so abruptly?'

'I've run through the scene in my mind over and over again. I spotted Adamsson's car. I recognized his personalized number plate. There was no one sitting in it. I looked around. Couldn't see him. Thought he might have gone into the swimming baths to visit the loo. Thought I'd wait for him. I used my phone to call his mobile, ask him where he was. No service. That was the last time I used my phone. I saw there were other messages on it, but none from him. Then something . . . Maybe I was subconsciously aware of being watched? I was uneasy. The back offside window of Adamsson's car was starred. Perhaps a pebble had struck it? That's all. If you say that's nothing, then I'd agree with you.'

'You think he's gone missing?'

'Once I got my pay as you go phones, I tried to contact

him. I've tried everywhere I could think of. There's still no service on his mobile. He lives with his father, but his father is not picking up. I tried his office. They say he's gone on holiday. Most unlike him, especially since we'd previously arranged to meet again later this week . . . though not at the swimming baths.'

Bea said, 'You don't think Adamsson's gone missing of his own accord, do you?'

'No, I don't. He's an irritating little man in some ways. He only exists to make facts and figures jump around, but he's straight as a die. The only time I've ever known him take time off before was when my brother gave him the sack and he lit out for France for ten days. But that was a misunderstanding, and he was reinstated immediately on his return.'

Bea took a deep breath. 'The police can find him if anyone can, but the sooner they know what you know, the sooner they can get started.'

It seemed to her that the police wouldn't take Leon's concern for Adamsson seriously. Yes, they might try to contact him, but that wouldn't be their first line of investigation. Orlando, however, was a different matter. His father had been killed. They'd think he would profit by his father's death.

Orlando was obviously thinking along the same lines. 'It looks like I'm for the high jump. I found my father dead but didn't ring the police. I have no alibi, and I can't prove I received any texts on my smartphone. The police will be bound to think I killed him for the title and the lolly, and that Mrs Whatsit was collateral damage because she happened to spot me doing him in. But, if he'd lived, I stood to gain a nice lump sum at the end of my six months' courtship of Dilys. As it is, I'll get diddly-squat and a title which I do not intend to use.'

'That's your best argument yet,' said Bea.

Dilys drifted into the kitchen to put some coffee mugs into the dishwasher, but this time she didn't drift out again. 'Have you decided yet, Orlando?'

Orlando put his arm out, and she came to stand beside him, placing her hand in his.

'Dear Dilys,' said Orlando. 'You know the best and the

worst of me. I don't know what I'd have done if you hadn't
given me shelter last night. Of course you're right, and I must
go to the police with what I know.'

Bea warned him, 'Be prepared, Orlando. They're going to
tear you to pieces and put the fragments under the microscope.
Leon, do you have a solicitor, and can you get him to go to
the station with you? And Orlando, do you have one?'

'I'm shaking like a jelly,' said Orlando. 'I've never needed
one before.'

Dilys said, 'Use mine. The family one, not the one for business. He's an old dear, used to sit me on his knee and pretend
he was a horse and jogged me up and down when I was little.'

He was probably a hundred years old. How like Dilys to
rely on someone inappropriate! Bea set her teeth, but Orlando
brightened up. 'Could I? What's his name? Can you give him
a ring?'

'Of course,' said Dilys, taking out her old mobile phone.

Leon got up. 'Bea, may I use your personal phone
downstairs?'

'You can use the one in what used to be Maggie's office.
It has its own outside line.'

She led the way downstairs, and he followed.

He wanted privacy. He was going to exclude her. For selfish
reasons, because he had always been a loner? Or because he
was trying to protect her from whatever danger it was that
threatened him?

Because he *was* in danger, wasn't he? The others hadn't
seen it, but she had.

Bea told herself to be calm. All this was taking time out of
her day's work . . . but the virus had already taken a chunk
out of her day, hadn't it? Downstairs in the main office, all
was quiet, if not exactly as per normal. Some of the girls were
on their mobiles, some busy with paper files. Carrie was talking
in a low voice to Keith, who appeared to be the calm eye in
the centre of the storm. Keith moved at his own pace.
Unflappable. Slow but sure.

Bea fetched the keys from her office, let Leon into Maggie's
room and indicated the whereabouts of the outside line.

Carrie met her as she came out. 'Keith's taking an age.'

Bea nodded. 'But you've got everyone working. Housekeeping. All very necessary. Any horrible hiccups?'

'Nothing that we haven't been able to reschedule. A woman failed to turn up for an interview with you at three—'

Bea clapped her hand to her head. 'I forgot.'

'Well, it didn't matter, did it? Keith thinks we ought to upgrade again.'

'Painful, but necessary. Can you discuss when he wants to do it?'

A phone rang. In Bea's office?

Carrie said, 'It's your private line. It's been ringing on and off all day. Someone wanting Mr Leon. I've tried to answer it as much as I could. They won't leave a message. I said he wasn't here at first, but now he's come . . .?'

'I'll tell him.' Bea made no move to do so.

Carrie said, 'Trouble? Can I help?'

'At the moment, no. But thanks for offering.'

Carrie stiffened her shoulders. 'About Dilys . . .'

'You'd prefer she didn't try to help any more?'

'Don't get me wrong. She's had a bad time, but she's not exactly clued up about modern technology, is she?'

'I'll try to keep her out of your hair.' Bea closed the conversation by walking off into her office. The phone had stopped ringing. She sat in her chair, looking at it. Then checked to see who had been calling. Holland Holdings. Of course.

She went to the window and looked out over the garden and up through the bare branches of the tree to the spire of the church beyond. A bright-blue sky, beginning to fade with the onset of the dusk. The afternoon had fled away, and soon it would be night.

She tried to pray, but her mind was such a jumble of impressions that she couldn't think constructively.

Danger.

Definitely.

Leon put his arms around her from behind. 'I've found out which police station is dealing with the problem and said I was coming in. My solicitor will meet me there. Keep some supper for me?'

FIVE

Wednesday afternoon

L eon contacted his solicitor and went to the police station with Orlando. And then there was peace and quiet. Comparatively. Bea stood by the window in her office, looking up at the sky, trying not to think.

Someone crept in behind her. 'Excuse me. Is it all right if I . . .?'

A member of staff looking for something? Bea nodded. Didn't turn round. Felt for a hankie. No pockets. Bother.

The phone tinkled. Stopped. Footsteps retreated.

She was alone again. Good. She found a pack of tissues in her top drawer, blew her nose. Sniffed. An alien scent. Medicinal?

Carrie came in. 'Have we the keys to Maggie's old office? The girl wanted to go in there, but I think Mr Leon must have gone off with them. I told her to do it next time.'

'What girl?'

'The one who came to disinfect the phones.'

Bea shook her head. 'I'm missing something here.'

'You know? The new service for cleaning phones. Protects us from cold germs and stuff. We used to have them do it years ago at my other place. I thought they'd gone out of business, but apparently not.'

Bea stared at Carrie, trying to think. Her brain was made of treacle, and thoughts swam slowly around and around. 'To the best of my knowledge, I haven't signed any contract with such a service. Not that it's a bad idea. Did you sign up for it on my behalf?'

Carrie shook her head. 'Why would I do that? I thought you had. The girl showed me her copy of the contract, and it's signed over our office stamp.'

Bea let herself down into her chair and looked at her shiny, just cleaned phone. It gleamed back at her. Potentially dangerous.

She said, 'I've just had a thought . . .' She indicated that
Carrie should follow her and led the way into the main office.
Most of the girls had gone by now, though a couple were still
putting on their coats while they discussed having a night out.
Dilys was tipping the contents of waste paper baskets into a
black plastic bag.

Keith was still there. He lifted his hand. 'Once more round
the Wrekin, and I can reset. Should be out of your hair in ten.
Maybe twenty.'

'That's great,' said Bea, watching the last two girls leave.
They climbed the stairs to street level and disappeared. Bea
beckoned to Carrie to follow them into the well at the bottom
of the stairs.

Carrie said, 'You wanted to speak to the phone-cleaning
girl? She must be long gone.'

'And left what behind? Can you get Keith to come out here
for a moment?'

'Why?'

'Just do it, will you?'

Carrie frowned, but did as Bea asked.

Close to, Keith was so large that he blocked out the light
from the street lamp nearby. And, wouldn't you know, Dilys
came too.

Bea said, 'A girl came to clean the phones this afternoon.
I didn't authorize her to do so. Do you think you could check
to see if she left something behind?'

Keith half closed his eyes. 'You're talking bugs? You think
someone wants to listen in on your conversations?'

Dilys squeaked and covered her mouth with both hands.

Carrie gave her a look, but refrained from comment.

Bea nodded. She hugged herself. It was chilly out there
without a coat. 'Could you check the phone in my office first?'

Keith plunged back inside, closely followed by Dilys.

Bea said, 'Carrie, we need to find out who used our agency
stamp on the authorization for the phone cleaning service.'

Carrie clicked her fingers. 'I wonder . . . Jennifer?'

Their newest employee. Bea recalled a thin, young to
middle-aged woman with knowing brown eyes, excellent refer-
ences. 'Why Jennifer?'

A shrug. 'I don't know. Yes, I do. Her eyes and ears are everywhere. She listens to other people's conversations but never joins in. Keeps herself to herself, as they say. Also, she wouldn't stump up when we were collecting for the girl who left when her husband got a job up north. I was going to say something to you about her not fitting in, but she's efficient enough and it didn't seem important. Do you want me to go through her desk?'

'Please.'

Carrie went back inside, and Bea followed her. It really was too cold to stand outside without a coat.

Carrie delved into the desk space that Jennifer used.

Dilys watched her, wringing her hands. 'Oh dear, I've brought such trouble on you! I didn't mean to, honestly!'

Bea forced herself to smile. 'Nonsense, Dilys. This has nothing to do with you.'

'If I hadn't let Orlando stay, none of this would have happened.'

'I'm not so sure about that.'

'The thing is, he's such a sweet person and his family treat him so badly so I . . .' She gestured, helplessly.

Bea could see that there might well be some fellow feeling between those two misfits. 'How are things between you two?'

'He did ask me to marry him. I didn't want to hurt his feelings, but I had to say "No". I don't love him like that. I think of him like a brother, sort of. Not that I ever had a brother. But he's been so kind to me, letting me talk and telling me about his family. You can't imagine what a relief it is to talk to someone who understands. It's helped me to get over things. He's nice to go out with now and then. Not often, of course. I don't really like being out late at night, but we go shopping for this and that, especially cheese, which he loves. He says he must have been a mouse in a previous incarnation, not that I believe in such things, and then we have a nice lunch out, nothing expensive, you know? He says he'd like to take charge of my wardrobe, too, but I couldn't let him do that because I know he'd spend far more than I can afford . . .'

The gentle moan went on and on. Bea stopped listening.

Keith appeared in the doorway to her office, holding

something up in his hand. 'It's safe to talk. This sort only picks up phone conversations. Can you spring to some overtime? I'd like to see what else has been left behind.'

Bea hadn't realized she'd been holding her breath. 'Overtime, plus a bonus. Yes. Thank you, Keith. I don't know what we'd have done without you.'

He seated himself at the first desk and attacked the telephone.

'Got it!' Carrie held up a form. 'Copy of the contract with the phone cleaning company. She's filled in the name of the company herself. She has a distinctive hand, prints everything. Someone has signed it with a squiggle which could be yours at a pinch, Mrs Abbot, if you don't look too closely. I suppose she copied your signature from a letter somewhere. Eureka!' She held up the office stamp. 'I keep this in my top drawer, which is always locked. I wonder how she got that.'

Dilys wiped tears away. 'Well, you do leave your keys in the lock on your drawer sometimes. I had to get at the cash box the other day to buy some more coffee. You were interviewing someone, so you gave me your keys and told me to leave them on your desk, so . . .'

Carrie paled. 'I did, too!'

Bea said, 'No worries, Carrie. We have to trust one another in here or life's not worth living. Dilys, you are splendid. You really do keep your eyes open, don't you? Have you ever seen Jennifer doing something that you thought wasn't right?'

'You mean, like when she stays behind at night and looks in other people's drawers? I was cleaning up one night and saw her. She said she was looking for her pen that she'd lent someone. Then she told me off for not cleaning the toilet properly, so I went back and did it all over again, though really I thought it was all right. But she's very fussy about such things, and you can't be too careful about hygiene, can you?'

Keith moved on to another phone. He frowned at Bea. 'Don't you have a proper cleaner, Mrs Abbot? I thought that Dilys was a relation of yours.'

Bea felt guilty. She really hadn't looked after Dilys properly, had she? 'Yes, Keith. You're right. Sort of. Carrie, what's happened to our regular cleaner?'

'Sprained her ankle or something. I was going to ring round, but Dilys offered to help out. I did try to tell you, but you were busy and it didn't seem important.'

'I like to help,' said Dilys.

Keith said, 'This phone's clean, but I'd better check them all, hadn't I?'

Bea thought of Leon's chauffeur leaving him without notice, about the brakes failing on the Rolls, and the courtesy car which had refused to start. Had their cleaner been got at, as well? And if so, did it mean the agency was now in the line of fire?

But why? Because Bea was friendly with Leon? Was that fact really sufficient for her agency to be targeted? Surely not. But, if it was the case, then what was going to happen next? Was she, too, going to be run down in the street? Gracious heavens, where was all this leading?

Finally, Keith said, 'I think these are all clean. I can't see any other bugs which might have been left at the side or under desk tops, but I'll have a quick scan round with my little machine. Then, if you can run to it, a cup of tea?'

Dilys said, 'I'll make it.' Then, hands to mouth, mumbling, 'Only, I haven't finished the cleaning.'

Bea winced. 'Leave the cleaning, Dilys. Carrie will find us another cleaner tomorrow. Someone we've used before and can trust.' She shot a look at Carrie, who had gone pink and who nodded agreement. 'What we need now is a council of war, with Keith.'

'Including me?' said Dilys, ready to be told that she wouldn't be needed.

'Definitely with you,' said Bea. 'Tea and biscuits in my office, as soon as Keith has finished. That is . . . Carrie, Keith? Can you spare the time?'

'Fifteen minutes,' said Keith, and was as good as his word.

Tea. Biscuits. Draw the curtains against the dusk.

'The thing is,' said Keith, taking two shortbread biscuits in one hand and waving his mug of tea in the other, 'telephone bugs are illegal.'

'I know,' said Bea, looking in her top drawer to see if she could find some aspirin. 'We really can speak freely now?'

Keith crammed the biscuits into his mouth and nodded. ''Effnittly.'

Carrie sipped tea, frowning. 'Someone wants to learn the agency's secrets. Planning to pinch our customers? Do you think that virus was all part of it?'

Dilys looked as if she were about to cry. 'Oh, but that was all my stupid fault and it was Orlando's phone it was on and he didn't know there was a virus, honestly.'

Bea gave up the search for her aspirin and rubbed her forehead.

Keith took another two biscuits, eyeing her over his mug of tea. 'Mrs Abbot, you are going to report the bug to the police, aren't you? Because if you aren't, I'm supposed to do so. And if I don't, I'll be in trouble.'

'Yes, I'll report it,' said Bea. 'I've got a detective inspector coming round this evening, and I'll tell him all about it. Perhaps you can give me a statement to pass on to him? He can contact you direct if he needs clarification.'

'What's it all about?' Carrie was not going to be put off. She wanted answers, but Bea didn't have any.

Dilys said, 'Do you think Daddy organized it?'

The others regarded her with open mouths.

Dilys blushed, but persisted. 'Well, I know Daddy doesn't like Uncle Leon coming here because he thinks Mrs Abbot is bad for him, but—'

'What!' from Bea.

Dilys gave a nervous start. 'Oh, I don't think you are, really, and neither does Aunt Sybil. But when Daddy gets an idea into his head . . . and everyone around him is so anxious to please that I thought . . . It did cross my mind . . . Though probably it's very silly of me, because I know I haven't any head for business—'

Bea said, 'You think your father might set out to bug this agency because he disapproves of Leon coming here? Really?'

Dilys wriggled. 'Daddy's not used to people standing up to him, you see. He's been such a powerful man for so long that . . . And Uncle Leon has only been back in our lives for a short time, and then there was the board meeting when they all turned against Daddy and Uncle Leon took over almost half of his companies, and Daddy was really, really upset about it.'

This was not how Bea had understood the matter. 'Dilys, your father's getting on in years, and he agreed that for the sake of his health he should wind down his activities.'

'That's what they all said—' with a dark look – 'but it was a fait accompli or a putsch or whatever it is that they call it, so he had to give in and pretend he liked it. But he felt it tremendously . . . Oh, not at first, when he was really rather relieved, but later, making a joke of it, pretending he didn't really care, but I thought he did, really. I'm sure Uncle Leon has done his best, but he doesn't understand that he's not up to the job.'

Bea wondered if she were dreaming. Leon's progress had been narrowly watched by the commercial press, who'd approved his innovations and consistently given his leadership the thumbs up. Leon's companies were thriving . . . but his brother still thought he was not up to the job? The old man must be off his rocker!

Dilys took a biscuit and nibbled at the chocolate on it, first one side and then the other. She appeared to have said all she wanted to say.

Bea prompted her. 'Dilys, I think I can see why your father might regret having to hand over some of his companies to his brother, but why would he want to bug our phones?'

'I suppose because he thinks you're a bad influence on Uncle Leon, that you encourage him to think he can run the companies on his own, without Daddy. I don't think he has a very high opinion of women in business . . . Auntie Sybil excepted, of course.'

Bea blinked. 'I wouldn't dream of advising Leon about his work. He doesn't confide in me about his business affairs, and that's fine by me.'

'Daddy used to be quite all right about it, but just recently he's got it into his head that if you hadn't pushed Uncle Leon into masterminding a coup, he'd still be in control. He told Sybil you were evil, and she laughed so much she had a coughing fit.'

'Goodness me!'

Dilys shook her head. 'It's not a good idea to laugh at Daddy. It only makes him worse. I blame the Welsh Dragon—'

'Who?'

'Oh. Sorry.' A flutter of fingers. 'Mrs Evans. His house-keeper. She's like his guardian angel. Or that's what he says. Some days she won't even let me into his rooms. She's been with him for ever, and she's got this extended family who sort of, well—' another wriggle – 'they make his wishes come true. She said to him one day that she could find out what lies you were feeding to Uncle Leon, and he said, "How could you do that?" and she said to leave it to her. I never thought she meant it. I thought she was just humouring him, and that she wouldn't really do anything about it.'

'But . . . Dilys, doesn't he realize that you're staying with me?'

'Well, actually, he probably doesn't. When Aunt Sybil told him she wanted to take me and Bernice off to America for a vacation, he told her that I wasn't to go because I was tied up with Orlando, and of course I was, in a way. I didn't say anything because I didn't really want to go to the States. Aunt Sybil is a bit overwhelming, isn't she?'

Yes, she was. 'You think your Aunt Sybil arranged for you to visit me, without telling him?'

'She said she didn't want to leave me alone in the house when she was away, and she thought it would be good for me to help you out here in the office, and I agreed because it is a bit lonely at the big house with Bernice and Auntie Sybil gone. And Bernice is so grown-up nowadays that I don't know what to say to her any more, and I had nothing to do and I don't even see Daddy nowadays for days on end. I suppose Aunt Sybil forgot to tell him. She's the only person I know who's not afraid of Daddy . . . except for Uncle Leon, of course, but I don't think they're on speaking terms at the moment. Oh dear, oh dear. Whatever is Daddy going to say when he realizes you've found his bug?'

Keith extended his mug for a refill. 'Mrs Abbot, the man's paranoid. You are going to report this, aren't you?'

Bea took a deep breath. 'Yes, Keith. I'm going to report it. Dilys, thank you for explaining.'

'That's all right. I don't think you're a bad influence on Uncle Leon. I think he's a bit of all right, and I think Daddy's being a bit silly, but I know better than to contradict him when he gets one of his fancies. I mean, I did tell him I didn't want to marry Orlando, and he still thinks it's going to happen. Orlando and I are agreed that Daddy's as bad as Lord Lethbury-that-was. Orlando's father.'

Keith leaned forward to pat Dilys's knee. 'Don't you let them push you around.'

A little colour came into Dilys's cheeks. 'No, I won't. Or rather, I'll try not to. It's a bit difficult when I'm so dependent on them. It would be different if I was capable of earning my own living. I've no money of my own, you see, and I'm absolutely useless in an office.'

Keith said, 'Can't Mrs Abbot find you a job as a housekeeper or cook? I'm sure you'd be great at that.'

Bea had to admit that Keith was right. In her own house, with her own equipment, Dilys would probably be fine.

Carrie looked to Bea for a lead. Meaning, shouldn't the agency try to find Dilys a good job?

Bea said, 'I should have seen it sooner. If that's what you want, Dilys, then we'll see what we can do.'

'Thank you,' said Dilys. 'I'd really like that. I need to live in somewhere, so that I can have Bernice with me.'

Bea nodded, while thinking that Bernice might not agree. Bernice had been introduced to a different way of life and was happy in her new, fee-paying school. Bernice was talking about going to a top boarding school. Her Aunt Sybil doted on her, and her Uncle Leon thought she'd make a good businesswoman one day. Suppose Dilys wanted Bernice to go to live with her in some small house or flat somewhere and attend a state day school . . . which way would Bernice jump? She was a nice kid and often seemed to be looking after her mother, rather than the other way round. Well, sufficient to the day.

Carrie cleared away the tea cups. 'So what do we do about Jennifer? And what precautions do we take to avoid trouble with Mr Holland senior?'

'I don't know,' said Bea. 'If we sack Jennifer—'

'You'd have to give grounds,' said Keith. 'Let the police

deal with it. You've found a bug. You tell the police. You produce my report. They visit in strength, question your staff. You produce the copy of the contract with the phone cleaning company, and they say they'll check for fingerprints. They take everyone's fingerprints. Jennifer – if it is she – will realize the game is up and disappear.'

Bea nodded. 'Or, alternatively, we could put the bug back and feed them misinformation, but I can't think what or how to . . . No, your way is best. And we might be able to get some useful information from her when she's confronted with what she's done.'

'Being straightforward is always best,' said Keith, looking sideways at Dilys. 'And Dilys? You'll find her a job she likes?'

Bea thought of trying to explain Dilys's complicated background and gave up. 'Yes, Keith. We'll do our best.'

Keith grinned. 'I'll do that report for you now. Dilys, you can find me a desk to write it on, can't you?'

'Follow me,' said Dilys, leading the way back into the main office.

Carrie looked at Bea, and Bea looked back.

In a hushed voice, Carrie said, 'He's going to ask her out. And she'll go!'

'And who is going to explain that to Daddy?'

'Is Leon Holland brave enough?'

At which both women began to laugh. Bea moaned, 'Oh, this is awful.'

Carrie shook her head. 'Keith's a good, kind man. He wouldn't hurt her.'

Bea said, 'He's been in and out of the agency for years, but I've never had anything much to do with him. What do we know about his private life?'

'Widowed. Tragic case. A car accident? No children. I think he's a Christian.'

'What sort of Christian? I don't mean what denomination. I mean, does he try to act in everyday life as a Christian should, or does he keep his religion for high days and holidays?'

'I don't know. I've never heard him swear, and he doesn't drink or boast about having women or tell the sort of jokes which make the girls flinch. He doesn't wear a cross or talk about going to church. I don't know why I thought he was a Christian. Maybe he isn't.'

'He looks old enough to be her father.'

'I don't think he's as old as he looks. But . . .'

'But, he's going to get hurt. Daddy has only to twitch his little finger and she'll run back to his side.'

'Agreed. But if her family really don't care what becomes of her and he's a good man who would look after her . . . why not?'

Bea sighed. 'You're a romantic, Carrie. The Hollands don't "do" romantic.'

Carrie gave her a sidelong look. 'Leon Holland does.'

'That's different. He can stand on his own two feet.' Bea knew she'd blushed.

'Right,' said Carrie. 'Back to basics. How do you want to deal with Jennifer?'

'Do nothing, say nothing. Act as usual. She has no idea we've tumbled to her little game. I'll get the police to arrive in force, and then we'll see which way she jumps.'

Dilys appeared in the doorway. 'Keith's hungry, and so am I. He asked me if I'd show him a good eatery around here. I've got my key, and I won't be late.' She disappeared.

Bea shut her mouth, which had dropped open. She reflected that for the first time Dilys's pale-pink jumper looked right on her.

Carrie laughed. 'She's got a date.'

'He's a fast worker, but as soon as Daddy hears about it—'

'If it gives her some self-confidence . . .?'

'Yes, I know all that. And, thank you, Carrie. I've kept you long after office hours.'

'Oh well. I haven't much on at the moment.'

Bea understood that. Carrie's history mirrored her own after a fashion, which was one reason why Bea had employed her. Carrie had brought up her son alone, doing a variety of office jobs to keep them both going. Her son had gone into the army and was presently serving abroad, which had enabled her to look around for a position with greater responsibility.

'I appreciate it,' said Bea. She looked at her watch, and

then checked with the clock. Nearly half past seven, and neither Orlando nor Leon had returned. What if the police didn't believe their stories? What if Orlando were arrested for his father's murder?

She told herself to stop worrying. And failed. Her friend the policeman would be arriving for his supper any minute, and she had nothing prepared for him. Now that was an emergency. She left Carrie to lock up the agency rooms and climbed the stairs to her own kitchen. She hadn't fed Winston since lunchtime. He would be ravenous. And yes, here he came plopping through the cat flap, smelling of chicken . . . Whose food had he been eating? He assured her he hadn't eaten all day and that she must remedy the problem straight away. Which she did. He was getting fat, but she had more to worry about than that.

The kitchen phone rang, and she answered it, wondering if it were bugged . . . But no, it couldn't be, could it?

The inspector. 'I'm running late. How important is it to see you tonight?'

'It's urgent. Lots to tell.'

'One hour.'

And where, oh where have my two little boys gone?

SIX

Half past eight. The inspector rang to say he was further delayed but would get there when he could. There were no further messages. The supper would be spoiled if the men didn't come soon. She thought of trying to ring Leon and Orlando. Realized she hadn't their current phone numbers.

A key turned in the lock on the front door as she was checking the potatoes, and Leon's arms stole around her from behind. She clasped his hands to her and leaned back against him. Closed her eyes. 'You think your brother's trying to kill you, don't you?'

He was dispassionate. 'That's ridiculous.'

'But that's what you suspect. The police kept you a long time. Didn't your solicitor turn up?'

'He did. I used the man I met this morning to make my will. The detective inspector kept me waiting for ages, then dismissed me, as if what I had to say was of no importance. I think she's going after Margrete Walford's husband. She believes Orlando and I are a side show and it was a coincidence that we were asked to meet where the woman was killed.'

'I wish I could believe that, but Orlando isn't back yet so they must be putting him through it.'

'I don't think Orlando's in any danger. I understand that Margrete's husband has been celebrating her death with a magnum of champagne. I've got an appointment at nine. Do I smell cooking? Did you keep any supper for me?'

Anxiety overrode caution. 'You will take care, won't you?' She wanted to add, *Don't take risks. You're important to me.* She stopped herself.

'Don't worry about me.' Her phone rang, and he released her.

She said, quickly, 'Don't answer that. Or not yet. I must tell you first that there's been an attempt to bug my phone in the office downstairs. I don't think this one is bugged, but I've just realized that it might be. I must ask Carrie if the woman was allowed to come upstairs to . . . No, she'd have said, wouldn't she?'

'What? Why should anyone want to—?'

'Dilys thinks your brother is mounting a vendetta against you. She says he now regrets passing some of his companies over to you—'

A gesture of annoyance. 'He didn't have any choice. He got over it.'

'I know, but Dilys says that he's beginning to think he shouldn't have done it. She says the people around him are feeding his paranoia and offering to help bring you down. Leon, I'm afraid.'

'I know what I'm doing.'

'Famous last words.'

The phone stopped. Bea got the casserole out of the oven and drained the vegetables.

The phone started up again. 'The phones downstairs have been quiet all afternoon. I suppose because Keith was monitoring them. I checked when I came up, and this one didn't have any messages on it then.' She looked at the number revealed. 'I think it's your brother. If it is, what do I say?'

An amused smile. 'Say you hate me. Try to make it sound as if you mean it.'

Infuriating man. She picked up the phone.

'Mrs Abbot?' The same sharp female voice as before. 'Angharad Evans, speaking for Mr Holland. I've been trying to get you for ages.'

'Sorry. Someone gave us a virus, the phones have been all over the place. We had to get a techie in to deal with it.'

'I understand Mr Leon is with you?'

Bea twitched a glance at Leon, who had seated himself at the table beside her. Could he hear the person on the line? He stared back at her, intent, half smiling.

Bea said, 'What precisely is going on, may I ask? I thought I'd made it clear that he was no longer welcome here, but he turned up again this morning and now just a few minutes ago with some sob story or other, as if I haven't enough to do without—'

'Can you put him on the phone, please?'

She raised an eyebrow at him. He shook his head.

She said, still watching Leon, 'He's in the loo at the moment, says he's going out again straight away. Can you please tell me what this is all about? I'm beginning to lose patience—'

'I have a message for you to give Leon from Mr Holland. He recorded it earlier. I will play it to you now?'

'If it doesn't take long. I've got—'

'If you please!' said the voice.

A short pause, and then a scratchy, bad-tempered man's voice said, 'Leon? I can't believe what you've done! Your treachery is unforgivable, and I've finished with you, do you hear?'

Bea watched Leon, who was watching her and not looking at the phone. Did he already know what his brother was going to say?

The woman's voice returned. 'Mr Holland is too distressed to continue, but he wants me to give his brother the following message: you are no longer his brother and you are no longer welcome in his house. He is calling a series of extraordinary general meetings and will resume chairmanship of Holland Holdings UK Division, which he should never have been persuaded to hand over to you. He has instructed that the locks be changed on the accommodation you've been using here, and that your belongings be packed up, awaiting collection at your leisure. The car you've been using has been returned to the garage and the lease on it terminated. All communications should be addressed to his solicitors in future.' The connection was broken.

Bea put the phone down and began to dish up the food.

Treachery?

He was watching her, waiting for her to make up her mind. Treachery? She shook her head. No, that wasn't in Leon's nature. Snapshots of his actions during the time she'd known him flicked through her mind. She homed in on the moment she'd answered an SOS to find him, careless of his own plight, fighting to resuscitate a half-drowned Dilys. At that time he'd

hardly known the girl, and she certainly hadn't done anything
to make him think kindly of her. She could easily have died
if he hadn't worked so hard to save her.

She said, 'Treachery? No can do. If you've angered him, if
he's trying to strip you of everything you've got, then it's
because you've crossed him in some way. Knowing him and
knowing you, you had words because he was trying to get out
of supporting Dilys.'

She didn't even make that a question. She put his plate of
food down in front of him and fished out a knife and fork.

The lines of strain eased on his face. He started on his food.
'This looks good.'

She put her own plate of food on the table, but didn't start
on it. 'You knew what he was going to say?'

The slightest of nods. 'The same message was on my smartphone voicemail yesterday, before I went out to see Adamsson.
I guess it's been sent to you so that you stop giving me the
time of day. May I congratulate you on your cooking, Mrs
Abbot?' He reached across to put his hand on the table beside
her, palm upwards.

She laid her hand over his. She could feel his pulse, slightly
faster than normal. Perhaps hers was faster than normal, too.

She said, 'If we were being old-fashioned, we could prick
our wrists and bleed into one another to seal an everlasting
friendship. Did you ever do that as a child?'

He shook his head. 'Eat up. Did you keep some back for
Orlando and Dilys? Where is she, by the way?'

'She's out for the evening. There's been a development
there. I'll tell you later. Back to your brother. Are his threats
empty?'

'Probably. He retained a few shares in all the companies
which he handed over to me, so technically, yes, he could call
a series of extraordinary general meetings to challenge my
way of doing things. But that would make headlines on the
financial pages, and our stock would plummet.'

She took a small mouthful and tried to swallow. Failed.
Took a sip of water and tried again. Got it down. 'You're the
darling of the media. Everyone applauds the way you've been
going on. And everyone knows he's past his best.'

'He doesn't think that way. He has billions in the bank, and they carry clout.'

'Are you concerned as to the outcome?'

'I'm concerned, yes. I've put all my money into redeveloping the companies he passed over to me, and I don't like the idea of a family feud.'

'What does your sister Sybil say?'

'She has some sympathy for him. She's much nearer in age to him than to me, remember. She thinks he's in the wrong, but she's not willing to interfere. She says she'll make sure little Bernice is well looked after, no matter what.' He cleared his plate. 'Seconds?'

She gave him another helping. She'd hardly touched hers. 'Sybil doesn't care what happens to Dilys?'

A shrug. 'No one does, much. You guessed correctly, by the way. I wanted him to set up a trust fund for Dilys. He said he'd made provision for her by marriage to Orlando, and that he's no use for whiners. She'd been upsetting Mrs Evans, interfering with his routine, questioning this and that. Trying to find a new role for herself, I suppose. It didn't go down well. She's no great brain, is she? He may be right in saying that we all, including Dilys, ought to make our own way in the world, but she's had a raw deal and isn't well equipped to join the rat race. Yes, Briscoe can be tetchy. I probably chose the wrong moment to champion Dilys's cause. He asked if I were questioning his judgement . . . and, of course, I was. Things escalated from there.'

'Dilys is one of the walking wounded, and she certainly isn't capable of earning her own living at the moment. At least, not in an office.' There would be time to tell him about Keith later.

He tackled his second helping with vigour. 'Let me explain how it is with Briscoe. He's always had to fight his corner, and he doesn't see why everybody shouldn't do so, too. Our own father was not interested in anything but business. A fine role model he was; a cross between a banker and a pirate. He married twice in order to get himself an heir and a spare, and I don't think he cared tuppence for either of his wives. His first wife gave him Briscoe, then took some years off to visit the South of France and have a good time generally before dying in giving birth to Sybil.

'It was ten years before he married again, and that marriage produced the desired "spare", in me. My mother was a much-admired beauty. She handed me over to nannies and left for another wealthy man when I was six. I never saw her again. She died a couple of years ago, left no note for me, no message, nothing. Not that I expected any.'

Yes, thought Bea. That still hurts, doesn't it?

He shrugged. 'Well, that's the Hollands for you. Bad pickers, you might say. Not good at sustaining relationships. Like Briscoe and Sybil, I was sent off to boarding school at the earliest opportunity. Sybil has married for money and status, three times. I settled into a long-term partnership but avoided marriage. My brother seemed to live only for making money. I think we were all surprised when he upped and married his then housekeeper and produced Dilys. I have sometimes wondered if he married her to avoid disruption in his routine. I don't think it ever occurred to him that his wife might bear him a child or that he should offer either of them any affection. So when Dilys's mother died in a car accident – nobody's fault, she took a bend too fast – the girl was sent off to boarding school.'

He cleared his plate again. Drained his glass.

Bea fetched a yogurt and fruit mixture from the fridge for him. She'd hardly touched her own plateful. 'Could you yourself set aside enough to provide for Dilys? He can't strip you of everything, can he?'

'You never know quite how things will go at extraordinary general meetings. There are always some malcontents with an axe to grind. The balance sheets are healthy if not startlingly good. I sacked a couple of the managers he'd appointed, for incompetence. They complained to him. He took their part, encouraged them to go to employment tribunals. I'll win, but it's something I could do without.' He hesitated, shooting her a sharp look. 'If I lose everything, you could always find me a job as a cocktail waiter, or a toy boy, couldn't you?'

She tried to laugh. 'You'd bounce back.'

'You believe in me?'

'Yes, I do.'

Silence, while they both thought about that.

He said, 'Marry me?'

She shook her head. 'You're not thinking straight.' She pushed her chair back. 'You were testing me, wanting me to hear your brother's message. How long have you known that he was going to try to destroy you?'

'He isn't.'

'I asked the wrong question. How long have you suspected that he would turn on you?'

'Ah.' He tilted his head back, looking up at the ceiling. 'Since last Thursday evening, when we disagreed about Dilys's future and he challenged me to return my companies to his control.'

'You took precautions. Don't deny it. Of course you did. Now, what would you have done? Consulted your solicitor, yes. Not the one Holland Holdings uses. You guessed he'd deny you use of the suite at the big house. You already have your bolt-hole in the Barbican. May I ask why you aren't using that?'

'It's bleak and cold. I prefer your company.'

'And my cooking?' She frowned. 'What else? You would have found and staffed another office.'

'At short notice, that was a bit awkward. I did wonder if you'd let me rent Maggie's old office here and find me a good PA?'

'Oh, no, you don't. Besides which, the timing's wrong. You've probably already rented a suite of offices in the City somewhere, with platinum blondes attached . . .'

He laughed, raised his hands in surrender. 'I'd been thinking of doing just that for work purposes for some time, because it was awkward administering Holland Holdings (UK) from Briscoe's home territory. So, yes, I did set myself up in another office. But, I hadn't wanted to stop living at the big house so soon because I wanted to keep an eye on Dilys and little Bernice. Plus my sister Sybil is always good company. Remind me to give you my new phone numbers. And what was that about the agency phone being bugged?'

'I'll tell you later. One thing I'm sure you did was to go to see Adamsson, your brother's head accountant. You didn't think he'd approve of the line Briscoe was taking and wanted his advice. And Adamsson said . . .?'

'He was distressed. He said he'd already tried to talk to my brother about Dilys. He warned me that Briscoe was planning to regain the companies which had passed to my control. He said my brother would use any tiny mishap at any one of my companies to cause me trouble; an infringement of health and safety rules, a slip-up on the balance sheet, a lowly employee dismissed without good cause. Any or all of these minor matters could be magnified into mismanagement on my part.

'He is an unassuming little man to look at, but he can be fiery in defence of his beliefs. Very black and white. Very small town accountant, carrying his Protestant torch of truth and light into the boardrooms of the mighty. Not the type you normally find at the top of the financial tree. To tell the truth, I feared for his future if he crossed my brother. I tried to suggest that he be circumspect, but he was one jump ahead of me. He told me he had considered resigning rather than follow orders which he would find distasteful. I was so enchanted by his courage that I became carried away and—'

'Said that if he resigned, he could have a job with you. Hence your brother's accusation of treachery.'

'Yes.' He stood up. 'You've hardly touched your supper. May I make some coffee? I have to go out in a while and may be back late.' He cocked his eye at her.

She smothered a grin. 'You've been angling to get into my bed for months, and you think I'll let you do so now? You are so wrong, Mr Holland. If you're desperate, you may return, but you and Orlando will have to make do up at the top of the house, and I'll have Dilys in the guest room next to me.'

'Dear me. Now I'd hoped that, seeing me in such distress—'

'No, you didn't. And Dilys needs a chaperone.'

He threw up his hands. 'You've lost me.'

She twitched a smile. Little did he know! 'Dilys has acquired a follower . . .'

The kitchen phone rang.

He said, 'It may be for me.'

She checked the number of the caller on the phone and

picked it up. A deep man's voice, one she recognized. 'Is himself there?'

'Yes, Lucas. You've been running errands for him, have you?' She passed the phone to Leon. 'Your taxi awaits.'

Apparently, Lucas was not just reporting for duty, but had something specific to say. Leon said, 'Mm,' at intervals. And finally, 'Thank you. Fifteen minutes?' And put the phone down. He said, 'I asked Lucas if I could retain him for a couple of days, double his usual take home pay. He agreed, so I suggested he took a trip out to the swimming pool car park, to see if Adamsson's car was still there. Lucas says the far end bay, where the murders were committed, has been taped off and police are still on the site. They were stopping all-comers to ask if they'd been there yesterday and what they'd seen. He said he was just a sightseer, and they let him peer over the hedge. Adamsson's car has gone.'

'I suppose he came back, looked around for the people he was supposed to meet, didn't see them anywhere . . . or perhaps he did see Lord Lethbury's corpse? And drove off?'

'Remembering that the back offside window was starred . . . I have a bad feeling about it. And why didn't he answer his mobile when I rang?'

'Perhaps he himself was never there, and his car was there as bait? After all, he's supposed to have gone off on holiday, hasn't he?'

A reluctant nod.

A peal on the front doorbell. 'Now who . . .?' said Bea.

It was Orlando, looking shrunken and miserable. 'Sorry. Forgot the key Dilys gave me. She said I had to turn off the alarm system, but I couldn't remember what the numbers were for the life of me.'

'Come on in,' said Bea, drawing him into the kitchen. 'We were worried about you. Have you been with the police all this time?'

'Don't you ever listen to the news? Margrete's husband, the banker or whatever he is, took fright and tried to get on a flight to Spain this afternoon. They arrested him at the airport. Charged him with her murder.'

'What? But your father . . .?'

'They tell me he just happened to be there, waiting for me, at the wrong time. He must have seen the banker killing his wife and been killed himself before he could tell the police.'

She switched on the small television that she kept in the kitchen and found a news bulletin. And there it was.

'A man has been detained in connection with the murder of . . . Arrested as he attempted to flee the country to . . .'

She felt as if she'd been hit on the head with a hammer. Could it really be a coincidence that they had all met at the car park at that time? Surely not, although coincidences could happen . . . But! No. She didn't believe it.

Leon had frozen into a statue.

She said, 'What about the fake texts which took you and Leon out there?'

Orlando slumped into a chair. 'The police think it was a coincidence, that someone was playing a joke on us, getting us all out to meet together. There's no trace of the texts on my phone. It's clean. Empty. Whatever.' He collapsed on to a chair and put his head in his hands.

'And on Leon's phone?'

Orlando said, 'They were hoax texts, I tell you!'

Leon half closed his eyes. He picked up his coffee cup and sipped. Watching Orlando, saying nothing.

Bea didn't know what to think. 'That's terrible. Your poor father. And you, Orlando, have you eaten?'

He shuddered. 'No, I couldn't. I keep thinking, my father didn't understand me, but he was my father, after all, and maybe we'd have come to some understanding eventually, but now . . . it's too late! If only I'd got there earlier!'

'You might have suffered the same fate,' said Bea, impatient with histrionics. And then, softening, 'Of course it's a blow, and you must feel it, terribly. So the police said you're in the clear?'

He sniffed. 'I suppose that's what they said. They were opening and shutting their mouths, but I don't think I took in a word of what they were saying. I know I said to my solicitor that I'd had enough. He agreed, we upped and left. They didn't stop us. I keep seeing my father. I look at him through the window. His eyes are closed. I knock on the window, I call

his name. Again. And again. And then I open the door and
. . . I'm never going to get him out of my head.' He rubbed
his eyes.

'Have you any other close member of the family? Wasn't
there a distant cousin? Someone you could stay with for a
while?'

'Oh, her. She hates me. The police said they'd contacted
her. I suppose I'll have to ring my father's solicitor at some
point, not that I'm expecting to benefit from the will . . . but
I don't even have a phone now. I left mine with the police,
not that they're interested, but . . .'

Leon delved into a breast pocket and slid a mobile over the
table to Orlando. 'Take this. Keep it. I've hardly used it. It's
pay as you go, and it's got nearly fifty pounds on it. Ring your
cousin. You may not like her, but families usually pull together.
You shouldn't be on your own at this difficult time.'

Another shudder. 'I know what she'll say. That if I hadn't
been the way I am, all this would never have happened.'

Was that true? Possibly.

Bea said, 'Why don't you ring your boyfriend, Charles, tell
him what's happened?'

Another shudder. 'Oh, I couldn't. I mean, he was so devastated when I told him about the arrangement with Dilys—'

'Which didn't work out.'

'No, but he might think . . . And I can't let Dilys down.
She's so fragile.'

Bea hid a smile. 'Don't worry about her. I'll see that she's
looked after.'

'Oh. Well . . .' He picked up the phone Leon had given him
and looked around. 'I'll take it upstairs, shall I? I mean, this
might take a while.' And off he went.

Leon put his empty cup down. 'I have to be off, too. I've
still got several pay as you go phones to play with.' He took
a small memo pad from his pocket, scribbled on it, paused
for a moment, concentrating . . . added another number, tore
the sheet off and handed it to Bea. 'You can get me on either
of those, but use the code as before.'

She followed him to the front door. 'Are you coming back
tonight?'

'I don't know that I ought to . . .'

They looked at one another, but didn't touch.

He said, 'Will you wait up for me?' He sounded uncertain.

She said, 'If you're not too late. Ring me.'

He nodded, picked up his coat, and left. She didn't go to the front door to see him off, but watched from behind the curtain in the sitting room as he got into Lucas's taxi and drove off. If the house was being watched, she couldn't see any sign of it.

And then there was peace and quiet.

Well, quiet. There was no peace for someone like her who could worry for England.

And, oh! She'd forgotten the rest of the food she'd cooked. If the inspector came now, it would be cold, wouldn't it?

SEVEN

Late Wednesday evening

Ten o'clock, and no sign of the inspector. Nor of Dilys. Nor of Leon.

Orlando had gone out, saying he was meeting Charles in a pub to have a good long talk. Well, that was all right, except that Orlando didn't seem to know what he'd done with his front door key, could not be trusted to deal with the alarm, and might or might not return at a reasonable hour. How late would she have to wait up for him? This was worse than being a landlady.

Five past ten, and the doorbell went.

DI Durrell. Worn out, and in a bad temper. He kicked the door shut behind him, flung down his coat and stalked into the kitchen. 'Don't speak to me. Don't even say, "Hi!" Feed me some carbohydrates and strong, sweet tea. I haven't eaten since breakfast, my wife's away with the kids at her parents and is angry because I'm not with them for their golden wedding anniversary, my DC has a filthy cold and has been sneezing all over me, and I've been handed a case I can't solve. What's more, I think I've stepped in some dog poo . . . Aargh!'

He seated himself, took off his shoe and threw it across the room.

Almost, she laughed. She'd saved him a plateful of food. She put it in the microwave to heat it up. She handed him a bottle of beer, an opener, and a glass. She remembered her mother saying, 'When the man comes home in a temper, don't argue with him. Feed the brute!'

The microwave pinged, she rescued his reheated food, stripped off the cling film and placed it before him. He poured the beer out too hastily. It was going to foam over the rim. She pushed a knife and fork at him, took the beer and the glass out of his hands, and poured it out properly.

He grumped at her. Which she took as a thank you.

He ate. She toyed with some yogurt. She didn't feel like solid food.

He pushed his plate aside. 'Don't think you can get round me with food. The case you talked about is dead as the dodo. Margrete Walford went to the car park to meet her lover, who is a swimming attendant at the pool. He never made it because he'd been held up by some minor mishap in the showers, alibi confirmed. Her husband got to her first, killed her and then killed the other one, who witnessed the crime . . . what was his name? Never mind, don't remind me, I don't need to know. Husband took fright, hared off to the airport and was arrested. End of story, good result, feather in what's-her-name's cap.'

She fetched some more yogurt and fruit out of the fridge for him, plus the container holding several different wedges of cheese. The inspector liked to eat cheese in chunks, without biscuits. There wasn't as much cheese as she'd expected. Had Orlando been having a go at it? Dilys had said something about Orlando having been a mouse in a previous incarnation. She sighed. As if . . .

The inspector drained his glass and set it down with a deep sigh.

She got out another bottle of beer for him, cleared away the dirty plates.

In tidying the table, she picked up the piece of paper Leon had left for her and thought she'd better put it somewhere safe. He'd written some gobbledegook at the bottom of the page after his telephone numbers. Letters and numbers. He was good with numbers. Could remember them better than most people. She tucked the paper under her telephone.

'Don't talk,' said the inspector, round a mouthful of cheese. 'I'm thawing rapidly, but I'm not there yet.'

She picked up the shoe he'd thrown across the room and took it to the sink. Yes, there was indeed dog poo on it. She donned rubber gloves and dealt with it.

'Aaargh.' He stretched. Sipped beer. Cut another wedge of cheese. 'As for the case I'm on, I can see I'm not going to get a result there. Black mark, Durrell. Conspiracy? Probably. But how to prove it?'

She angled an eyebrow at him. An invitation to confide.

'A beauty parlour, so called, with hairdressing at the front and cubicles for tanning, electrolysis and how's your father at the back and downstairs. It's got a high-sounding name, but I've got a sensitive nose and my nose tells me it's a hotbed of intrigue, not to mention a knocking shop after hours. Heavy breathing and soft music. Coloratura arias from staff and customers. I know who killed the stylist in the middle of a busy afternoon – or at least it has to be one of two people – but can I break their alibi? They've all got alibis, you see. Every single person was otherwise engaged when Lavender Lou got shafted with a pair of scissors.'

She filled and switched the kettle, preparing to make some coffee.

'The suspect was having her nails done, right? Next door to where Lavender Lou was supposed to be taking time out after a heavy massage session with a client. There was coming and going galore. Up the stairs with this, and down the stairs with that. The receptionist was trying to deal with a woman who'd been complaining about a recent hair-colouring session, and Kitty Kitten, who'd been spending a serious amount of time recently with Lavender Lou . . . yes, that sort of time . . . was giving an old client a manicure.

'Kitty Kitten says she heard nothing. Client agrees. They heard nothing, saw nothing, and will say nothing except how devastated they both are that lovely Lavender has stopped breathing and will no longer be playing false and loose with pretty Kitty Kitten. I got there in record time, by the way, with my new DC. She's not a bad driver, though a trifle sharp on the brakes. I thought it would be a doddle to work out who'd done it. My instincts started twanging as soon as I saw the layout, but can I break the alibi? No way, Jose. And thanks but no thanks. No coffee or I won't sleep tonight. Not that I'll get much sleep, with my wife and the kids out on the coast, which is where I ought to be.'

Bea said, 'Was it a good manicure?'

'Mm? How should I know? It looked all right to me. She took off her gloves to show me. One of those with dots and stripes in different colours. My wife treated herself to a special manicure like that for her last birthday. Very expensive it was, too.'

Bea put her chin on her hands. 'Describe it. Give me lots of detail.'

'What on earth for?'

'Indulge me.'

'Well . . .' He concentrated. 'White tips with a black edge. Stripes in different colours with glitter on them. How am I doing?'

'She took off her gloves to show you?'

A nod. 'One more piece of cheese, then I must go.'

Bea teased the piece of paper out from under the phone. Leon had written two telephone numbers, followed by the registration number of a car. Adamsson's car? How like him not to tell her outright what he wanted her to do. 'If I tell you how to break that alibi, will you trace a car for me?'

'Consider me incapable of speech. What have I missed?'

'It's what your DC has missed. I take it she doesn't normally get her nails done professionally?'

'Lord, no. She bites them. Urgh. So?'

'The sort of manicure you describe takes ages to do. You have to let each layer dry before the next is put on. You don't put your gloves on for hours and hours afterwards because the varnish might still be tacky and you would worry about smudging the design. Anyway, if you look around you, you'll see that very few women actually wear gloves nowadays. I'm wondering why the client wore them . . . perhaps to avoid getting blood on her hands when she killed Lavender Lou? You see, if the manicure had been completed just before you arrived, then it is most unlikely that she would have put her gloves on straight away. I don't know if the client killed Lavender Lou because she wanted to please Kitty Kitten, or if she was covering up for the girl herself, but if you can—'

'—get the receptionist to tell me when the manicure was supposed to have started—'

'And how long such a design should have taken?'

'You think the manicure had been finished some time before—?'

'Perhaps the day before. Or that morning at some other

establishment? I don't know which of them actually did the deed, but you should be able to play one of them off against the other.'

He leaned back in his chair. Burped. 'Mrs Abbot, I kiss your hands and feet. Metaphorically speaking.'

'Yes, here's your shoe. I'll just puff some air-freshener on it—'

'And what do I have to do in return? You said, find a car?'

She copied out the number. 'This car was spotted in the car park where the multiple homicides took place.'

'Oh, no! Not my case.'

'Certainly not. You are enquiring about an entirely different matter. A stolen car. It's no longer in the car park. It could be anywhere. In a breakers' yard, perhaps. Or at one of the airports. I think it's been dumped somewhere. But I may be wrong.'

'Why hasn't the owner reported it stolen?'

She smiled sweetly. 'Because he's missing, too. Adamsson by name. Head accountant to Holland Holdings (Overseas). Supposedly on holiday in France. But if he went to France, what was his car doing at the swimming pool?'

'Who says it was?'

'Leon Holland.'

The inspector had met Leon and formed a favourable opinion of him. He took out his notebook, sighing heavily. 'Start at the beginning . . .'

She wrinkled her nose. 'Not sure how far back to go. One thing you might also like to think about is that the outside line in my office has been bugged. I've a report here from the engineer who dealt with it. Also, I suspect someone's watching the comings and goings in this house.'

Bea paced the floor. Eleven o'clock, and no sign of Dilys, Orlando or Leon.

She was physically tired but unable to rest. Round and round in her head went the events of the day; the things that had gone wrong, that could go wrong, and what she might be able to do about them.

In the past it had been amusing to try to work out what Leon was up to. Today he'd been more open with her than usual . . . or had he? She ought to be able to guess how he was dealing with the situation at Holland Holdings. He could be a Tricky Dicky. He didn't care much about making money for himself. He'd made a fortune of his own before he was dragged back into the Holland family business. Since then he'd put his money into the companies he'd been allocated in the carve-up of Briscoe's empire.

He didn't believe Briscoe was trying to kill him.

No, that wasn't right. He suspected Briscoe was trying to kill him, but he was trying not to believe it.

He'd quarrelled with his brother over making provision for Dilys.

He'd been thrown out of his suite of rooms and his office at Briscoe Holland's headquarters in his big house in the country.

He'd set himself up in another office . . . where? She must remember to ask him.

Now, one of Leon's companies was still situated in the grounds of the Holland estate: the Holland Training College for domestic staff. Although Leon had taken it over along with the other UK companies, the college maintained the big house and grounds by supplying Briscoe with housekeepers, nurses, cooks, maids, cleaners, security guards, chauffeurs, gardeners and handymen. Etcetera.

Briscoe required a constant supply of personnel to keep himself in the manner to which he had become accustomed. It must be a constant source of irritation to him that control of the training college had passed to Leon, particularly since his younger brother had appointed a new head, sacked some of the old staff, and reorganized the schedule.

Conclusion: the training college would be the first of Leon's companies to be targeted. Leon would have understood that. So what precautions was he taking?

Bea pressed both hands to her forehead. She couldn't think straight. What if Leon had been followed when he left her house and been run down in the street? What if he were lying in a hospital bed somewhere?

She stopped that line of thought. Worrying about far-fetched possibilities wouldn't help.

Thinking constructively might.

Sybil. His sister. She'd shot off to the States at short notice, taking Bernice with her. Why? Had she taken herself out of the firing line because, although she sympathized with Leon, she wouldn't want an altercation with her brother? Sybil had wanted to take Dilys, too, but the girl had refused, partly out of fear of the unknown, partly from inertia, partly because her daddy had told her to stay.

But, Dilys had been rubbing Briscoe up the wrong way, trying to interfere with his domestic arrangements. So what had Sybil done? She'd arranged to get the girl out of the house, to stay with Bea Abbot.

Oh dear, what was Sybil going to say about Keith?

Stop worrying! Keith may not have impressed Dilys. Dilys may not see anything in him. They may never see one another again.

Bea twitched the curtain over one of the windows at the front. She couldn't see anything amiss, but she was beginning to wonder if there might be a CCTV camera in the street, monitoring whoever called at her house. There was no other explanation she could think of, to explain how Briscoe knew when Leon was, or was not, visiting her. It was rubbish to say that Jennifer or one of the other agency girls might have been feeding the information back to Briscoe, because they'd long since left the premises. Yet, as soon as Leon had arrived for his supper, Briscoe had known about it and made sure Bea knew that he knew.

Perhaps another bug had been placed somewhere in the house on the ground floor? A bug which might pick up their conversations?

But who could have planted one in the main body of the house? Had there been any callers that Bea didn't know about? Bea made a mental note to ask Dilys if she'd let anyone in without telling her.

It was clear that Briscoe thought Bea was helping Leon. Well, she was.

And that Briscoe resented that fact? It sounded like it.

If so, was Bea herself in danger? Mm. Not proven.

What could he do to attack her?

Ah. Well. Yes. He could attack her through her only and much-loved son, Max.

Bea checked the calendar. Max, his wife and delightful children were out of town until Friday. Max was a hard-working politician, a member of the House of Commons, who thought he knew best about everything. Max thought it was his responsibility to guide his fragile mama through life's turbulent waters. Max could, on occasion, be a right pain.

Max had been made a director of the Holland Training College some time previously. On the basis of this one appointment Max fancied himself as an entrepreneur who could speak with authority on all aspects of business in the House.

Bea considered him a child in such matters, but didn't say so. She was fond of her son and hoped he reciprocated.

So, if Briscoe wanted to attack Bea, he might try to get at her through Max. Which would be unpleasant, but not necessarily difficult to deal with, because . . .

Because Leon would have foreseen the problem and dealt with it. He was probably out somewhere, at this very minute, dealing with it.

How? Mm. Mm. She clicked her fingers, threw back her head and laughed.

Oh, Leon. Clever boy. If she were right . . .

The phone rang, and Leon's voice, said, 'Is that twenty-nine something?'

'Twenty-nine eleven. Have you finished wining and dining her?'

He sounded shocked. 'Would I? After the meal you gave me? She'd like a word with you.'

On to the phone came the very person Bea had been thinking about.

Anna, the recently appointed head of Holland Training College. An appointment which had been made through the Abbot Agency.

'Mrs Abbot? I've been swept off my feet. I don't know whether to laugh or cry.'

'He takes me that way sometimes, too.'

Anna was the fortyish, single mother of two teenagers, now away at university. She was maxi-efficient, with a streamlined look; fair hair swept up into a knot, sharply-tailored suits, killer heels. At one time Bea had speculated that Leon might be interested in Anna other than for professional purposes. But, apparently not.

Anna said, 'He said you knew all about it, otherwise I wouldn't have accepted, not without checking with you. It is all right, isn't it?'

'It's very much all right,' said Bea, pleased to find her suspicions verified. 'Otherwise, we'd have had you back on the agency's hands looking for another job.'

'I can't tell you how much it means to me. I'd been worried sick about what was going to happen. There were grumbling noises from the big house when I first took over, because I'd sacked two of the previous tutors. One was a man we'd found dipping his fingers in the till, and the other had been caught exposing himself in the car park.

'The gossip was that Mr Briscoe was going to encourage them to take us to employment tribunals, even though they hadn't a leg to stand on. Mr Leon kept telling me it was going to be all right, that I must hold my nerve, and I trusted him, which was just as well because when I braved the lion in his den – I mean, Mr Briscoe – he couldn't have been more charming, said he thought I'd done things the way he'd have done them. It's being so close, you see, we get gossip going both ways, and I must admit I don't like the sound of what's going on there now, not at all.'

'How did you hear, and what did you hear?'

'One of my girls was working temporarily for Mrs Evans, the housekeeper up at the big house. The one they call the Welsh Dragon, and apt the nickname is, too. Anyway, the girl told me . . . No, I'll tell you later, perhaps. Not on the phone.'

'Right. But the training college is now doing well?'

'Indeed. We tightened up the rules and did some reorganizing of classes which has made all the difference. I think I might still have to sack one of the kitchen helpers, but that's a minor matter. The atmosphere used to be so grey and murky, but now it's positively upbeat. We really had begun to pull together, but I had no idea . . . When Leon asked me to . . . Well, you could have knocked me down with a feather!'

Bea was amused. Evidently, Anna wasn't able to 'read' Leon as well as Bea.

Anna gulped. 'He said, had I a pound coin to give him, and I wondered why he'd need one. So I found one and gave it to him, and he said . . . he said I'd just bought the bulk of his training college shares! Just like that!'

'With the proviso that—?'

'Yes, of course. We've to make Dilys a non-executive director so that she gets an income from us. Pour soul. We've all been so sorry for her, what she's been through, and her father wanting shot of her. I was sworn to secrecy until we'd got everything signed and sealed at the solicitors, which we did yesterday. Still I couldn't tell anyone, but I helped him arrange a finger food and drink celebration for the tutors and the staff tonight with outside catering, everyone to dress up for it, and they all wanted to know what was going on, and I had to be mysterious and say they'd find out in due course. And that's when Leon announced it. He made a perfectly splendid speech, and there was a formal handover, with the press and photographers and everything. I did wonder if you'd be there as well, seeing as you probably put the idea into his head—'

'He thought of it all by himself. Selling you the college means you can develop it properly, you can continue to supply staff to the big house where appropriate, and Dilys's future is secured.'

'Leon is clever, isn't he? Not that I . . . I mean, well, you understand, he's not exactly my . . . I'm not exactly up to his weight.' She was telling Bea she wasn't interested, romantically.

'You mean, you'd never know what he was up to?'

Anna laughed, relieved. 'Mr Briscoe still has some shares, of course, but not many. Not enough to upset any decisions I want to make. One or two other people have a few shares – I think your son does, doesn't he? Leon's kept a few, and he's giving some to Dilys, but I now own the bulk of them. Leon said I could go to him if I ever wanted advice, but that he didn't think I'd need it. He'd asked me before if I meant to work till I retired, and I said I certainly did. At my age, I'm not likely to put my future into the hands of any man who might leave me stranded, as my first husband did. Not that I mean that Leon would . . . Sorry. That was out of order. I've had too many glasses of champagne.'

'Make the most of it,' said Bea. 'My blessing, for what it's worth. Some day soon you and I will get together and work out how we can help one another. You will train the staff, and I will find them jobs, right?'

Bea was amused. How many years was it since the college had been trying to get a link with her agency? She had resisted because she hadn't been able to trust their manager. Now, at last, she would be able to do so. Clever Leon.

Anna was happy about it, too. 'Yes, I'd like a proper arrangement with the agency. We must talk about it, soon. Oh, he's here, wanting a word.'

Crackle. Pop. Leon's voice. 'So, Bea. May I come home now?'

Home? He thought of her house as home?

She blinked. What sort of home had he ever had? He'd grown up in the charge of hired help. His mother had hardly ever been around. He'd gone out into the great wide world as soon as he could and had won through to some sort of stability with a partner who'd upped and died on him last year. He'd owned a millionaire's dream of a house and sold it. He had a pied-à-terre in the Barbican, which he said was bleak and cold. And lonely? He'd been thrown out of his rooms at the big house.

Of course, he could go to a hotel, but he was saying that he needed the comforts of home. She hesitated.

'Or,' he said, in a flat voice, 'we could meet somewhere in town. At the Ritz, perhaps? I hear their bedlinen is the finest in the land.'

That put her back on track. 'Forget it,' she said, briskly. 'I can't leave because neither Dilys nor Orlando have returned, and I don't think either of them have a key.'

'I do,' he said, and broke the connection.

Half laughing and half angry, Bea put the receiver down. 'Now what have I done!'

Half past eleven

Dilys rang the bell. Bea turned off the alarm to let her in, and the girl drifted past her into the hall, saying, 'Sorry, I forgot my key. Are you all right?' She didn't wait for an answer, but disappeared up the stairs before Bea could question her.

There was colour in Dilys's cheeks, and her eyes were bright, so Bea deduced that the evening had gone well.

Orlando followed shortly after, also bright of cheek and eye but nowhere near as happy. 'Don't talk to me about Charles!' he said, and stormed off up the stairs before Bea could say anything.

Bea went into the kitchen to feed Winston for the last time that day and to make herself a cup of cocoa.

A few minutes later Leon's key turned in the lock. He let himself in, saying, 'The alarm isn't on. Shall I do it for you? You'd better give me the number.'

She sang it out to him, and he dealt with it for her. He was good with figures, wasn't he? He deposited his coat and travel bag in the hall, saying, 'Whatever you're making, is there one for me, too?'

He was wearing another charcoal grey business suit. He went into the living room, taking off his golden silk tie and loosening his collar. He looked stunning, but tired.

She took him a mug of cocoa and sat beside him on the settee. She tried to work it out. He'd had a hard day, what with spending time with the police and all. He'd had an early supper with her, gone somewhere to get changed, driven out to the college, overseen the transfer of authority and driven back. Or had Lucas driven him? Yes, probably.

She said, 'Congratulations. You've saved the college, provided for Dilys's future, and avoided war with your brother.'

'All in a day's work, ma'am.'

'"A man's got to do what a man's got to do." Will you regret what it cost you to avert the war?'

He sipped cocoa, set the mug aside, and lay down with his head on her lap. 'My mother used to say, "Don't upset your brother, there's a good boy."' He lifted her hand and placed it on his forehead, closing his eyes. 'Say it, Bea. Say it.'

She stroked his forehead. 'Yes, you have been a good boy. A very good boy.'

She hadn't realized how tense he'd been until that minute.

Muscle by muscle, he relaxed. His breathing slowed. She continued to stroke his forehead.

He said, 'I may have won this battle, but what of the next, and the one after that?'

'You'll manage.'

'You know why I didn't tell you what I was doing?'

'Oh, yes. You thought that if I knew, I'd be worried about Max getting involved. But he's not due back in London till Friday. You can leave me to deal with him. If you haven't already done so.'

'You know me so well.' He smiled to himself at some thought he was not prepared to share with her.

'You've given him something to keep him quiet?'

'Mm. I don't think I've got the strength to climb the stairs. May I sleep here?'

'I'll fetch a duvet and some pillows.'

But she didn't move yet. She'd heard that women needed to be mother, wife and child to their man, at different times. She could do the mother bit all right. The wife bit? Maybe, but not yet. The child . . .? Women usually stopped feeling like children after their parents died, but men didn't. Or, some didn't. Leon still had a child inside him, wanting his mother, trying to please her, even after all these years.

She said, 'You're a very good boy,' and kissed his forehead . . . only to find he'd fallen asleep.

And how was she to get out from under him, pray? She was not, repeat not, going to spend the night sitting upright on her settee. As soon as he was deeply asleep, she'd move.

EIGHT

B ea leaned on the banisters as she slowly made her way downstairs. She'd woken at gone midnight, still on the settee, shivering. Leon had been deeply asleep and hadn't moved even when she wriggled out from under him. She'd thrown a rug over him and departed for her own bed, without attempting to read her Bible or say her prayers.

She hadn't attempted it this morning, either.

In the old days Maggie had brought her a cup of tea in the mornings. Dilys didn't seem to have thought of it. Bea missed Maggie, a lot. They kept in touch by phone, but it wasn't the same as being able to tell one another the details of the day . . .

The house seemed very quiet. Bea picked the newspapers up off the mat and listened, but couldn't hear anyone else moving about. The first thing Maggie used to do in the mornings was to turn on both the radio and the television. Maggie liked to surround herself with sound. Dilys was quiet as a mouse.

Coffee. Essential. Breakfast. Something for a slight headache. She felt eighty in the shade that morning. Nice, bright morning. Birds chirruping. Winston the cat yowling. Ugh!

And here came Dilys, chirpy as a sparrow. Singing to herself. Singing!?

'Good morning, good morning,' sang Dilys, all smiles. 'What do you fancy for breakfast this morning? Shall I pop out for some fresh rolls or something? It would be no trouble, I assure you. I'm finding my way around like nobody's business now.'

Bea shuddered. 'Sit down, Dilys. We need to talk.'

The girl looked at her watch. 'Yes, of course.' She didn't

sit but clattered plates and mugs on to the table. 'Can you lend me a couple of quid? The battery on my watch has run down, and Keith says he'll show me where I can get another fitted at lunchtime, but I'm a bit short of the readies so—'

Bea tried not to shriek. 'Dilys, please. Sit down. I have something important to tell you. Your Uncle Leon will explain it all to you later, but you need to know—'

'Is he here? Did he stay the night? Daddy said he was sweet on you, but that you had more sense than to get married again at your time of life.'

Bea took the girl by the arm and steered her to a seat. 'Please. Sit. Listen carefully to what I have to say because it's going to affect everything you do in future. Your uncle—'

'Did I hear my name mentioned?' Leon appeared in the doorway, still dressed in his business gear, looking rumpled. ''Morning, Dilys: we need to talk. Bea, may I use one of your bathrooms?'

Dilys squeaked. 'Oh, what a fright you gave me! Do you want some cereal for breakfast?'

Leon rolled his eyes. Bea wondered how long it would be before he regretted giving away so much of his capital to ease this silly little girl's path in life.

Bea said, 'Leon, you may use the guest room's en suite, on the first floor. You want a full breakfast, I assume?'

He nodded and went off up the stairs with his travelling bag. Bea made a cafetière of coffee, trying to work out where Leon was keeping his clothes at the moment and who was doing his laundry. Was he still using Lucas's house as his base and getting Lucas's wife to look after his clothes? Well, that was his affair and nothing whatever to do with her. She said, 'Dilys, your uncle has—'

Orlando appeared, not looking rumpled. He was dressed in his freshly laundered bright-pink shirt, jeans and boots, and carrying a denim jacket. Had Dilys got up early to attend to his clothes?

Orlando said, 'Oh, thanks. A quick cup of coffee is just what I need. The office want me to check out some barn or other near the airport. I know there's a tithe barn somewhere out there, but can't remember exactly where it is.'

'Good morning, Orlando.' Dilys dimpled at him, pouring coffee into mugs. 'So you've still got a job? I'm so glad.'

'No thanks to Charles. He's throwing me out of the flat.'

'Well, you can always stay here,' said Dilys, handing him a mug of coffee. 'There. Black and strong, just as you like it. No sugar for you. Two for me.'

Bea clenched her teeth and counted to ten. Well, to five, actually. She said, 'Orlando, you are welcome to stay here one more night, but I do think you should make your own arrangements for the future.'

'Don't worry, Orlando,' said Dilys, helping herself to cereal. 'My Uncle Leon's moved in as well, but that still leaves the two bedrooms upstairs.'

Orlando ignored Bea to speak direct to Dilys. 'Well, I suppose I could fetch all my kit from Charles's place and bring it here this evening. Unless you could go and fetch it for me?'

'Sorry,' said Dilys. 'Otherwise engaged. Keith's meeting me for lunch, and then—'

Bea broke in. 'Have you got Keith's phone number on you, Dilys? Would you ring him, now, this minute? I need him to check if we've got a bug on my landline up here in the kitchen. I'd also like him to see if there's a camera trained on our front door to monitor who's coming and going. Urgent.'

The two children looked at her, horrified. They'd managed to escape reality for a little while. And she'd most unkindly brought them back down to earth.

Dilys put her spoon down, slowly. 'Keith's got another job on this morning, but . . . yes, I'm sure he'll come.' The sparkle had gone out of her.

Orlando bleated, 'But the police arrested Margrete's husband.'

'I don't think this bugging has anything to do with the police,' said Bea. She could hear the toilet flush upstairs. That would be Leon. She could also hear movement down below as the girls arrived at the agency for the day's work. She was running late. Leon would be down for his breakfast soon. 'I'm going to make scrambled eggs for breakfast. Any takers?'

Dilys shook her head. She fished her phone out of her pocket and went off with it. So Keith had given her his number already?

Bea tried to gentle her voice. 'Well, Orlando: how did you get on when you rang your elderly cousin? Don't you want time off to meet her, see to the arrangements?'

An empty look. 'She doesn't need me. She said so, in so many words. She said my father always said I'd be the death of him. She says he wouldn't have wanted me to have anything to do with his funeral . . . Not that we can have the body for a while yet.' He swallowed. 'I told her I had every intention of doing the right thing by him and by her, but it didn't go down well. There's family for you! Or not, in this case.'

He'd been disinherited by his father and slagged off by his cousin. Oh, the pain of it. Orlando wasn't coping as well as Leon had . . . but Leon had been shown the door at a younger age and was made of stronger material.

Orlando shook his curls. Brightly smiling, he said, 'The coffee was fine. I really must get going. I'll bring my things round later, if that's all right with you.' He didn't wait for a reply but slid out of the kitchen as the phone rang.

Bea picked it up, warily.

'Another wild goose chase.' The inspector. Still in a bad temper?

'Good morning to you, too,' said Bea. 'You found the car, then?' The coffee in the pot had all been drunk, and Leon would soon be down, needing sustenance. Multitasking, she switched the kettle on. 'Where did it turn up?'

'Burned out, in a back street on a housing estate. If you parked a strange car there, it would be stripped and burned out within the day.'

Bea emptied out the coffee grounds from the cafetière and poured in more ground coffee without bothering to measure it. 'Was Adamsson in it at the time?'

The inspector made a noise like a boiling kettle. Or perhaps it was the kettle, boiling. She filled the cafetière to the top.

'No, Adamsson was not in it. There was no body in it.'

'In the boot, perhaps?'

'No. Empty.'

'Then he's still missing?'

'Tcha! Missing? No, he's on holiday.'

'Who says so?' She pressed down on the plunger.

'His office. Apparently, his car had been stolen the morning he was due to go off on holiday to France. He hadn't got time to report it to the police and asked them to do it – which they forgot to do. Adamsson told them he was going to rent a car and be on his way. I suppose it was taken by joyriders. They would have used it for a couple of days and then dumped it.'

'At the swimming pool? You're joking! Are we sure that Mr Adamsson junior is abroad? Can his father contact him?'

'I sincerely hope you're not asking me to spend any more time on this.' Click. He'd broken the connection.

Leon arrived to put his arm around her and kiss her cheek. 'Why does your coffee smell better than anyone else's?' He was wearing a different grey business suit and a fresh-from-the-packet shirt, this time with a light-blue satin tie. He looked well-barbered and ready for anything the world might throw at him. Captain of Industry, and the rest. Tra la.

She ladled muesli into a bowl, added milk and set some bread to toast. 'Adamsson's car has turned up, burned out. No corpse inside. His office says he reported to them that his car had been stolen, and that he intended to tour France in a rented car. My policeman refuses to help look for him. Orlando's gone to work; Charles is throwing him out of his flat. Dilys and Keith have become an item. Oh, Keith is our computer techie, who—'

He picked up the newspaper. 'Tell me all that again in ten minutes' time. I may look awake, but I'm not. Ah, coffee . . .!' He reached for a mug.

'Scrambled eggs?'

No reply. He'd turned to the Business section of *The Times*.

She dumped the bowl of muesli in front of him.

One hand came out to connect with the spoon, scoop up a mouthful of cereal and disappear behind the paper.

She said, 'This is like a cartoon. Man too busy with world affairs to communicate. Woman hovers, waiting to be noticed. I should have ordered a copy of *Hello!* magazine to entertain myself with.'

'Mmh? Have you got the *Financial Times*?' He held out his hand for it.

She did not have the *Financial Times* delivered. Did he really expect her to provide it, just like that? Or to run out to the shops to buy him one?

She considered hitting him over the head with a frying pan. She considered giving him the money and telling him to buy one for himself. She thought of telling him that he snored, which would be a knockout blow for any would-be lover. But, he didn't, much. His soft purr was acceptable.

She wondered if this were not another test. Last night she'd played mother to the little boy hidden way inside him. She could go on treating him like a little boy. But, no, that would not be a good basis for a long-term relationship.

She said, 'Your brother told Dilys I was far too sensible to take you on board. How right he was.'

The newspaper was slowly lowered. Narrowed eyes surveyed her.

She said, brightly, 'I am not your mother, your housekeeper, your mistress or your wife.'

He raised the paper again. Pushed the empty cereal bowl aside.

She collected the toast and found the butter. Started to beat up some eggs. 'Scrambled eggs coming up.'

From behind the paper: 'With smoked salmon?'

'Not unless you've ordered a delivery of it.' She swished the eggs into a pan, seasoned and stirred. 'Did you take in what I said earlier about Adamsson and Dilys?'

The newspaper was carefully folded inside out and laid aside. 'I have a video conference meeting at my new office at ten.'

'You'd better get a move on, then.' She placed a plate of scrambled eggs on toast before him. 'Would you like me to cut the toast up into soldiers for you?'

She wasn't sure if he'd be offended, or laugh. He didn't seem sure, himself. Then, he grinned. 'We've turned into Beatrice and Benedict. Two people attracted to one another, but set in their own ways.'

'It's probably too late for either of us to change.' She poured him a second mug of coffee. 'Did you hear what I said about Adamsson's car?'

A nod. He was eating now. Fast. A glance at his wristwatch. 'Where's Dilys?'

Now that was indeed a good question. She'd gone out of the room to ring Keith . . . ages ago. 'Dunno. Any instructions for today?'

'If your policeman refuses to look for Adamsson, I'll have to see if I can trace him myself. Here.' He produced a simple cellphone. 'You might need this to contact me direct at any time. You'll set up a meeting with Anna to discuss a closer cooperation with the training college?'

'Yes, we've agreed that already. Is your brother going to have a tantrum when he finds out what you've done?'

'Evans the Welsh Dragon was lurking there last night, tight-lipped, in the background. We should get the fallout any minute. I've got meetings all day. I'll try to find out what arrangements have been made for keeping in touch with Adamsson. Take you out this evening?'

'Dilys,' she said, reminding him. 'Orlando.'

His phone rang. 'Yes,' he said, answering it. 'I'm coming.' A last gulp of coffee. 'Lucas is outside. I'll leave it to you to deal with Dilys. Ask her to come out to supper with us tonight. As for Orlando: don't let him move in. You'll never get rid of him.'

He was off, collecting his travel bag and overcoat in the hall as he went. He'd taken her newspaper as well. Bother.

Dilys drifted in, smiling. She'd actually got some colour in her cheeks for once. 'Keith's nice, isn't he? I told him about being married to Benton and how awful it had all been, and about losing my two boys. Keith was so lovely that I cried, but only a bit. He thinks he's too old for me, but I told him he's only got into that way of thinking about himself because he hasn't had anyone to look after him since his wife died. He said he thought I was as pretty as a spring flower, and that made me laugh, because no one has ever said that to me before. And I told him so, and he said . . .'

Bea tuned the rest out as she cleared the table, only to take notice when Dilys concluded, '. . . and he's promised to have his hair cut before we go out to lunch.'

Bea reminded her: 'Did you ask him to check this phone for a bug?'

Dilys reddened. 'I forgot. I'll ask him at lunchtime. You don't mind my having a few hours off, do you?'

Bea fought back an impulse to slap the girl. 'Sit down, Dilys. This is important.'

Her sharp tone reduced the girl to a dither. Her colour fled, and she bit her lip, ready to cry.

'It's all right, Dilys,' said Bea, trying to reassure. 'It's just that you need to know that you don't have to go out with anyone you don't like—'

The lower lip quivered. 'But I do like him.'

'Yes, yes. He's a nice man. But you need to know something else too. Your Uncle Leon has made a considerable sacrifice to ensure you a decent income in future. You will be able to rent and furnish a home for yourself and Bernice. You won't be a millionaire, but—'

'Oh, that's wonderful!' Hands clasped, eyes shining. 'Then I can set Keith up in business, he can take on someone to help him, and . . .'

Bea groaned, but Dilys wasn't listening. The girl jumped up, pulling out her mobile. 'Just wait till I tell him!'

'Dilys!'

The girl was off.

Bea sat down and closed her eyes. You just couldn't help some people, could you? Give them a sack of gold, and they fritter it away. Dilys had signed everything she possessed away to that toad Benton who'd gone through a pretence of marriage with her. Now she was going to part with all that Leon had given her.

There was only one possible bright spot on the horizon, which was that Keith was a very different sort of man from Benton. If it were explained to him properly, Keith might well decline to take what the girl was offering. Well, he might. But it would take a man of iron rectitude to look a gift horse in the mouth, wouldn't it?

Bea said, 'May the good Lord preserve me from idiots.'

And, talking of idiots, it was more than time for her to go downstairs and see what other problems the agency had to face that day.

Thursday afternoon

Keith had done his job well. All the phones were back on. All the computers were in working order. All the girls, including Jennifer, were back on schedule. And what was Bea supposed to be doing about her? The inspector had said it wasn't his department and she was supposed to take the bug into the local police station. Hmph. And when was she supposed to do that, may she ask? It would have to be after she'd shut the agency down for the day.

Carrie flitted to and fro, checking on this, commending that. Bea was too busy to leave her office in order to make lunch upstairs, and sent out for sandwiches instead. She did spend a minute worrying about what she'd got in the fridge or freezer for supper until she remembered that Leon was supposed to be taking them out.

Dilys was nowhere to be seen. Bea was grateful for that at first. And then she worried what the girl might be up to. The phone rang. For her. A customer wanting the moon. The moon and sixpence. Wasn't that a film? She couldn't remember. A demanding customer, anyway. Bea forgot about Dilys for the time being.

Keith didn't appear. She thought about phoning him direct. Her phone rang. Another query. She let Keith slide out of her mind.

Anna rang, asked if she could drop in to see Bea that evening some time to discuss the future of Holland Training College. Agreed. Perhaps she could join them for supper?

A bottle of wine was placed on her desk. The inspector. Smiling, for a change.

Bea swivelled round in her chair. 'You cracked the mystery of the lovelorn manicurist?'

'When the gloves came off, tears followed. Kitty Kitten done it. Her client was her very own older sister, who'd had a manicure that morning at another salon but was prepared to provide an alibi. They're both in custody as we speak.' He seated himself, leaned back, and gave a long, long sigh. 'I suppose I ought to apologize. My wife says so, anyway. She says I make scandalous use of your brains and that, whenever she's out of town, I impose on your good nature to cook for me. She's right, of course.'

Bea narrowed her eyes at him. 'Apology accepted. So what brings you here today? Don't tell me. Adamsson's turned up. Dead.'

A tinge of colour came into the inspector's cheeks. 'He's touring in France. And it's not my case.'

Bea ignored that. 'Let me guess. The dead woman's husband – what's his name? Walford? He's got a good solicitor, and he's produced an alibi for the time of Margrete's death? He wants out of custody. The powers that be are uneasy. They thought they'd got an open and shut case. Husband kills cheating wife, and then goes on to get rid of the unfortunate Lord Lethbury who happened to be a witness. All other theories were discounted because, bingo! They'd got the husband bang to rights.'

'He probably used a hit man.'

Her face must have expressed amused doubt, because he shifted uncomfortably in his chair. 'I'm sure they'll find a connection.'

'You've come to see me, which means that you aren't convinced. You remember only too well that first impressions might be misleading. Lord Lethbury might have been the intended victim, and Margrete Walford the inconvenient witness. You've remembered that the peer's son, who was at odds with his father, was the one who discovered the body but didn't report it, and that Leon Holland had also been lured to the car park under false pretences.'

'It's not my case.'

Carrie put her head around the door. 'Everything all right? Do you want me to stay late tonight?'

'Come in for a moment, Carrie. Inspector, I told you last night that we found a bug had been placed on my telephone yesterday and you told me to take it to the local police station today – which I haven't yet had a chance to do. We also have a report from the engineer who found it for us. Do you have a minute to interview the girl who made the bugging possible?'

'Not my scene. You know perfectly well you have to go through the usual channels.'

Carrie said, 'I could ask Jennifer to stay behind, and you could have a word.'

'No, no. I—'

Carrie wasn't letting him get away with it. She stepped back into the main office. 'Where's Jennifer? She hasn't gone already, has she?'

Voices were raised. 'She said she'd got a tummy ache and went off a few minutes ago.'

Carrie relayed the bad news to Bea and the inspector. 'Shall I check to see if she's cleared her things out of her desk?'

Bea's phone rang.

Leon. 'Is that twenty-nine something?'

'Eleven. Yes.' She wasn't sure she wanted the inspector to overhear whatever Leon had to say.

'You've got someone with you?'

'Yes.' She turned to her diary, flipping pages, making out that she was speaking to a client. 'Go ahead.'

'Something someone . . . It's been bothering me. I tried to check it out. Adamsson. You know I said I tried his mobile and it didn't ring or go to voicemail? I've tried again. There's no service on his mobile. It's dead. Today is Thursday. A week ago today I met Adamsson at my office in town. We arranged to meet up again when I got back from Birmingham and pencilled an appointment in for *today*. A week on. He said nothing about meeting on Tuesday, or about going away on holiday. So—'

'Someone is lying. I have an interested party here. The inspector. Leon, I think it's time you reported Adamsson junior as missing.' She handed the phone to the inspector. 'Leon Holland saw Adamsson last Thursday and arranged to meet up again today. He spotted Adamsson's car, unattended, in the swimming pool car park. His mobile is not in service. His car has turned up, burned out. Leon wants to report the man missing.'

For a moment she thought the inspector would decline to

take the phone, but then he shrugged and did so. She left him to it. Carrie met her in the doorway, lifting her hands in despair. 'Jennifer's cleaned out her drawer. She kept a pair of slippers here to wear at work. They've gone, and so has her umbrella. It doesn't look as if she means to come back.'

Bea tried to look on the bright side. 'Well, at least we don't have to pay her this last week's wages.'

NINE

Thursday evening

The inspector slammed the phone down. 'For the umpteenth time, This Is Not My Case!'

'I know that,' said Bea, dropping into the chair behind her desk. 'But what am I supposed to do? Leon and that poor creature Orlando were lured out to a car park by false text messages. Orlando was supposed to meet up with his father to discuss a financial deal cooked up by him and Briscoe Holland. Leon was due to meet Mr Adamsson, Briscoe Holland's chief accountant. Leon spotted Adamsson's car, unattended. He'd already had someone attempt to run him down. He was on bad terms with his brother, the head of the company. He suspected a trap, so he turned tail and left. Orlando was not so fortunate, or so wary. He didn't spot Adamsson's car, but found his father and a woman unknown to him, dead in their cars. He panicked and fled. On his way out he spotted Leon entering the car park, watched him try to make a phone call, and then leave.

'Now, whichever of the two was originally meant to be the victim, doesn't it seem odd to you that both Leon and Orlando were sent to the car park by text messages with a Holland Holdings connection?'

The inspector threw up his hands. 'Someone was playing a practical joke on them.'

'Why were Lethbury and Adamsson present? Were they, too, misdirected, and if so, by whom? Was Lethbury the intended target? Were Leon and Orlando led there to direct suspicion to them?'

Despite himself, the inspector was drawn into the mystery. 'You haven't proved Adamsson was there. His office says he went to France, and they should know.'

'Leon says they were due to meet up, and *he* should know.'

The inspector winced. 'I suppose getting Leon and Orlando there would certainly confuse the issue, if Adamsson wanted to kill Lethbury. In that case, Margrete's murder is collateral damage.'

Bea waved that aside. 'I can't see that mild little man Adamsson as a double murderer. Why should he want to kill Lethbury, anyway? Nor Orlando. And certainly not Leon who, in any case, is given an alibi by Orlando.'

'Provided you believe Orlando.'

Bea played with a pencil. 'I suppose the police have looked at what's on Lord Lethbury's phone?'

'I imagine so. It's NOT MY CASE!'

Bea went on: 'Leon is sure someone is trying to kill him.'

The inspector snorted. 'I suppose he thinks it's his brother, the Lord High and Mighty head of Holland International.'

'No,' said Bea. 'He's been given every reason to think so, but he doesn't. As I told you, my phone here has been bugged. Fortunately, we discovered what had happened before any major damage was done. As soon as Leon returned, the phone rang and I was asked to listen to a recorded message from Leon's brother, accusing him of this and that, and threatening to destroy him. In spite of this, Leon doesn't believe his brother wants to kill him, and I trust his judgement. But, how did they know Leon had returned, because we'd already removed the bug on the phone?'

The inspector threw up his hands again. 'What do you want me to do?'

She tried to think clearly. 'If Margrete's husband has managed to throw doubt on the original theory that his wife was the main target, the police will go back to thinking it was Lord Lethbury. I imagine whoever is in charge will want to have Orlando in for questioning again.'

'I think you can take that as read.'

'Leon thinks Adamsson is missing. Do you agree with me that there is more to his disappearance than meets the eye?'

'But you don't think Adamsson is the murderer.' He laughed. 'Don't tell me . . . You think Adamsson is dead as well!'

'His car is. Very.'

'You are trying to make out that the original target was

Adamsson, and that the others were collateral damage?'
Incredulous.

Bea threw up her hands. 'I don't understand what's going
on. If it isn't Briscoe Holland who's behind the I Hate Leon
brigade, then who is?'

'It's not unknown for victims of assault to declare that their
nearest and dearest couldn't possibly be behind the attack,
even though there is ample evidence to prove that they were.
Brothers have been known to fall out before now.'

'Leon grew up away from his family. He doesn't have any
romantic views about them.'

'Nevertheless,' said the inspector, getting to his feet, 'that's
what it will turn out to be. Sibling rivalry. The old buck
resenting the young stag who's challenging his right to rule
the herd.'

'But—'

'Look, I think I've been very patient, but enough is enough.
Have you personally witnessed anything to do with the
murders? No. You're feeding me hearsay, and you know
perfectly well that That's Not Admissible As Evidence!' He
almost shouted the last words at Bea.

Bea suppressed an urge to shout back. She looked down
and away from him, thinking that he hadn't used to be so
bad-tempered. They'd always been able to have a laugh about
the case in the old days. What had caused this change?

She said, 'We've known one another for quite some time.
Is anything wrong?'

He thumped her desk. 'Nothing's the matter!'

Bea caught sight of Carrie's head appearing round the door.
Bea signed to Carrie, *Not now!* Carrie's head disappeared. Bea
tried to remember what appointments she had that afternoon
but couldn't think straight. Well, whoever it was must wait.

The inspector stayed where he was, head down, leaning on
her desk with both hands.

'Tell me,' said Bea, in her softest voice.

He turned away from her, reaching for a handkerchief in
his pockets and not finding one. He took a tissue from the
box on her desk, walked away to the window. With his back
to her. 'I spend my time trying to take criminals off the streets,

trying to make everyday life easier for the majority. I deal with the scum of society. I see things, hear things which would scare the living daylights out of the man in the street. I make jokes about my work because otherwise I'd go mad. But sometimes, just sometimes, it gets me down and I think about taking early retirement.'

Bea drew in her breath. She was shocked and dismayed.

He said, 'My wife says I'm heading for a nervous break-down, and she's right. I'm going to put in for some leave tomorrow.'

She was ashamed of herself. The inspector was a good man, on the side of the saints. He'd been showing signs of strain, and she had refused to see them. He was a strong man, up against the forces of evil. He dealt fairly with everyone. He hadn't complained about his lack of promotion in recent years, but she had understood he was not always fairly dealt with in that respect. He deserved a break.

Leon would cope. She thought of him, stoically accepting his family's rejection of him . . . and Orlando trying to come to terms with the same thing. They'd cope, because they were innocent.

A twisty thought entered her head. It isn't always enough to rely on innocence when evil is at work.

She set that thought aside. The inspector was her very good friend. They'd been through a lot together. He'd asked her for help, not always in so many words, but implicitly. She must try to comfort him. She couldn't cuddle him as she would a child. She couldn't put her arms around him. He wasn't her husband.

But somehow she must show that she felt his pain. She went to stand beside him, almost touching. She prayed, *Lord, give me the right words to say.*

She didn't know what she was going to say till she said it. 'Hold fast.'

'Easier said than done. You say you're a Christian, but I can't believe in a God who allows so much evil into the world.' He was hurting. His fists were clenched. He might hit her, or the window . . . or leave the building and walk straight under a car.

She said, 'It doesn't matter how little you believe. He said he'd always be there, waiting for you to remember that he loves you. Standing beside you.'

'Don't tell me that you can see him?' Angry, trying to joke.

She didn't reply. No, she couldn't see him, but she did believe that he was always beside her, waiting for her to turn to him for guidance, for comfort, for peace. Most of the time she believed that, anyway.

He blew his nose. 'Well, I can't stand here talking all day.' He looked at his watch. 'You'll forget what I said, of course.'

'No. I won't forget. I'll remember.'

He turned a blotchy face on her. He was still angry. But also, perhaps, touched. Calmer. A joking tone, 'You'll pray for me? Is that what you mean?'

'You know I will. Get a babysitter and take your wife out for the evening. Make plans for your holiday.'

He was putting himself back together again, ignoring his moment of weakness. 'Well, as I said, it's not my case. Tell Leon to report whatever it is he's worried about himself.'

'I heard you.'

She saw him out. The agency rooms were deserted, except for Carrie shutting down the system and getting ready to leave. Carrie was fidgeting, darting looks at Bea. Wanting something. Bea was too tired to find out what it might be. That talk with the inspector had taken it out of her. All she wanted was a quiet sit-down while supper was being cooked – preferably by someone else. They were going out, weren't they? And Anna was expected, too. Bother. She could do with an early night.

But, Carrie was still fidgeting.

Bea made an effort. 'You wanted me for something, earlier?'

'Dilys came back with Keith. She's been out with him all afternoon.' An even tone, concealing irritation. 'Dilys says she wants to replace a button on his shirt and that she's sure you won't mind her raiding your sewing basket, so she's taken him upstairs.'

Bea nodded, but didn't comment.

'This box arrived for you.' Carrie indicated a hefty cardboard box on her desk. 'I thought it could wait till tomorrow, but the man who brought it said you'd ordered it for delivery today.'

'I haven't ordered anything. I suppose we'd better see what it is.'

Carrie produced a pair of sharp scissors, and together they prised up the lid and tackled the bubble wrap inside.

'Eeeek!' Carrie stumbled back against her desk.

Bea's mouth dried.

Her hands shook as she pulled apart the last layer of packaging.

Soft black fur.

Winston? Their cat?

He didn't often come down into the agency rooms but, if someone left a window open, especially in the summer, he did venture in to be stroked, given titbits and made much of.

The cat in the box was very, very dead.

Bea felt for a chair and slumped into it.

Carrie pulled herself upright. She managed, 'A glass of water?' And went off to get it.

Bea put out a hand, with care, to touch the soft fur. The cat was curled around itself. Winston usually lay stretched out at full length. He was a very big cat.

Perhaps he'd died somewhere on the street, met with an accident, and someone who knew where he lived had thought fit to return him to Bea? To be opened immediately.

She felt numb. Shock.

She stroked him. His fur was cold and . . . not quite right. Too short. And, he seemed a lot smaller in death.

She tried to lift him out, thinking in a fuzzy sort of way that she must bury him in the garden . . . and let him fall back into the box.

Carrie brought a glass of water and handed it to Bea. 'Drink up.'

Bea was shaking. She took the glass of water and drank it off. Cold, cold. That was good.

At the second attempt, Bea lifted the cat out of the packaging. She realized with another shock that this cat was too light, far too light for Winston.

The cat mewed. Bea fumbled and dropped it back into the box.

Carrie stifled a scream and backed away.

Bea closed her eyes. Her heartbeat had gone into overdrive.

She picked the cat up again. It was a pretty little black puss. A toy cat. With a mechanical 'mew' when you touched its tummy.

A joke, Mrs Abbot. Someone is playing a practical joke on you.

She firmed her voice. 'It's a toy, Carrie. It's not Winston.'

Stop shaking, Mrs Abbot. Take it in your stride. Yes, you know and I know that this has been sent to you as a warning, to let you know that at any time they could kill your real, live cat.

She put the toy cat up on the shelf. 'The girls will enjoy stroking him and making him mew, just like a real cat.'

Stop shaking, I tell you!

She said aloud, 'It gave us quite a shock, didn't it? Are you all right now, Carrie? Thank you for the water. I was quite taken in for a moment or two.' She pushed the packaging back into the box and set it aside. If she could get the police to pay attention to her problems, she'd give them the box to look at.

Carrie had her hand to her heart. 'What a fright . . .!'

'Yes.' Bea tried to smile. 'That's enough shocks for today, I think. Time to pack up. Are you all right to face the rush hour traffic? I must go and feed Winston. He always wants food at this time of day.'

She was still shaking, though not as badly as before. She couldn't wait to get rid of Carrie so that she could look for Winston.

Carrie said, 'Well, if you're sure . . .?' And tried to laugh. 'Luckily, I'm staying in town tonight, meeting an old friend for supper.'

Bea saw Carrie out, switched on the separate alarm system for the agency. She took the inside stairs, locking the door which led from the basement to the ground floor behind her. She made an effort to remember what she was supposed to be doing that evening. They were going out to eat somewhere, weren't they?

It would be an informal occasion. She'd bought a new dress

the other day, which she was looking forward to giving an
outing. It was midnight blue with a sequinned bodice and lace
sleeves. Rather fetching. But, considering all that was going
on, a warm jumper and a woollen skirt would be more appropriate for a family-type get-together. She was looking forward
to seeing Anna again. Hopefully, she'd have some worthwhile
gossip about Briscoe to report.

Would Briscoe really have bothered to send her a toy cat
which could be mistaken for Winston? She couldn't think
straight. Because if he had done that, then he would be capable
of trying to kill his brother . . . or would he?

She must tell Leon about it, ask his opinion. Now, where
was Winston? She couldn't rest until she'd found him and
checked that he was all right. Ought she to keep him indoors
in future? No, he wouldn't agree to that.

And then there was the inspector. She switched off her cares
to pray for him. *Dear Lord, forgive our foolish ways. He's a
good man, pulled down by the dreadful things he has to deal
with. You have always said that we will not be given tasks too
hard for us to manage, but sometimes we need time off to
recuperate. If he doesn't get away soon he might resign from
the force, and that would be a great loss . . . besides which,
what would he do with the rest of his life? Please be with him
in this, his dark hour.*

She was conscious of people shouting as she mounted the
stairs. There were lights on in the hall. Wait a minute, wasn't
Dilys supposed to be . . .? And whose were all those bundles
and suitcases in the hall?

Orlando's? Oh, surely not.

Men's voices, shouting. In the living room. Lights were on
in the kitchen, as well. And someone was cooking. Now who
would that be?

Thump. More shouting.

Winston came streaking out of the living room, ears flat-
tened. In the hall he paused to give his bib a lick. He spotted
Bea and changed direction to wind around her legs. I'm
starving, feed me, I love you, I need food. Now!

She picked him up to give him a cuddle. The great big
lummock! The stupid, big, furry thing! How dare he give her

such a fright as to pretend to be dead and delivered in a parcel! Well, not him. Obviously. But someone.

Winston's tolerance for being cuddled was minimal. He wriggled around, jumped down to the floor, gave her a look of offended dignity, and stalked off into the kitchen . . . from which came the aforesaid cooking sounds and smells.

Curry?

Keith, swaddled in an apron, was wielding a wooden spoon while tasting something which was cooking in one of her largest saucepans. He'd got the radio on, playing softly. Dilys was seated at the table with a sharp knife, paring cooking apples and laying slices in a pattern into a pastry-base in a flan tin.

What a delightfully domestic scene, and how annoyed it made her feel! And, weren't they supposed to be all going out for supper tonight? But if the meal was already being cooked . . . and it would be less stressful, wouldn't it? She must act pleased that Keith and Dilys were preparing the meal.

Dilys saw her first. 'Apple tart for supper, Mrs Abbot. Keith's favourite.'

'Sounds delicious,' she said.

On seeing her, Keith dropped the spoon and looked sheepish. 'Mrs Abbot, I hope you don't mind. Dilys said something about checking your landline up here and looking out for a camera which might be recording your movements. Then young Orlando arrived with his luggage and needed help bringing it in, and Dilys said you could do with something cooking for supper, and invited me but . . . Sorry. I ought to have checked with you first.'

Bea didn't know whether to laugh or cry, so concentrated on feeding Winston. 'Thank you, Keith. That's most kind of you. Is the phone up here all right?'

'Yes, but there was something in the porch. Dilys said someone seemed to know who was coming and going, and I found a tiny camera trained on the front door. Someone close by must be monitoring it, in another house, or in a parked van, perhaps. Can't be far off. Probably still in the street. Do you want the camera put out of action, or removed, or what?'

'Put out of action . . . No, wait a minute. Can you skew it

so that it only covers people going down to the agency rooms? Then whoever put it in might think the wind had shifted it and not realize we'd discovered it was there.'

'I'll do that straight away.' Keith still looked uncomfortable. As well he might, thought Bea. She'd deal with him later.

She said, 'So who's in the living room?'

'Orlando,' said Dilys. 'Keith said he'd help him hump his stuff up the stairs, but we didn't get far before Orlando had to take a phone call from Charles. His best friend, you know?'

Keith's eyebrows rose, wanting to know if Bea shared his opinion of 'the friend'. He picked up the tale. 'When Orlando got off the phone to Charles two policemen arrived, wanting Orlando to go down to the station again. I don't know why. The poor wee lad doesn't seem to know what time of day it is. I was going to fetch you to sort them out, but Dilys said Orlando must learn to stand on his own two feet.'

Footsteps in the hall. The front door opened. And shut.

Silence.

Had the visitors gone? Bea went into the living room, which was empty of people. The lights had all been left on. Just like men, switching things on and forgetting to turn them off. But, the curtains hadn't been drawn. She drew the curtains. In a dull sort of way, she wondered whether or not she ought to be doing something to make sure Orlando had called his solicitor, but it was all too much trouble and she'd had enough trouble that day . . . not to mention that she was really worried about Leon. He'd said he had meetings all that day . . .

Keith mumbled himself in, shutting the door behind him. He'd forgotten to take off the apron he'd been wearing. 'Camera turned away from the front door. You really ought to report its existence to the police.'

She stared at him, thinking that yes, she ought to do so.

He said, being helpful, 'Shall I report it for you? I mean, it's not urgent to get it off or anything, is it? But they ought to know.'

She nodded.

He cleared his throat. 'If convenient, might I have a word?'

She nodded again and indicated that he should take a seat, hoping he wouldn't be long. She sat, too.

He was uneasy. Fingering that stupid beard of his. She wondered what he'd look like without it. He plucked at his jeans. Realized he was wearing an apron, and tore it off. Flushing. Embarrassed. 'Mrs Abbot, I don't want you to think that . . .' His eyes were everywhere, but not on her. He shifted in his chair. Started again. 'Dilys is the sweetest little . . . I want you to know that I wouldn't ever take advantage of . . . I mean, she's told me all about her bigamous marriage to that man, and how it ended. I can see how it might look, her inviting me for supper, but I can assure you that . . . What I mean is, you can trust me. I wouldn't harm a hair on her head.'

Bea made herself smile. 'I know you wouldn't.' She was so tired . . .

He crunched big knuckles together. 'She was saying she comes from a family with money, and that she'd like to put money into a business for me, but of course I wouldn't, ever. Honestly. I need that like I need a hole in the head. I've been there, you see. Done that. Had my own business, worked it up nicely and sold it. I like putting things right, and helping people with their IT stuff on a one to one basis, but admin . . .' He shook his head. 'Not for me. I've already got my own house, not up to her standard, but it's worth a bit now and . . . What I mean is, I know I'm too old for her. I'll look after her for a bit, if you like, just till someone her own age comes along.'

Bea said, 'What would a girl like Dilys do with a man her own age?'

The big hands spread out in a gesture of renunciation. 'I expect she'll meet someone suitable one day.'

Bea might not have continued this conversation if she hadn't been so tired and worried. 'What you mean is that you spent last night dreaming of coming home to a bright, cosy house and supper waiting for you, with Dilys flitting about, telling you what she'd heard from a friend, or seen at the shops. You thought about how good it would be to drop into bed beside her, and you even wondered if she'd mind giving you a child. Then this morning you woke up, looked in the mirror, and told yourself you were too old for her, that there was no fool like an old fool.'

Crimson in the face, he nodded.

'I think,' said Bea, 'that you are exactly what she needs. Her own father has never been interested in her, has been throwing her in the way of anyone likely to take her off his hands. Like Orlando.'

The big hands clenched. 'Orlando's all right, I suppose. But to think of him with her . . . That's not right.'

'Dilys needs a home where she'll be cherished and can blossom as a wife and mother. You do know she has a daughter still?'

'The one who's gone to America?'

'Bernice has made herself a new family and, although Dilys may not yet realize it, the girl may never return to live with her mother. Bernice is no fool, and she's a good judge of character. She'll take one look at you and see what I see; a good, kind man, who is offering a loving home to her mother.'

He blushed again. 'It's too soon. I'm sure Dilys hasn't thought of me that way.'

'Nonsense,' said Bea. 'Consciously or otherwise, she made a beeline for you. Didn't she invite you to supper?'

'But her family—'

'The only one you have to worry about is her Uncle Leon, who is setting up a trust fund for her. She'll have an income for life, and you will make sure she's never again targeted by charlatans out to fleece her.'

He stood up, awkward, bumbling. 'I'm sure you're wrong. She wouldn't want someone like me, except perhaps in emergencies.'

Someone rat-tat-tatted on the door. A key turned in the lock.

'I'll get it,' said Bea. She flew into the hall and Leon's arms. And burst into tears.

TEN

'Hey, hey! What's all this?' Leon held her tightly. 'Tears?'

'Stupid me,' said Bea, trying to disentangle herself and reach for a hankie at the same time. 'Things have been happening, and I was so worried about you, and the inspector's burned out, and the police have taken Orlando in again for questioning, and yes, that's all his stuff that he's brought in and . . . you are all right? Still got all your fingers and toes?'

'I've been skinny dipping in the piranha pool, but emerged with all the essential bits in working order. So, what's going on?'

'Supper,' said Bea, withdrawing from his arms. 'Here. Dilys and Keith have been cooking for us. And Anna's coming over later. Is that all right with you?'

Dilys sang out from the kitchen doorway, 'Come and get it!' She was flushed and laughing. 'I really think I've mastered this oven at last. My flan looks wonderful!'

Leon registered Dilys's newly acquired air of happiness and rubbed his chin, looking sideways at Bea.

Keith called out from the kitchen, 'I've laid the table in here. Is that all right?'

'What?' said Leon, checking with Bea. 'Who?'

'Keith, our Mr Fixit computer man,' Bea said, touching Leon's cheek to reassure herself that he really was there and apparently in perfect health. Her fears now seemed childish. What on earth had she thought might have happened to him? She said, 'I'll explain later. Do you think we ought to do something about Orlando?'

Leon shook his head. 'Surely he'll have had the sense to contact his solicitor? Let's eat first. If he's not back by the time we've finished I'll phone around, see where they're holding him.'

They ate in the kitchen. Bea was conscious that Leon was putting Keith under the microscope, as if interviewing him for a job, which in a sense he was. Keith did seem to understand what was going on and, though his colour rose a little, he was secure enough in himself to cooperate. The curry was good, and the apple flan was delicious.

When they got to the coffee stage, Bea spotted Winston trying to climb on Leon's knee. 'Don't give Winston anything. He's had his supper already. Which reminds me that someone sent me a toy cat today, and for one awful moment I thought it was him.'

The phone rang, and Bea reached for it.

'Mrs Abbot, sorry to trouble you. A small problem.' Anna, from the training college. She was speaking in the clipped voice of someone fighting off a panic attack. 'My car won't start.'

'What!' Bea swivelled to look at Leon, saying, 'Anna's car won't start.'

Leon reached for the phone, but Bea fended him off. 'Where are you? You won't try to walk to the station, will you?'

'I came back into the college to look up a taxi number and . . .' A long intake of breath. 'I can smell gas. And I can't get out. The front door's jammed or something.'

'You have keys?'

'Yes, but . . . you know the security people up at the big house used to check the college buildings after I'd left at night? A routine inspection. They used to put a chain round the handles to the front and back doors and padlock it. That all stopped when Leon took over, and they don't come round here any more. Or aren't supposed to. But I think that's what's happened now. I've rung British Gas, but . . . I just wanted you to know that . . . If anything happens . . .'

Bea tried not to shout. 'Break a window or a door. Get out of the building.'

'Yes, of course. How silly of me . . .' A pause. And then, 'Will you hold on while I . . .?'

Bea said to the others, rapidly, 'Anna's got herself locked in the college by mistake, and she can smell gas. She's called British Gas, but it's miles out in the country and—'

'I'm on my way,' said Leon, taking out his phone. 'I'll get

Lucas to take me out there in his taxi, but he'll have to get here first to pick me up.'

'I'll come, too,' said Keith, pulling on his jacket.

Dilys launched herself at Keith. 'Don't go!'

Bea shouted, 'Stop! Both of you! You're not thinking straight. It would take you nearly an hour to get there. And what for? It's a trap!'

Leon grimaced. 'You're right. It was Anna herself speaking?'

'Oh yes,' said Bea, still holding her phone to her ear. 'I can hear her trying to break some glass. She's coughing. Why don't you phone the police!'

Keith had his mobile out. 'What's the name of this place? The postcode?'

Leon had his phone out, too. 'Can we get hold of your friend in the police, Bea?'

'No,' said Bea. 'He's not available. Keith, give the phone to Leon when you've got through. This place is way out in the sticks, but a local policeman could—'

Dilys shrieked, 'Ring Daddy, for heaven's sake. He can get someone out there quicker than anyone.'

Keith spoke into his phone. 'Which service do I want? Police! Hurry!'

Leon hesitated. She could see him thinking it would do no good to ring Briscoe, if it was he who had set the trap for Anna. But worth a try? 'You're right. If I can get through to him . . .' He turned away to make the phone call.

Keith was not panicking, but he was near it. 'Yes, a woman, trapped in a building, locked in by mistake. It's . . . Dilys, what's the postcode?'

For a wonder, Dilys was able to cope. She took the phone from Keith and gave the code. Keith put his arm around her shoulders saying, 'Clever girl!'

Dilys, breathlessly giving information to the police, kept checking with Keith, making sure he thought she was doing the right thing.

Leon was barking into his phone. 'I must speak to him! He needs to send the security guard out to the college! There's someone trapped in . . . No, I know the college hasn't anything to do with my brother now, but—'

'Hello?' Anna was back on the phone, sounding groggy. 'I've broken a window, but I'm feeling more than a bit odd—'

'Get close to the window,' said Bea. 'Or lie down by the front door if there's a gap there. The police are on their way, but—'

'The thing is . . .' said Anna. And repeated herself. 'The thing is . . . my car's just been serviced, so it should have started first go.'

'Anna! Stay with me!'

Dilys said, 'The police want to talk to Anna. What do I tell them?'

Bea said, 'Tell them that they'd better hurry if they want to catch her alive. She's fading out on me. Anna! Anna . . .!'

Leon clicked off his phone. 'They won't put me through to Briscoe. They say the college is nothing to do with them any more.'

Dilys held Keith's phone out to him. 'The police say they're sending someone as quickly as possible. Shall I try to get through to Daddy?'

'You can try,' said Leon, stabbing at his phone. 'What's the British Gas emergency number, anyone?'

Bea tucked her phone under her chin and dived for the telephone directory she kept in the kitchen. 'I think I've got it somewhere. You want to check they're on their way?'

Dilys got out her own phone and keyed numbers. Waited for a response. 'I've heard that one spark and a building can be blown up.'

Bea found the book, thumbed pages, couldn't find the number. 'It should be here, somewhere.' And, into her phone, 'Anna, stay with me.' No reply. Bea slid into a chair. 'Anna?' She pushed the book over to Keith. 'Anna . . .?'

Keith took the phone book from her, leafed through it, found the right page and held it up for Leon to see.

Dilys spoke into her phone. 'May I speak to Daddy, please . . .? No, I do understand he has to go to bed early, but it is rather important . . . No, it can't wait till morning. There's a lady who's been locked into . . . Oh. Yes, I see that, but when it's a question of life or death, surely . . . Yes, yes. I understand. Thank you.' She put the phone down. Was she going to cry?

Bea said, 'Anna, can you hear me?'

Someone rang the front doorbell. Keith said, 'Shall I go?' and went to answer the door . . . returning with a bedraggled Orlando, who was in no mood to hear about other people's troubles.

'I thought you were going to take my things upstairs for me? I've had the filthiest day imaginable, and . . .'

Keith took him by the shoulders and pushed him out of the room. 'I'll help you up with your things. Don't bother Mrs Abbot. There's a bit of a crisis on. Here, let me take the heaviest bag.'

'Crisis?' They could hear Orlando complaining as he creaked his way up the stairs. 'What do you think I've been up to . . .?'

'Anna?' said Bea, more to herself than to the phone.

Leon paced backwards and forwards into the hall and back again, trying to get through to British Gas.

Dilys bit her nails. An unattractive habit.

Winston leaped on to the table, and for once nobody shouted at him.

'Anna!' A crash at the other end of the phone brought Bea to her feet. 'Anna, is that you?'

A man's voice, faintly, came along the phone line to Bea. 'Hey, there she is. You got her, right?'

'Hello! Hello!' Bea shouted into the phone. 'Is someone there?'

A tinny voice said, 'Looks like she was on the phone.' Crackling noise as the phone was picked up. 'I'll answer it, shall I? Hello, is anyone there?'

The gas people? The police? Bea said, 'I was on the phone to my friend. She said she smelled gas, but she got locked in by mistake.'

'My mate's just lifting her out. She's still breathing.'

'Is she going to be all right?' Bea signalled to Leon, who suspended the phone call he'd been making.

The voice on the phone said, 'Hold on a mo, while we get her into the fresh air.'

Heavy tread of feet. Noises off. Voices saying something about propping doors open to clear the gas. Where would the gas be coming from? The kitchens? Was the central heating at the college run on gas?

Bea hung on to the phone, waiting.

'They've found her?' That was Leon.

'Is she all right?' Dilys, wringing her hands.

The voice returned, sounding perturbed. 'Some stupid whatsit has left the gas taps on in the kitchen at the back here. We've turned them all off and opened some windows, but it'll be some time before the gas clears. In fact, we'd better get out . . . now! Phew!'

Bea said, 'Is Anna all right?' No reply.

Keith clattered down, collected some more of Orlando's belongings and toted them back upstairs. Dilys dithered, then disappeared to help him.

The voice on the phone returned. 'Look, no one should come back in till we give the all clear. We'll be back in the morning to check things out.'

'What about my friend?'

'She's coming round, but we're taking no chances. Straight to hospital.'

'Can I speak to her? Which hospital?'

The line went dead. Bea terminated the call and laid the phone back in its rest. 'Leon, you heard? She's come round, but they're taking her to hospital. Gas taps had been left on in a kitchen at the back. I don't understand. I thought they were all fitted with fail-safe knobs nowadays.'

'They are,' said Leon. He dropped into a chair beside her. 'Someone must have turned them on, waited a while and blown out the flames. They meant the building to go up, didn't they?'

'And Anna with it. Don't tell me she was locked in by mistake. The police will have to take notice now, won't they?'

Keith and Dilys came down the stairs. He had his arm around her shoulders. 'You did good there, girl.'

Dilys blushed with pleasure.

'Now,' said Keith, 'would someone like to tell me what this is all about?'

Everyone looked at Bea, who took a deep breath and said,

'I'll give you the highlights as I know them, but I can't pretend to understand what's really going on here. A couple of days ago two people were murdered in a car park in West London. It was in the news. One was Orlando's father. Another was a woman going through a bitterly fought divorce.'

Keith nodded. 'I do read the papers.'

'Leon and Orlando were lured to the site with false text messages and . . .' She ended up saying, 'No one is sure who the primary target was. There is another complication. When he was in the car park, Leon spotted Adamsson's car. There wasn't anyone in it. That car later turned up, still empty, burned out in a run-down council estate. Mr Adamsson's office says it was stolen that morning and that he has rented a car and is off on holiday in France. The police think a joyrider stole the car from wherever it was, that it was in the car park by coincidence, and that said joyrider then took it away and burned it.' She took another deep breath. 'All right so far?'

Keith nodded, frowning. 'I don't like coincidences.'

'Neither do I,' said Bea. 'Though I know they can happen. On to the next phase. Dilys gave Orlando shelter. He handed her his smartphone and asked her to charge it up. She did so, and infected the agency system with a virus . . . which we asked you to clear for us.'

'So the smartphone you gave me to clean up was Orlando's? The one with the virus on it?'

Bea said, 'It looks as though whoever sent the text messages to Orlando and Leon followed it up by sending their phones a virus to wipe out everything on them. This meant they couldn't prove they'd been asked to go to the car park.'

Leon nodded. 'I gave my smartphone to the police, with all the messages on it. I have no idea whether or not they managed to ignore the virus and retrieve the texts which took me to the car park.'

Keith said to Bea, 'So infecting your system was an accident?'

'Yes. A lucky one for us, because you were on the spot to help us when one of our agency staff arranged for a bug to be placed on my phone . . . which must be a separate matter. Mustn't it?'

'Why target you?'

Bea felt herself colour up. 'Either because I had given Orlando refuge or because I was offering support to Leon.'

Leon got up. 'Excuse me. A phone call to make . . .' He went off into the hall.

Bea said, 'That's not all. This afternoon I was sent a box containing a toy cat who looked like Winston . . . Winston! Get off the table! You naughty boy! Give him some more of his biscuits, will you, Dilys? . . . The cat in the box looked like him, only smaller, and it gave me a horrible fright. It was addressed to me personally. Now you could say that I'd upset a client who'd sent it to me by way of revenge but, added to the other "coincidences", I don't believe it. Someone is trying to frighten me and, I'm ashamed to say, they're succeeding.'

Dilys gave a squeak of distress. Keith put his arm around her shoulders.

'Consider what's just happened,' said Bea. 'A friend of mine who has just taken over the running of one of Leon's companies – one which used to belong to Briscoe Holland – couldn't start her car, was locked into the building, smelled gas and has ended up in hospital. And the building itself, which employs dozens of people and trains hundreds, has been put in danger. Is that a coincidence, too?'

Leon came back in, shutting up his phone. 'I didn't want to bring in the heavy squad, but I can't see any alternative. My immediate reaction on hearing that Anna was safe was to rush out there to make sure she was all right. Also, to check on the building, because its front door is currently open to all-comers. Then I had second thoughts.'

Bea noted that Leon was not holding it against Keith for putting his arm round Dilys.

'I wondered if whoever is orchestrating this vendetta might well think it a good idea to hang around, waiting for me to show up. So I decided against it. I have a decent regard for my skin and don't want to end up in hospital. The taxi-driver Lucas gave me the name of a man who supplies bodyguards for film stars and politicians. I had a long talk to him earlier today, and I've just been on the phone, asking him to check things out for me. He'll go out straight away to make sure the college building is secure.'

Bea had her head in her hands, thinking hard.

Leon said, 'Bea? What have I missed?'

'So much has been happening that doesn't make sense. I'm beginning to question my own judgement. Suppose . . . no, how could it be? But just let's suppose for one moment . . . who was it who picked up Anna's phone and told me she was coming round and that they were taking her to hospital?'

'Well . . . the British Gas people,' said Leon.

'The man didn't identify himself. Aren't they supposed to do so, straight off? And to ask me who I am? Suppose it wasn't someone from British Gas?'

Silence.

Then, 'The police?' from Keith.

'Could they have got there in time?'

Leon frowned. 'I suppose they could. Couldn't they?'

Bea lifted her hands. 'I'm imagining all sorts of things. Suppose the person I spoke to was in fact the security man who'd put the chain on the door after Anna went back into the college.'

Keith said, 'But if it was him, why did he go in again to get her out?'

'Perhaps because he saw her smash the window and use her mobile to call for help? Perhaps because he hadn't realized he'd locked her in and wasn't prepared to let her die?'

Leon grabbed the phone book. 'What was that number for British Gas again? I'll ring them, ask them for an update on our emergency call—'

Keith keyed numbers. 'I'll check with the police, same thing.'

'And I,' said Bea, 'will try the hospitals. If she's been taken to one and is fit to be discharged, we could go to get her. I think Windsor might be the nearest.'

Dilys said, 'If we can find where she is, Keith and I could drive out there and rescue her. After all, she does know me.'

'Yes, indeed,' said Bea. 'Good thinking, Dilys.'

Orlando stumped down the stairs and into the kitchen,

looking aggrieved. 'Did anyone think to save me some food? I've had the worst day of my life and—'

Dilys put her finger to her lips. 'Shush! I'll get you something in a minute.'

His voice rising, Orlando said, 'I don't see why I should hush. If you'd been badgered by the police all day as I have, you'd—'

Dilys pushed him on to a chair. 'Just shut up. You're not the only one who's had a bad day. A friend of ours was locked into a building that was going to get blown up any minute!'

Oh, thanks, Dilys. Nicely put. And how about Dilys telling Orlando off? Dilys is flexing her muscles, isn't she!

Bea rolled her eyes at Leon, who was otherwise occupied. Bea got through to directory enquiries. 'Can you give me the numbers for hospitals in the Windsor area? A friend has been in an accident and I want to find out where she could have been taken . . . Yes, I'll hold.'

Winston jumped up on to the table again and plumped himself down, furrily, in the middle of it. Clearly, he thought some more food might be forthcoming and wanted his share. Bea pushed him off. He got back on again. She gave up and let him be.

Leon held his phone aloft. 'British Gas say they're trying to get an engineer out to the college, but they're currently suffering a heavy demand for their services, etcetera. They want to know if we've vacated the building, leaving all doors and windows open. I said we had. They said they'll get there as soon as they can. Tomorrow morning, probably. So it wasn't them who rescued Anna. I'll ask them to get there as soon as possible.'

Keith was taking longer on the phone to the police. 'Yes, yes. I understand. Yes, that's the postcode . . . You've sent someone out to have a look? Good. Yes, I'll hold on, but if you could give me a contact number . . .?'

Orlando said, 'What's going on? If it hadn't been for the fact that I don't benefit in any way from my father's death, I'd be locked up in a cell right now.'

Dilys handed him some bread. 'Tell you in a minute. Pop it in the toaster for me, will you?'

Directory enquiries gave Bea the numbers of hospitals in the Windsor area. She scribbled them down and tried the first one. 'Can you tell me whether a friend of mine has been admitted to . . .?'

Leon walked out into the hall, still talking on his phone.

Dilys scrambled eggs.

Keith hung on to his phone. 'Yes, I'm still holding . . .'

Bea ended her call. 'She's not there. I'll try the other. They say there are only two hospitals which would take people from that area.'

Dilys rescued the toast, buttered it, poured on scrambled eggs and plonked the plate down in front of Orlando. 'Eat.'

Keith shut off his call. 'The police are ringing back.'

Leon returned, looking grim. 'Suppose whoever Bea spoke to – and presumably they were the people who set the trap – but suppose they didn't really bother to turn the gas off and open the windows, but have let the building continue to fill with gas? Any spark could send it sky-high. I've warned the heavy squad.'

Bea replaced her receiver. 'Anna has not been taken to either of the hospitals in that area. Our only hope is that the police have taken her to the nearest station in order to take her statement.'

Keith's phone rang. He listened. Closed his eyes, momentarily. Said, 'Yes, thank you.' He put the phone down. 'The police say we've been wasting their time. They think we've had too much to drink. They've been out to the college, which is deserted. In the dark. There are padlocked chains on the front and back doors. One broken window in the foyer. No other windows broken. No smell of gas. And no sign of Anna.'

ELEVEN

Leon pounded the table. 'Where is she?'

Dilys looked as if she were going to cry. 'Do you think she might . . .? Wouldn't they have taken her to the big house when they found she was alive? It's nearest. Shall I try to ring Daddy again? Mrs Evans said he'd gone to bed, but it is an emergency.'

'You can try,' said Leon, 'but if Anna did wake up, why doesn't she ring us? Answer, because she's being prevented from doing so. If only the police—'

Keith said, 'Sorry to interrupt, but three of you have had your phones interfered with already, right? You must know that a hacker can arrange to listen to calls and read emails on smartphones. You asked why, if it were the security men who'd set the trap for Anna, they then went back to rescue her. It is possible that her smartphone had also been hacked, and that they were listening to her asking British Gas and then Bea for help. Anna dropped that phone when she passed out, and they picked it up, didn't they? Now why would they do that? Answer, because it could be used in evidence against them, if they are indeed the hackers. I doubt very much if it's still in her possession.'

Leon said, 'I can't believe my brother would have authorized the security guards to kill someone. I simply can't believe it.'

You don't want to believe it, Bea thought. Neither does Dilys. But who else could have set this up?

Bea said, 'Can you think of anyone else who might have had it in for Anna, or for the college? Is there any other explanation of the facts?'

Silence. They shook their heads.

Orlando said, 'You're all mad! First you say your friend's locked into a building that's going to get blown up. Then you say she's disappeared, but the police report there's no sign of her or of the building being blown up. She was having you on!'

Bea muttered to herself: 'Hearsay. People make statements but, when you try to check them, the facts disappear into the mist.'

Leon said, 'You think Anna was pulling Bea's leg? That she wasn't in any danger? But . . . what about the man's voice on the phone that Bea heard?'

'And where is she now?' said Dilys. 'Is she safely in the big house?'

'Dunno about safe,' said Leon. 'Some of my brother's staff strike me as being a bit rough.'

Dilys nodded. 'Some of the security men, yes. A couple of them are a bit fierce. I was always frightened of them when I was little . . .'

And still are, aren't you?

'. . . but one of them's a real sweetie, as soft as you like. If she's been taken to the big house, they'll be looking after her, of course they will. Keith and I will go out there tomorrow and pick her up.'

'Hearsay,' muttered Bea. 'But, how to check?' She looked around. Since Dilys had so chirpily announced her faith in her father's retinue, and since it was logical that it was the security men who had rescued Anna – whether or not they'd set the trap in the first place – then it was equally logical that they'd taken her to the nearest place of safety, which was indeed the big house. Common sense indicated that Anna would be all right there. Wouldn't she?

'I'll ring her,' said Leon.

'Keith says she may have lost her own phone,' said Dilys.

'Trust me,' said Leon, checking his notepad before keying in a number. 'I've been handing out simple pay as you go phones to everyone in sight for emergency use. And this is an emergency.'

They could all hear the phone ringing. And ringing. And ringing. And then . . . 'Hello?' Tentatively. Anna's voice? And background noises.

'Anna? It's Leon here. Where are you, and are you all right?'

'Leon? Yes, I'm all right. Sort of.' She cleared her throat.

She didn't sound quite as positive as usual. 'I was on the phone to Bea, wasn't I? Then I passed out. Two of the security men from the big house rescued me. They've seen to the gas leak, so that's all right. My car still won't start, so they've put me on to the train for home.'

'What train are you on?' Leon was keeping his head in admirable fashion.

'It's a slow train, stopping everywhere. I don't know what time I'll get into Paddington, but I'll get a taxi home from there. I might be a bit late getting in to work in the morning, what with having no car and all, but at least the college is safe.'

'Is there anyone at home to look after you when you get in?'

'The boys are both away at uni. But I'll be all right.'

'Can you find out what time you stop at the next station, and where it will be?'

Pause, while Anna enquired of someone in the carriage with her. 'Ealing Broadway is next. Then Park Royal in about ten minutes, they say.'

'Right. Get out at Park Royal and wait to be picked up. You can come here to Mrs Abbot's for the night. That way you'll get a good night's sleep and we can see you get to work on time in the morning.'

'Oh, that's too much trouble . . . but if . . . I must say, I do feel a bit shaken. Yes, thank you very much. And thank Mrs Abbot for me. I hope I'm not going to keep her up too late.'

'Ring me if anything goes wrong.'

'What could go wrong now?' A laugh with a wobble in it. Anna clicked off.

'Thank goodness for that.' Keith spoke for them all. 'Dilys and I will collect her—'

'I'll organize a taxi to take you and pick her up,' said Leon, on his phone again.

Bea said, 'Now, who's going to sleep where?'

Keith was on his feet already. 'I'll go back home, of course. It won't take me long. Dilys, you'll need a coat. It's cold outside.'

There was colour in Dilys's cheeks. 'I won't feel safe, if you desert me.'

Orlando eyed her with disfavour. 'Well, I was here first, and I'm staying in the boy's bedroom up top. You can't expect me to walk the streets.'

Bea tried not to giggle. 'No, Orlando; of course not. Keith, can you make do on the settee in the flat upstairs? It's a decent size. Anna can have the spare room next to me and Leon—'

'Taxi's waiting outside. Keith, have you enough cash on you?' Leon reached for his wallet.

Keith shook his head. 'I'm all right. Come on, love. Mustn't keep Anna waiting . . .' He disappeared into the night with Dilys in tow.

Leon said, 'I'll ring the heavy squad and tell him to stop looking for Anna. Then I'll take a taxi to a hotel for the night.'

'That's good,' said Orlando. 'Everybody taken care of. Phew, I'm bushed.' He went up the stairs, pulling on the banisters, making the point that he'd been hard done by.

Leon got on his phone again, while Bea put the supper things into the dishwasher and set it going. It had been a long day. She wished she could go up to bed, too, but she had to wait up for Anna.

She went into the living room, made sure the grilles were locked over the windows and the curtains closely drawn. Leon followed her in and subsided on to the settee, closing his eyes.

She thought of all that had happened that day. Dilys had found a new role for herself in life, Keith and Leon had come to respect one another, and Orlando . . . well, Orlando had survived another day at the police station. Briscoe Holland had scored another try. And the inspector . . . *Dear Lord, look after them all.*

Leon looked tired. She wouldn't tell him so, though. Telling people they looked tired only made them feel worse.

She said, 'A hard day at the coalface?'

He loosened and took off his tie. 'Writs flying everywhere. Conferences with solicitors. Holland Holdings under attack on all sides. I won't go under without a fight, but it seems that a fight there will have to be.'

She left one side lamp on. 'You'll sleep here tonight?'

'Unless I get a better offer?'

It would be so easy to let him come into bed with her. No

need for sex. Just the pleasure, the deep pleasure, of going to sleep with a man's arms around her.

But not yet. No.

'When this is over?' he said, his narrowed eyes glinting at her.

Mm. Perhaps he did still have sex on his mind. She shook her head at him. 'I'll fetch you a duvet and pillows.'

'Promises, promises.' He patted the seat beside him. 'Come and sit here for a moment.'

He wanted to put his head in her lap and be soothed? Well, why not. She sat beside him. He put his phone on the table beside the settee, eased off his shoes and let himself lie down. Closed his eyes.

He said, 'At one point I was going to offer Keith the use of my electric shaver, but then I thought he needed to decide about his beard himself.'

She stroked his forehead. 'I think Sybil will see the point of adding Keith to the family.'

'Mm. Bernice has been texting me . . . wants to know if her friend Maggie is pregnant yet. She wants to be godmother.' He relaxed into a smile. 'I like my great niece.'

She smiled, too. 'Will Bernice appreciate Keith? Sybil has widened Bernice's horizons beyond the Greater London area. A pony and a boarding school would probably be next on her list. And, although I'm not a betting woman, I'll bet Dilys gets pregnant again within the month.'

'Or the week.' He took her hand and laid it across his eyes. 'Don't let me go to sleep. I've got to take the call from Hari yet. He's going to ring and tell me what the situation is once he gets to the college.'

'Harry? The heavy squad?'

'His name is Hari Silva. Of mixed ancestry and many talents including kick-boxing.' He sighed and nestled closer into her lap. 'When this is all over, if I'm left with more than a couple of pairs of boxer shorts, I'm going to buy you a socking great diamond. Not a ring. I notice you're still wearing the engagement ring your husband gave you . . . possibly as a defence mechanism? Warning me you're still not free? No, I fancy a diamond drop on a fine chain, to hang around your neck.'

'As a sign of ownership?'

His lips curved in a smile. 'Who could own you? This house
. . .' He gave a contented sigh. 'It's like a fortress, sheltering
those who have been wounded by the world. You take us in,
feed us, and solve all our problems.'

She thought about that. Was her house really a place of
refuge? Sometimes. And yet she could remember days and
nights when she'd raged up and down, refusing to believe that
her dear departed husband was going to die. She remembered
lying awake night after night, alone in the big bed, aching for
the act of love. There'd been other days, too, when she'd been
at her wits' end to know how to handle her son Max, who was
a dear good boy and a hard-working member of parliament,
but who had a distressing predilection for blondes other than
his ambitious wife, and who overestimated his financial acumen
. . . and that was putting it mildly. Max would be back next
week. Would he be drawn into the fight on Briscoe Holland's
side? Mm. Possibly, because he had bought himself a few
shares in the training college, which had now become the latest
battleground. Well, she'd deal with that when it happened.

Which reminded her she hadn't been out of the house for
some days now. She must try to find time for a good long
walk in the park tomorrow.

Did the enemy think of her house as a fortress to be stormed?
And if so, how would they attempt a raid? By stealth – as
they had done through Jennifer, sending her in to spy on them
and help bug the phone – or by frontal assault? Getting the
police to re-interview Orlando? Where would the next attack
be directed? Mm. Through Max? Oh well, she'd steered him
back to the straight and narrow before now and would probably manage to do so again. She must put in a spot of prayer
about that, too. *Dear Lord, you know . . .*

She was too tired to think what words to use.

Would it be helpful if Sybil returned to help Leon? Mm. It
might.

She was about to ask Leon if he ever prayed when she
noticed that he had begun to purr. It wasn't exactly a snore,
but it showed he had dropped off to sleep. Just as on the previous
night.

She eased herself off the settee, found a duvet to put over him, and was about to turn out the light and leave him when she heard a mobile phone ring. Leon's, which he'd left on the side table. She shook his arm, but he was far gone.

Oh well. She took the phone out to the kitchen, where the dishwasher was swishing away and Winston was waiting for someone to feed him. She flicked the phone on. 'Hello?'

'Is Leon there?'

'He's asleep.'

'Is that Mrs Abbot?'

'Indeed. Do you need me to wake him?'

'Nah. He said as he could trust you if you can complete the following figure. It's twenty-nine—'

'Eleven.'

'Right. Well, the college. Looks OK on the surface, but it doesn't add up if you get my meaning.'

'Enlighten me.'

'Place deserted. It's raining. There's an alarm system, but it wasn't switched on. No security light over the front door. Bulb smashed. Front door, chain and padlock. New padlock. Common type. I have all those keys. No sweat. Heavily greased so that key would turn easily. Not been there long. Broken window to the left of the front door. I tacked a piece of plywood over it because, as I said, it's raining.

'Inside the hall. Trace of gas in the air, but not much, which is why I risked the plywood, right? Door to interior propped open with large stone. Corridor. Faint whiff of gas. Not enough to worry about. Kitchen at back. That's where they prepare food for the canteen, right? Gas taps all shut up, nice and tight. More whiff of gas. Windows all open a crack. You'd hardly notice from the outside. I checked. I opened the windows a bit more, to be on the safe side. Back door, same chain and padlock.'

Bea tried to work it out. 'When the police got there, they said the only window that was open was the broken one at the front. They ought to have noticed the lack of security light, for a start. You did.'

'I've a suspicious mind, me.'

'What do you think happened?'

'I think there were three lots involved. The first lot dealt with the lady's car. That could have been done any time after she arrived to work that day. Possibly just malicious damage. Petty stuff from a petty mind. They wanted her to be upset and annoyed. To make her get a taxi to the station, or to walk there in the rain. They didn't know there was a plot to sabotage the building.'

'You think the building was the real target, and she got in the way by mistake?'

'I do. The second lot, now, they're serious about it. They go along after the lady leaves for the night. They have no idea she's been held up and will need to return to the building. They have keys to the front door. They go in, turn off the alarm, open the gas taps. They ensure the door from the corridor into the hall is propped open, switch off lights, turn the alarm back on and leave by the front door, smashing the security light as they go. Five to ten minutes, max. The trap is set. At some point during the night or early morning something would automatically switch on – like the central heating – and the building would go up.

'They return to base. Then they have second thoughts. They have no idea the lady is even at that moment trudging back to the building, but they remember that someone else, a cleaner, possibly, is due to come in early tomorrow and might get there before the building explodes. They hadn't bargained for bodies. Bodies mean a heavy police presence instead of an insurance claim. So, they tell a third lot – who don't know diddly-squat about the plan to blow the place up – to go out there and secure the front and back doors with padlock and chain so no one can get in. They ought to have done it themselves, but maybe their shift is over, maybe they want to give themselves an alibi, maybe because it's cold and raining, they pass the job on.

'This new lot put the first padlock on the back door while the lady is getting back into the building to phone for a taxi. She lets herself in, turns off the alarm, switches lights on, smells gas. But this new lot, being thick, obey their orders to the letter and padlock the front door with her inside! The bulb in the security lamp above the door has been smashed, and there's a light on inside but that's no business of theirs. They have no orders about lights. It's as much as their job's worth to do anything about that. They ignore it. They prepare to withdraw. It's a nasty old night, isn't it? They want to get back to base, out of the wind and the rain.

'The lady smashes the window, and that saves her life. The new lot realize someone is still inside. They look through the broken window, are horrified to see a figure on the floor. They take off the padlock and chain, get her outside, and in all innocence air the building so that no one else can get done by the gas. Then when the air has cleared they leave the windows at the back open a crack, switch off all the lights and get out, padlocking the chain on the front door behind them and taking the lady away with them.'

'You think the second and third lots were from the big house?'

'Not for me to say. But I did do a recce up there. Security lights, everywhere. Alarms, all active. Two blokes on guard by the gates. They were under cover, but they had their eyes peeled. Two more came out of the house as I was watching, and there was an argy-bargy. I couldn't tell you what was said, being some distance off, but they were not on good terms. Lots of shouting and menacing body language. The first lot went back up into the house so I went over to the college car park to check on the lady's car. She wouldn't have noticed, in the dark and it raining, but there's no battery under the hood.'

'Batteries are heavy. Someone took it out and dumped it nearby?'

'Agreed. But, in the dark and the rain, I couldn't spot it. Maybe someone whipped it into the back of his or her own car and removed it. I'll get another first thing tomorrow, fit it and have the car checked over, brakes and all. Right?'

'Thank you. You heard that the lady was put on a train back to London? We're bringing her back here for the night. I expect Leon will be in touch with you first thing tomorrow.'

'Sure. Tell him I'm dossing down in the college for the night to make sure there's no more gas leaks. He can ring me any time. Right?'

As Bea clicked off the phone, someone rang the doorbell. Dilys and Keith, supporting Anna, who looked very unlike her usual polished self. There was a bruise coming up on one side of her face, her hair was all over the place, and her jacket and skirt were mudstained. Shoes ditto.

She was saying in a bright, brittle voice, 'I'm perfectly all right! Honestly, you'd think I was a child, the way you're treating me! Mrs Abbot, tell them I'm perfectly capable of . . . And it was entirely unnecessary for you to send someone to meet me. I'll be . . .'

Her eyes closed, and she went limp. Keith and Bea caught her between them.

'Shock,' said Keith. 'Far too bright. Tears before nightfall.'

Dilys said, 'Do you think we should take her to hospital?'

They'd obviously argued about this in the taxi, for Keith said, 'Her breathing's fine. Apparently, she knocked herself out wrestling with a heavy door, and that's why her face is bruised. If we take her to hospital, we'll be there for hours, and then they'll send her home with some painkillers.'

Anna was coming round. 'Where . . .? Oh . . .!' Tears. 'I'm so sorry. How stupid of me. I'll be perfectly all right after a good night's rest.'

Possibly.

Anna struggled to her feet, helped by Keith.

Bea said, 'Keith, would you help her up to the guest room? First landing, door on the right.'

Keith nodded and started up the stairs with Anna protesting feebly in his arms.

'I've got her handbag,' said Dilys, following them. 'She kept dropping it. She was sort of all right on the train, people were very kind apparently, but I'll get her undressed and into bed, shall I? She can borrow one of your nightdresses.' She followed the others upstairs.

Bea considered waking Leon up. Decided against it. Heated up some hot milk in the kitchen, refused to feed Winston again, and carried the hot drink upstairs to find that Anna had been efficiently washed, brushed and was now being inserted into bed by Dilys.

As Bea entered, Anna stretched out a hand to her. 'I'm so

sorry. What a fuss about nothing. It's good of you to give me a bed. I'll be perfectly all right in the morning.'

Probably. Anna was tough. Dilys said she'd be upstairs if Anna needed anything, and disappeared.

'Want to tell me about it?' Bea set the drink down on the bedside table. 'Or would you like to go straight to sleep?'

'I'm too wound up to sleep yet. It sounds so stupid. I was working late. Everyone else had gone. I locked up—'

'Chain and padlock?'

'No, why would I do that? There's a mortise lock on the front door.'

'Security light? Alarm system?'

'What do you think I am? Of course I set the alarm and made sure the security light was on. It was dark outside and raining. My car was round the corner in the car park, but it wouldn't start. I tried waiting, thinking I might have flooded it, but it was no go. I was going to ring for a taxi but hadn't the number on me, so I went back to the college—'

'Was the security light still on over the front door when you went back?' Bea handed Anna the mug of hot milk. 'Drink up.'

'Come to think of it, probably not. I was in such a state. It was getting late, it was raining and cold, and dark. I got inside, turned off the alarm, put the lights on, and smelled gas. That's when I rang the gas people, and they said to get out of the building, so I tried, and couldn't. Then I rang you and you said to smash the window, which I did. I did it with the big stone that we use to prop open the door to the corridor. I was going to shut that door when I suddenly felt so dizzy . . . That's when I passed out. Luckily, some of the security men from the big house were just passing by. They had heard me smash the glass and came to my rescue. I don't know what would have happened if they hadn't.'

'You recognized them, of course?'

'Oh yes. Nice men. Both very concerned for me. They gave me a hot drink and said they'd take me to hospital to be checked out, but I didn't want that. I could just imagine the fuss, and the questions about who had left the gas on. At first they wanted to take me up to the big house to get checked over, but I could see they were in two minds about it because they didn't think Mrs Evans would have made me welcome, and I agreed with them. All I wanted to do was to go home, but I wasn't fit to drive so they put me on the train. So good of them. They even paid my train fare for me. Is the building all right? What happened when the British Gas people came?'

'Everything's fine. Leon's got someone sleeping there tonight.'

'Oh, good.' Anna slid down the pillows. 'I'm going to give that kitchen helper the third degree tomorrow.'

'You think it was a member of staff?'

'A slovenly, sloppy kitchen helper, on her third warning. Leon won't be pleased, I'm afraid, but I've put up with enough cheek from her to—'

'It wasn't one of the tutors you sacked?'

'It might have been, I suppose.' Anna was so relaxed now that her eyelids were dropping. 'I'll sort it, in the morning.'

Bea patted her hand. 'We'll both give them hell, tomorrow. We'll get Leon to devise a particularly nasty punishment for them. And reward the security men. Do they still have your phone, by the way?'

'I'm not sure. I looked for it when I got on the train, but I suppose I must have left it on the floor at the college. I was so surprised when another phone rang in my handbag, because it wasn't the usual tone . . . and then I remembered Leon had given it to me for emergencies. You say the college is safe?'

'Absolutely.'

Bea turned the light off and sat at the side of the bed. Maybe Anna would still be too wound up to sleep? But no, her breathing was getting deeper . . . and, yes, she slept.

Bea left the room, leaving the door a crack ajar and the landing light on. If Anna woke in the night, she wouldn't be totally in the dark. Bea stood on the landing, thinking about each and every person under her roof that night.

Dear Lord, keep my friends safe. You know everything. You know the secrets of our hearts, our fears and our hopes for the future. Give them a good night's sleep. Each of them is grieving . . . or in distress . . . or in pain. We seem to be involved in a fight for our lives. You've kept us safe so far.

Well, comparatively safe. Anna is a tough one, but she could easily have died tonight.

I don't understand what's going on. I listen to what people say and can't decide who's lying, or at least who's not telling the whole truth. Is Hari Silva – what a name! – right in thinking the security men at the big house were responsible for trying to blow up the college? Or was Anna right in thinking someone at the college has got it in for her?

Mind you, I think Hari's right. That trick with the car sounds more like the temper tantrum of a sacked member of staff than part of a well-thought-out plan to destroy the college. But probably not a woman. Those batteries weigh a ton.

Something furry wound around her legs. Winston, who'd given up all hope of another meal and was indicating he'd like to go to bed, please.

She picked him up, checked that the light in the hall had been left on to reassure Leon if he woke, and made it to her own bed. At last.

Winston lay on the bed, waiting for her to stroke his tummy before he went to sleep.

Dear Lord, I'm dumping the whole lot in your lap for tonight. Perhaps in the morning you'll tell me what to do next.

TWELVE

Friday breakfast

Bea was up early. She reached for her bible, and her phone rang. No, not her phone. Leon's, which she seemed to have taken up to bed with her.

'Hari reporting. Who am I speaking to?'

'Twenty-nine eleven.'

'Good. Is himself up yet?'

'It's half past six, Hari. Do you want me to wake him?'

'No need. All quiet here. Birds singing. Rain pattering on the leaves. Quite poetic, if you like that sort of thing.'

'You slept well?'

'On the couch in the lady's office. One eye and one ear open. Nothing to report. Gas all cleared away. I've closed the windows that were open at the back and confiscated the padlocks and chains that were on the doors. Thought they might have fingerprints on them, though probably they wore gloves. I mean, I would, wouldn't you? Don't answer that, Mrs Abbot. I understand you're the law-abiding sort.'

'Just so. I expect British Gas will be out at some point to check for the leak.'

'I cancelled that. Rang and said I was a private contractor who'd been called in because they couldn't get here quickly enough. Said I'd located the leak and dealt with it. How about the lady?'

'Slept soundly. She hopes to come in today, though I'm not sure she'll be fit enough to do so. What about her car?'

'I'll wait till some of the staff arrive to take charge, then pop over to the nearest garage and get another battery. An amateur did that, don't you think?'

'Yes, I do. Maybe the gas leak as well. They've one or two disgruntled members of staff who might have wanted to strike back at the college.'

'The lady is partly at fault. She should have changed the alarm code and the locks when she took over.'

'You're right. I'll remind her to deal with it when she gets back to work.'

Hari killed the call. Bea threw back her curtains and opened a window.

Blenched. Shut the window again. The birdsong was far too loud for her frayed nerves. The sun was breaking through. Ugh. Another fine day.

Another fine mess you've got me into, Lord.

He seemed to laugh. 'Put on the armour of God . . .'

A cream coloured blouse, conservatively cut. A dark-grey skirt. High heeled court shoes. Make-up. She let the events of the past few days slither through her mind one by one. She was missing something. She knew it.

Dear Lord. I think you put me on earth to help other people who are not as well off as I am. I don't mean 'well off' in the money sense, but . . . You know perfectly well what I mean.

Not that I'm trying to teach you your business. That would be silly.

Oh, dear. I'm getting in a muddle. As if I could teach God his business!

All right. Will you sort this out, please? You know what's best.

But, if you want me to act in this matter, please give me clear guidance. Amen.

Winston was no longer on her bed but had gone looking for something to eat. Sometimes he visited the kitchens of other houses and begged for a taste of this and that.

She shuddered. It might have been him in the box yesterday. It might be him next time.

She firmed her shoulders. Let battle commence.

She checked on Anna, who stirred when Bea called her name and then went back to sleep. Good. Sleep was the best thing for her.

She checked on Leon; still asleep. She put his mobile on to the table beside him.

Kitchen. How many for breakfast?

Dilys drifted in, smiling to herself. Colour in her cheeks.

And who's been sleeping in my bed? Bea didn't enquire. Dilys said she'd had breakfast upstairs but had run out of milk so might she borrow some? She said she'd tried to wake Orlando, but apparently he was giving work a miss that morning so she'd left him to it, right? She drifted out again, humming to herself.

Bea had the kitchen to herself, apart from Winston. Ah, peace and quiet. Breakfast with the papers. At seven, Leon appeared. He grunted, kissed her cheek, picked up her newspaper and hid behind it. She served him with orange juice, cereal, toast, and a couple of boiled eggs. She made him a cafetière of coffee. She reported what Anna and Hari had said the previous night and suggested Anna take some time off. Could Leon alert Anna's second-in-command to take over? Bea wasn't sure Leon had taken it all in, but he didn't ask her to repeat herself.

Folding the newspaper inside out, he managed to say, 'No *Financial Times?*'

She ignored that. 'I'll keep Anna here today, shall I? Do you want to inform the police about the attempt to blow up the college?'

In other words, would he want to accuse his brother of trying to destroy him?

'No police. I think I can see how to deal with this without involving them. I rang Hari. He says he's spoken to you already. He's fitted Anna's car with a new battery and is going to leave it at the railway station. I'm going to make some more phone calls in the other room, all right?' He didn't wait for her assent but picked up the newspaper, poured himself a second cup of coffee and went out.

Dilys returned, saying she'd done her best with Anna's clothes and they wouldn't look too bad once they'd been ironed and her shoes had been polished. Should she take a cup of tea in to Anna?

'No,' said Bea. 'Let her have her sleep out.'

'I offered to make breakfast for Keith, but he said I'd got enough to do without bothering with him, so I'll get on with ironing Anna's clothes, shall I?'

Bea could hear the first of her staff arriving in the agency rooms below. And there she was, tied to the kitchen stove instead of attending to business. Grrr!

Keith descended, fully dressed. He didn't look as if he'd slept well. Had he slept alone . . . or with Dilys? Alone, definitely. 'What day of the week is it? Thursday? Friday? I can't remember where I'm supposed to be. Is Anna all right this morning?' His voice was croaky.

'Sleeping it off. Dilys is attending to her clothes.'

A long, long sigh. He gazed out of the window. Birds chirruping. A fine rain moistening new leaves. Crocuses a-springing. Here comes the first of the good weather.

He said, 'I'd best get out of your way. Get back to earning my living. Customers depend on me, and it'll be one less for you to feed.'

'Could you manage breakfast? Bacon and tomato? Possibly with an egg?'

'I usually avoid mirrors, but today I made myself look. I'd been thinking about shaving off my beard, having a haircut, getting some new clothes. Fantasy time. I've been kidding myself. I'm overweight, going bald on top. Far too old for Dilys.'

'She doesn't think so, and neither do I. Neither does Leon. There's some orange juice in the fridge. Help yourself to some while I cook.'

He obeyed as to orange juice, but refused to be comforted. 'I'll be off straight after breakfast.'

'Leaving Dilys to the mercy of whoever it is who set out to kill Anna?'

He groaned. 'It was her father's security guards, wasn't it? She wouldn't stand an earthly if they came after her. You don't really think her father sent them out to blow up the college just because it's passed from his control?'

She dished him up a plateful of sausage, egg, bacon and tomato, and handed him a knife and fork. 'That's what it looks like.'

'We can't just sit still and let him get away with murder. I know the police didn't find anything wrong last night, but—'

'Evidence,' said Bea. 'Find me some. You can't abandon her to her fate.' That was a bit over the top.

He nodded. 'I see I'll have to stick around for a bit. Maybe she'll come out on my rounds with me today. She enjoyed that yesterday and was most helpful.' He consulted his iPhone. 'Now, where am I due this morning . . .?'

Dilys dashed in. 'Keith? There you are! Take off that sweater, at once! I told you, you really mustn't go around like that with a hole at the neck. It won't take a minute. And I suspect your socks have got holes in them, so you'll have to buy some more. I can mend most things, but I don't like darning socks.'

Keith blushed crimson but pulled off his jumper and handed it over. 'I was thinking I ought to get back to work today—'

'I wish I could come with you. It was fun yesterday, wasn't it? I really enjoyed it. Can we meet for lunch? I'll have to stay here this morning to look after Anna, because Mrs Abbot will have to get to work.' She whisked herself away.

Keith met Bea's eye with a sheepish grin. 'She's quite something, isn't she?'

Bea nodded, trying not to laugh. 'Could you check on that camera in the porch before you leave?'

'Would you like me to disconnect it altogether? I could let it dangle loose, so that it looks as if it's come adrift by accident, but doesn't transmit?'

'Excellent idea. Thank you, Keith.'

Carrie toiled up the stairs from the agency. The kitchen door was open, but she knocked, nevertheless. 'A word, Mrs Abbot? That Jennifer, who arranged for our phones to be bugged, she's turned up bold as brass, saying she's got something you'd like to hear, and that it's urgent.'

Bea poured herself a cup of coffee. 'Which, being translated, means—'

'She thought she'd earn a packet by spying on us, but we got rid of the bug so whoever hired her to do us a power of no good has refused to pay her and—'

'She's hoping we'll recompense her, for informing on them in turn? Maybe she'll even ask for her job back?'

Carrie snorted. 'Fat chance. I've made out a cheque for what we owe her, but I thought you might like to speak to her first.'

'I would, indeed. Keith, I'm off downstairs. Don't forget to disable the camera.' And to Carrie, 'He's turned it so that it points to the agency steps which means—'

Carrie laughed. 'That the baddies will know by now that Jennifer has arrived to spill the beans to Mrs Abbot.'

'We won't tell Jennifer that, though,' said Bea. 'At least . . . not yet. Keep her waiting a while, Carrie. I want to tape our interview.'

Down the stairs they went. Jennifer was sitting near the door to the stairs, looking meek and mild. Quietly dressed in shades of brown, flat shoes, neat hairdo. The other agency staff were busying themselves with work, but they all knew what Jennifer had done, and you could have cut the atmosphere with a blunt butter knife.

Bea drew back the curtains in her own office, booted up her computer, checked the latest batch of emails and dealt with the most urgent ones. She was about to lift the internal phone to ask Carrie to send Jennifer in, when her phone rang.

'Mother?' A male voice.

Her son, Max. Of course. 'Yes, dear. What's the weather like up with you?'

'It's fine, which is more than I can say for . . . Mother, this is confidential information, keep it to yourself. A little bird informs me that Holland Training College is about to go bankrupt. He knew I had shares in it so . . .'

Ah, yes. Was Briscoe working through the list of shareholders, to spread alarm and despondency? Probably.

She said, 'It's quite all right, Max. One of the tutors was caught with his fingers in the till. He was dismissed and is now trying to stir up trouble. A storm in a teacup.'

'It's more than that.' Urgent. Alarmed. 'The thing is, I've been advised to offload my shares, and I thought that if you had any, you ought to—'

'Max, did your informant specifically ask you to warn me?'

'Yes, he did. But I would have done so in any case.'

'There's nothing wrong with the company now it's been sold off. Anna will take it onwards and upwards. Check it out in the *Financial Times*, if you don't believe me.'

'You are so naive, Mother. Of course they'll say that!' He slammed the phone down.

Bea took a deep breath and let it out slowly. She switched on her recording machine, asked Carrie if someone might make her a cup of coffee, and said to send Jennifer in.

The woman wore a bright smile which was nervous around the edges. 'Mrs Abbot, I expect you may be surprised to see me—'

'We thought you'd left us.'

'A misunderstanding, which I wanted to clear up. I don't suppose you realize it, but someone has got it in for the agency. I'm very much afraid that your outside line has been bugged!'

Bea leaned back in her chair. 'Really?'

Jennifer became agitated. 'I tell you, Mrs Abbot, you are in danger . . . and so am I for coming to warn you!'

'Suppose you start at the beginning. Who recruited you to spy on us?'

Jennifer's hand fluttered around her neck. 'I don't know his name.'

'You agreed to spy on this agency without knowing who wanted you to do it?'

Colour rose in Jennifer's cheeks. 'My instructions came over the phone.'

'Nonsense.'

'Well—' reluctantly – 'I knew he was employed at the big house.'

'What "big house"?'

A wriggle. 'You know. Holland Holdings. The big house.'

'In what capacity was he employed?'

'I don't know. Honest.'

Bea reflected that when people say 'honest' like that, it means they're lying. 'Try again.'

'He'll kill me.'

'I doubt it.'

'Well, he's head of security. Mr Denver. He called me into his office and—'

'You had a job, working at the big house?'

'In the maintenance department. I thought I was going to get the sack.' The woman gained confidence as she moved on to the story she'd prepared. 'Mr Denver said that Mr Briscoe was working to get his properties back, the ones that had been

stolen from him by his brother. It was criminal what Mr Leon
had done. He said—'

Bea checked herself. It would do no good to interrupt at
this stage.

'—that as my job was going to be merged with someone
else's I could do him a favour by getting information about
where Mr Leon was going, and who he was seeing. I said,
"How was I to do that?" And he said that Mr Leon had shacked
up with his totty – meaning you, no disrespect, Mrs Abbot,
but that's what he said – and you'd taken his side and were
helping him to evade justice – and I believed him because,
well, I'd been working for Mr Briscoe for quite a while and
. . .' Her voice faded away.

Perhaps Bea's stony expression had caused her to falter.
'And . . .?'

'Mr Denver suggested I apply for a position here. He said
you were always looking for girls who knew what they were
doing. He said there was no need to be too friendly with the
rest of the staff, but I should listen and pick up what gossip
I could.'

*How long had that camera been advising the enemy of Bea's
visitors?*

Bea said, 'But you soon learned that Leon was not living
here?'

Another wriggle. 'He said I hadn't tried hard enough. He
said I needed to step up my game or he'd give me away to
you, that I'd be out of another job and that he wouldn't have
me back. And I've an elderly mother to look after.'

*What, only one elderly mother? What about the usual three-
children-under-five and an incapacitated husband who all rely
on your wages?*

'So, you upped your game by stealing the office stamp and
forging my signature on a contract so that someone could
come in and bug the telephone?'

A despairing glance around. 'It didn't sound so bad when
he asked me to help him. You must see I didn't have much
choice.'

'What on earth did they – whoever "they" are – hope to gain
from bugging my phone? Leon doesn't use our facilities.'

'They said—' she twisted and untwisted her fingers – 'that you were behind his attempt to bring Mr Briscoe down. That without you, he'd have to give up.'

Bea cast her eyes up to the ceiling. 'They don't know either me or him very well, do they? And, who are "they?"'

'I don't know, exactly.' There was a note of desperation in her voice. 'Mr Denver, of course. He talked about "orders from above". It wasn't Mr Briscoe. I thought it was and asked Mr Denver, and he told me not to be so stupid. He said, "Why would Mr Briscoe have to concern himself with such a trivial matter?" I thought he meant Mr Briscoe had asked someone else to get him to work on it. Mr Denver called it Operation Tabasco, although I haven't a clue why.'

Bea said, 'So, Keith discovered the bug, we found the forged contract and you took to the hills. You didn't mean to come back, did you?'

'No.' A small voice. 'I realized you were on to me.'

'So you hightailed it back to Mr Denver, admitting your failure. And . . .?'

'He said I was on my own, that he'd never suggested I work for you, and that he'd deny it if I said he had. He refused to give me the bonus he'd promised and said I shouldn't try to see him again. He was horrid! He had those other great apes with him—'

'His security guards? How many of them does he have?'

Jennifer counted on her fingers. 'They do it in shifts, two at a time. Eight . . . no, seven at the moment. One is off sick. But two of them were there in the office when I saw him, and they were all laughing about something they were going to do, I don't know what, and they crowded in on me till I felt quite frightened, and then they marched me out and told me not to come back. I had to walk all the way to the station to get a train back to London, and they didn't even give me my fare!'

Bea felt a moment of pity. 'So what are you going to do now?'

A toss of her head. 'My information's worth something, isn't it?'

'Not a penny. Carrie has a cheque for the wages that are due to you. Collect it on the way out.'

A sniffle. 'You wouldn't give me my job back, would you?'

'No,' said Bea. 'You knew I wouldn't. You'd best go to the police with your story. I'm sure they'd be interested to hear it.'

'You know I can't do that. If Denver found out, he'd crucify me.'

Well, they wouldn't crucify her, as that particular punishment had gone out of fashion some years ago, but the camera in the porch would have told them that Jennifer had returned to the agency and they might well conclude she'd been trying to play both ends against the middle. They might beat her up? Denver and his security guards wouldn't baulk at that. Anna had been extremely lucky last night to have been rescued by two members of the team who still had a conscience and a regard for life.

Bea said, 'Who gets the pictures from the camera in the porch, and where are they based?'

She watched Jennifer work out the implications of Bea's knowing about the camera.

Jennifer fluttered her eyelashes. 'I don't know anything about a camera.'

'Try again.'

She tried to sound indignant. 'Isn't it illegal to spy on people like that?'

'Yes. It was supposed to cover the front door, but it's now trained on the agency steps. Which means they know you are here.'

Jennifer bit her lip. 'That's . . . awful.' Her eyes skittered around the room. She was going to lie. She had known about the camera. She was nervous, but not scared. Which meant that she didn't care who knew she'd returned to talk to Bea. Which meant that Denver had instructed her to return.

The woman fought to produce a reasonable explanation. 'I didn't know about the camera, honest. I suppose they thought I wouldn't always know when Leon arrived and left. You mean, it's now covering the agency steps?'

'We could put it out of action completely, of course. But, why should we? We have nothing to hide.'

'Yes, but . . .' Jennifer tried to smile. 'What am I going to do?'

'Go to the police.'

'And tell them that I agreed to borrow your stamp and copy your signature? No way. You've got to help me. Find me somewhere to hide, out of London . . . anywhere.'

'What about your elderly mother?'

'Who?' Jennifer shook her head. 'Oh. That. I lied. I've no one to look after . . . or to look after me. My mother's dead, and I never knew my father.'

'Tell you what I'll do. I'll ring the police and tell them you want to confess what you've done. They'll ask you to go into the nearest police station to file a report. We have our copy of the contract for which you forged the signature, and the bug you arranged to put on my phone, by way of evidence. If you do that, Carrie will see if we can find you a temporary live-in job out of town.'

Tears spurted. 'You can't abandon me.'

'After what you've tried to do to us? Be your age, Jennifer. I'm offering you a way out of the tangle you've got yourself into.'

Jennifer turned on the self-pity. 'If you knew how hard it is to work for a living.'

'I do,' said Bea, who did indeed know. 'Now, do we have a deal?'

Jennifer dabbed her eyes with a hankie. She clicked her handbag open and shut, considering her options. She straightened in her chair, ran a hand over her hair.

She's going to refuse. She thinks she can continue to play both sides against the middle. She's going to go back to Denver to tell him we know about the bug and the camera.

Jennifer stood. 'I'll be off, then. I can find my own way out.'

Bea watched Jennifer stalk into the main office, collect and sign for her cheque from Carrie and leave, taking the stairs to street level.

Carrie watched, too. 'Where's she going?'

'I've got her confession – if you can call it that – on tape, but she refused to take my advice and go to the police with what she knows and what she's done.'

'Keith says he's put the camera out of action. It's dangling in the breeze at the moment. He thinks that's safest.'

'What a blessing that man is.'

'He says that the range of such cameras can't be great. He thinks someone's getting the pictures close by, perhaps in a van in the street, or in someone's front window. I suppose they send them on to . . . wherever.'

Bea was worried. 'When they realize the camera has stopped recording what they want to see, what will they do?'

'They'll come to see what's happened. Keith's put a buzzer under the doormat in the porch. If anyone stands on that, we'll hear it down here. Also, he's fixed us up with a mirror at the bottom of the stairs, so we can see who's in the porch. Oh, and Mr Leon came down for a minute. He's carrying it off well, isn't he? Full of jokes. He said if you had a minute, he'd like to see you upstairs.'

Leon full of jokes? Ah, he was putting a good face on it, wasn't he? Bea took the tape out of her recording unit and took it upstairs with her into the sitting room. Leon was standing at the window, hands clasped behind his back. His laptop was on the big table, filling up with email messages. All from the same person? It looked rather like it.

'Don't read them,' he said.

Too late. She read out, 'You're a dead man.'

And another: 'This is your last day on earth.'

A third: 'You're nothing but scum. You deserve to die.'

He sounded amused. 'Death threats. I've never had those before. Have you?'

THIRTEEN

Death threats? Bea steadied her voice. 'How very . . . unusual.'

He swung away from the window. He was smiling, his eyelids crinkling. 'A new experience a day keeps the nerve specialist away. Or so they say.'

'You have to involve the police now. You can't keep on protecting your brother.'

'I doubt if he's doing it personally.' A gesture of defeat. 'You're right, of course. I can't stay holed up here all day. I have to go out. But if those threats are to be believed, I will be targeted the moment I step out into the road.'

'Tell the police to come here.'

'I could do that, but I have conference calls and meetings I have to attend in person. I have rung the police. I have to take my laptop in to show them. Then I have a meeting at the bank. Briscoe has stirred up so much trouble in that direction that I may have to lodge some more of my assets with them, to keep them happy.' He shut down his laptop, checked that there were no messages on his mobile phone. 'I think this is where I move out to a hotel, isn't it?'

Her knees were giving way. She sank on to a chair by the table. 'This is all so sudden.' Despite herself, her voice went up into a squeak.

He sat beside her, placing his hand over hers on the table. 'I feel like Alice in Wonderland. The cards are all falling on top of me and, though I shout at them to stop, they keep on coming. My flat in the Barbican was attacked last night. Petrol poured through the letterbox and set alight. Fortunately, someone saw the blaze and called the fire brigade before any great damage was done. But, it's uninhabitable. I have a suite reserved for me at a hotel nearby. I'll go there this evening.'

She tried to speak lightly. 'I'd prefer you under my roof.

Suppose, at the hotel, you answered the door to someone you thought was room service, but wasn't?'

'I'll have Hari with me. He can open doors and check taxis before I get into them. You're not wearing your engagement ring.'

'I forgot.'

'Good.'

'I want you to come back here tonight. You're safe here.'

'You want to share my danger?'

She had to smile. 'No, I don't. I'm a coward in a physical sense, but I won't have a minute's peace till you get back. Surely, this must stop sometime? Jennifer turned up this morning, and I taped the interview with her. She confessed she'd helped to get my phone bugged, acting on instructions from Denver, head of your brother's security. I think the death threats are coming from the big house, too. Briscoe's office staff have been primed to think you stole your brother's companies and are acting accordingly. You'd better take the tape with you when you go to the police.' No need to mention the pressure from Max.

He shrugged. 'As for dividing up the Holland empire, everything was done legally and with Briscoe's full consent. He said at the time that it was a relief to get rid of some of his companies. We dined together several times. We played chess. He agreed he might even come out with me in the car one day. He hadn't been out of the house for months. He seemed almost affectionate.'

'Until . . .?'

'I had to be away for a couple of days. Almost a week, as it turned out. I rang when I got back, asking if I might drop in to see him. He said he'd got a cold, had to take to his bed for a bit. I'd brought him back a box of his favourite chocolates. I wasn't allowed in his bedroom so I handed them over, only to have them returned to me next day, with a message that he wasn't eating chocolate any more. A couple of days later he sent for me. I thought he looked poorly. He was up and sitting in a chair by the window but not dressed. He started on me as soon as I got in. Said I was as bad as Dilys, wanting to hustle him into the grave. That's when I made my big

mistake and asked him to do something for her. He told me
to get out, and after that he refused to speak to me even on
the phone. You heard the message he sent me, saying I was a
traitor. I'm beginning to wonder if he's going round the twist.
He didn't show any signs of Alzheimer's, but I can't think of
any other explanation for the way he's been behaving.'

She put her free hand on top of his. 'Do you want any more
money? I can mortgage this house.'

'No. If I go down, I'm not taking you with me.' He went
to look out of the window. 'I rather think our snooper is holed
up in a van halfway down the street, on the other side. Facing
this way. The florist's van, with an aerial on top. I think it was
there last night, too. Vans aren't usually parked in this street
overnight, are they?'

'Certainly not. Purely residential. My agency is the only
commercial premises in the road and that's a historical
anomaly, because my husband's family started it way back in
the last century.' She joined him at the window. 'Yes, I see it.
You've been standing in the window so they can see you're
still here?'

'So long as I am here, you're in danger. I'm trying to work
out how to draw them away from here without risking my
own skin. Hari rides a motorbike. He'll be here soon, and can
park the bike nearby. I was thinking he and I could then leave
by taxi. If they follow, I could leave Hari in the taxi, stop
round the corner and run down into the Underground. That
would make it difficult for them to follow.'

'Nonsense. The police station is a couple of roads back
here, further up the hill. That's where you have to go first,
isn't it? But, you'd have to cross two streets to get there. If
you were on foot and they tried to mow you down . . . Take
no notice, I've a vivid imagination.'

'So have I.'

'Got it!' She clicked her fingers. 'We borrow some of
Orlando's gear. How do you fancy wearing pink jeans, a
Hawaiian shirt, a shaggy fur jacket and a beanie cap? Oh, and
bovver boots? You hop on the back of Hari's bike, and off
you go. They'll think you're Orlando and leave you alone.'

His face was a picture. 'What!' Surprise was followed by

horror, followed by consideration, followed by a reluctant grin. 'Do I have to carry a handbag as well?'

'A leather satchel slung over your shoulders, with your ordinary clothes and your laptop inside.'

'I draw the line at the boots. Anyway, they wouldn't fit me.'

'I don't suppose any of it will fit you too well, but if it gets you off and away safely, it's worth a try.'

'But if they think I'm still here, they might try attacking this house.'

'Not if we send Orlando out soon afterwards, wearing equally colourful gear. Hopefully that will give them double vision. Have you ever ridden pillion on a motorbike?'

'In the dim and distant, yes. But now, at my age? Have you?'

'Yes,' she said with a reminiscent smile. 'It was both frightening and exhilarating. And getting where I wanted to go in a hurry saved a life.'

He groaned. 'What happens if I fall off?'

'I visit you in hospital. I'll go and persuade Orlando to help us out.'

He caught her wrist. 'What about Anna? I asked Dilys, who said Anna was fine and still asleep. She said I wasn't to go in and upset her, so I haven't. I feel badly that she's the one who's got hurt.'

'I'll put my head round the door and see if she's awake. Come on. Work to do.'

As they went out of the door, his phone rang. Bea pushed him up the stairs ahead of her, while he took the call. He nodded, said a few words into the phone, and signed off. Only for it to ring again as they reached the landing. He said to Bea, 'I like to check with all my managers every morning at the moment.' And into the phone, 'Yes . . . yes. Good. And tomorrow you'll . . .?'

As he clicked off that call, another came in. Bea left him on the landing and continued up the stairs to winkle Orlando out of bed and explain what was needed. Dilys arrived, not wanting to be left out of the fun.

'What a laugh!' was Orlando's comment. 'But, no one could ever mistake him for me.'

'Oh yes, they could,' said Bea, determined not to listen to reasonable comment. 'Long enough for us to get him away from here, anyway. Then shortly after, you can leave, too.'

'I'm not working this morning.' But he got out of bed and starting rummaging through his bags of clothes, holding this and that up, shaking his head and throwing it down again. Dilys picked up everything he discarded, hung some up in the wardrobe, but retained a few items she thought might be suitable.

With an armful of clothing, Bea and Dilys descended on Leon, who had strayed, still talking on his phone, into Bea's bedroom. They dressed him between them. The jeans were on the short side: a virulent pea green and, with a belt on, they hung low on his hips. The T-shirt was bright yellow and clung tightly where it should drape. The long-haired fake fur waistcoat was a brilliant fit, and the over-the-shoulder leather bag had a deep fringe to it. They didn't bother with the boots.

'No, no . . .' said Leon, still on the phone, 'that's good news. I'll speak . . . Yes, yes. Good.'

'A beanie?' said Dilys, holding up a woollen cap.

Bea reached up to pull one on to Leon's head. Both women then doubled over with laughter. Leon looked like an ageing hippy, except that his hair was well cut and he had no beard. Nor a paunch, come to think of it.

'What!' said Leon, catching sight of himself in Bea's long mirror. He reddened. Total mortification. 'I can't go out like that!'

'It's great!' Dilys gasped. 'Oh, my! Oh, oh! Uncle Leon, whatever do you look like!'

Bea wiped away tears. 'Think of it as fancy dress.'

Orlando appeared, clutching a mobile phone. 'Lucky I invested in another phone yesterday, and this one's got a camera.' There was a flash of light as he snapped Leon in his new guise. 'Meet the new you.'

Leon swung round on him. 'Delete that, or I won't be responsible for the consequences.'

'All right, all right!' said Orlando, ironing out a grin. 'You must admit, it would be good blackmail material for the future.'

'If there is a future,' said Bea. 'Orlando, stop winding Leon up. Leon, calm down. We won't try any make-up.'

'Make-up?' Leon glared. 'If you think . . .! What will the bankers say if I turn up like this?'

'The bankers will think you're bonkers, but you can change somewhere before you get there. Dilys, can you pack his ordinary clothes in the bag for him, not forgetting his laptop and the tape I made earlier. They're on the dining-room table. Orlando, any suggestions?'

Orlando had come down in his pyjamas, which were paw-printed black on white. He walked all around Leon, shaking his head. 'No one would ever mistake him for me.'

'Thank the Lord for that,' said Leon. His phone rang again. He took the call, said, 'Yes, five minutes. Don't be surprised when you see how I look. Keep the bike running. I'll get on behind you, and we'll go straight round to the police station. That is, if no one follows us. Otherwise, I trust you to weave around till we lose the tail, and then go to the police. You can come into the station with me to make sure I don't get molested . . .' To his credit, he tried to grin.

Bea patted him on the arm and tweaked the woolly cap to a better angle. 'That's the ticket. Be brave, be bold, be daring. Come back safely when you've conquered the ogre.'

Dilys said, 'Do you mean Daddy? He's not an ogre.'

Leon tightened the belt around his hips. 'If my trousers fall down in front of the police, I'll be arrested.'

'You've got to get there first. Come on!'

Down they went. The landline phone was ringing, and Bea picked it up.

It was Carrie on the phone. 'Mrs Abbot, there's a man in the porch tinkering with the camera. Can't you hear the buzzer? What do you want us to do about it?'

Bea thought rapidly. Leon's disguise wouldn't fool anyone close to. The man in the porch had got to be got rid of. 'Does he realize you're on to him?'

'He might. We went out and checked it was a stranger. I suppose he's putting the camera back where it was.'

In which case it would give the person in the van a close up of Leon leaving the house, and that wouldn't do, either.

'Where's Keith? Oh, he's out on one of his own jobs, isn't he? Let me think.'

Leon had his phone out again. 'Hari's arrived. Parked three cars along to our right.'

Dilys hoisted the leather bag on to his shoulder. 'I think that's everything.'

Bea said, 'Orlando, go into the living room, see if you can get a shot of the man who's in the porch on your camera: now! Leon, wait for me to get rid of him. Dilys, stand by the door, open it when I say, but not before.'

She dashed into the kitchen and turned the taps on, filling the washing-up bowl with water. She pulled a mop out of the cupboard and handed it to Leon. 'Hold that till I ask for it.'

He said, 'I need to tell you something. No one outside London seems to have been bothered. No hooliganism has been reported anywhere else. I'm not sure of the significance of—'

'Stand back!' Bea rushed past him, crying out to Dilys, 'Open!'

Dilys opened the door wide.

Bea threw the contents of the washing-up bowl over the man who was standing on tiptoe, re-fixing the camera under the porch. Woosh!

'Whaaa . . . t!' The man staggered back.

'You silly man!' raged Bea. 'What did you want to get in the way for? Can't a woman clean her front steps without having some homeless person get in the way?' She reached back to grab the mop from Leon and swung it at the intruder. 'Scoot! Shoo! I will not have tramps trekking their dirt into my porch. Out! Out, I say! Or I'll have the police on you!'

The man, off balance, tottered backwards down the steps and ended up on his backside in the street. Bea flourished the mop in menacing fashion. He scrambled to his feet and made off as fast as he could . . . towards the florist's van. Limping, she was pleased to see.

Description: medium height and build, all in black, wearing a hoodie. White trainers.

She waved the mop around her head. It looked like a gesture of triumph, but it happened to connect with the camera, and turned it sideways till it was pointing up to the roof. 'Go, Leon! Go!'

Leon went. Down the steps, holding up his jeans. Hari drew up outside on his bike. With a hideous grimace, Leon got his leg over the pillion and off they went, passing the florist's van at speed.

Bea leaned, panting, on her mop. The florist's van was facing the wrong way to follow Leon. But it pulled out to follow him, and then stalled. They weren't sure it was him, were they? The driver, white, shaven head, burly build, lowered the window, looking back to where the motorbike was turning into the main road. He'd missed a gap in the traffic. He hesitated, half in and half out of the parking slot.

What about Bea's would-be camera-fixer? He reached the van and tugged on the driver's door – stupid man! – which failed to open. He was shouting. To be let in? Oops! A car looking for a parking space nearly ran him over!

The passenger door of the van shot open, and a skinny figure emerged on to the pavement, screaming at the camera-fixer, gesticulating for him to get into the back of the van, fast! Without waiting to get his accomplice on board, the driver of the van accelerated out into the traffic but, not having waited for a clear space, was hit by a large carpet-fitter's van. Bang!

The driver of the carpet-fitter's van – also shaven-headed and burly – descended into the road to the accompaniment of expletives undeleted.

The traffic built up behind them. Horns blared. Drivers shouted. The driver in the florist's van tried and failed to get his door open. His skinny passenger's arms waved wildly, clearly suggesting that he pull back into the parking slot. The carpet fitter reached into the driver's window, took hold of his jacket by the collar and shook him about as a terrier shakes a rat.

Bea flourished her mop. 'Thus perish all evil-doers! That's going to take the traffic cops to sort out.'

Dilys had her hands over her mouth, knees bent, in a paroxysm of laughter. Orlando snapped away at the scene in the street. 'Got them. All of them.'

Bea suddenly realized she was standing on the mat, which

was still buzzing, and that Carrie and another of her staff were standing at the bottom of the agency steps, looking up. She called out to the girls downstairs, 'It's all right. Panic over.' She turned to Dilys. 'Do you recognize any of the men in the florist's van?'

Dilys peered down the road, where a number of drivers had abandoned their own cars to try to sort out the traffic block. There was a lot of shouting and gesticulating. Several people were on their mobiles, either explaining the hold-up to their workplace, or yelling for help.

Dilys said, 'I'm not sure. One of them . . . but no! It can't be, can they?'

'Say it,' said Bea, drawing the girl indoors. 'Orlando, come inside!'

Dilys looked ready to cry. 'Is it . . . No, I really can't be sure, but he does look like one of Daddy's security guards.'

'Thought as much,' said Bea. And to Orlando, 'Go and get dressed, at once. You've got to be seen to leave the house very soon to complete the illusion.'

Orlando started up the stairs. 'I was going to take the morning off. Suppose they follow me?'

Bea crossed fingers and toes. 'When they're sure you're not Leon, they'll leave you alone.'

Orlando reached the first landing. 'Tell you what, nobody who had a good look at Leon would mistake him for me. I wouldn't be at all surprised if the police don't arrest him for causing a breach of the peace, going about dressed like that.'

'Agreed,' said Bea, but she said it under her breath. Then grinned. She rather hoped Orlando hadn't deleted that photo of Leon in Orlando's clothes. If they all came out of this alive, Leon would probably pay a considerable amount for it to be erased. Perhaps she'd get just one copy printed off for her archives, to look at when she needed a good laugh.

An unkind thought? Mm. Yes. Slap on the wrist. But, fun.

She shot into the living room to see how the ruckus outside might be proceeding. Dilys was already there, half concealed behind a curtain.

'Progress?'

'They've descended to fisticuffs. The carpet fitter is getting

the better of it. Oh, now the police have arrived. Do you think
they'll breathalyse the ones who've been fighting?'

'Do you think they'll want to know why one of them is wet
through?'

'He won't be able to say, will he?'

They were both grinning. Bea realized that they were
communicating as equals for the first time. 'Well done, Dilys.
You keep watch while I put the mop and bowl back in the
kitchen. Then I'm going up to see how Anna is getting on.'

Anna was sitting on the edge of her bed, looking frail. The
bruise on her face had ripened nicely, but she tried to smile at
Bea. 'Sorry, I'm a bit slow today. Any idea what happened to
my car last night? I can go in by train, but it takes a lot longer.'

'First, Leon has seen to everything. Your deputy is in charge
of the college today, and you are not expected back until after
the weekend. The battery had been removed from your car,
which was why you couldn't start it last night. An amateur at
work, don't you think? The car has been put back into working
order and left at the station for you to pick up when you're
ready to go back to work. The college buildings are safe. The
only damage is to the window you broke, which has been
boarded over.'

'But who . . . and why . . .?'

'We think two of the security staff from the big house
started the gas leak and left, thinking that an automatic switch
would trigger off an explosion and destroy the college
building.'

'But it was they who got me out! They were really upset
that I'd got locked in. They rescued me and put me on a train
back to London.'

'Either the two who got you out didn't know about the plot
to blow up the building, or they weren't prepared to let you
be killed. Take your pick.'

Anna made a wobbly dash for the bathroom. Retching noises.

Bea was annoyed with herself. She'd said too much, too
quickly.

She helped Anna back to bed. 'Could you stomach some
tea? Herbal, perhaps? Some bread and butter?'

Anna looked ghastly, but resisted being tucked in. 'I've got to get back. I've got to find out who started that leak—'

'Either you get back into bed properly or I send for an ambulance to take you to hospital, which is what we ought to have done last night.'

Tears flowed. 'No hospital.'

Bea handed Anna a box of tissues. 'You've been very brave, Anna. No one's doubting your courage or your willingness to be a martyr—'

'A martyr!' Blew her nose. Twice. Allowed Bea to pull the covers over her. 'Herbal tea. Lovely. I'm going to sack that kitchen assistant.'

'Revenge is a dish best served cold. Now, what shall we do about that bruise on your face? Have you any arnica? How did you get it, by the way?'

'Struggling to get the inner door closed, to stop the gas flooding into the hallway. I sort of pulled it into me.'

Bea turned it into a joke. 'You mean, you walked into the door? The eternal excuse of a woman who's been landed one by her husband.'

A weak laugh. 'No one but myself to blame.'

'Tea coming up. Give yourself permission to take the day off, right?'

'May I borrow some shampoo and a hairdryer? I feel so frowsty.'

'When you've had another little nap, you may borrow what you like from my bathroom next door. Now let me tuck you in, as our mothers used to do.'

Anna allowed herself to be tucked in. Before Bea left the room Anna had closed her eyes and was breathing more deeply. Good. Rest was the best doctor she could have at the moment.

Down the stairs Bea went to find Orlando, dressed to kill in fawn suede, admiring himself in the big mirror. 'Is the coast clear?'

Bea opened the front door and looked out. Nobody seemed to be taking any interest. She nodded. 'Ring me when you get to the tube station, to say you're safe.'

Off he went down the road. No one seemed to be following him. Was that good or bad?

She went back to the kitchen. Dilys was there, switching the kettle on. Good for Dilys. How many were there going to be for supper, and what had she got in the freezer which might do for them? Dilys was on her mobile. Talking to Keith? Yes. All lit up and rosy. All right for some.

Bea told herself she was becoming a sour old maid, resenting Dilys's happiness. Didn't the girl deserve a bit of luck?

Bea was in the middle of her search for food when Orlando rang to say, 'All safe so far. I'm going on to the office, may be back late, all right?'

Distraction. I'm being distracted.

Bea recalled Leon saying that he felt he was like Alice in Wonderland, fending off the cards. That the situation wasn't real.

No, it wasn't, was it?

Over the last couple of days her office phone had been bugged, a cat toy had been delivered and a camera planted in their porch. Leon had had to leave the house in disguise, his flat had been burned out, the college buildings endangered, and Anna had narrowly escaped death. Don't forget the hate mail, either. Bea thought that these incidents had been organized by a number of different people and had probably originated in the maintenance department of Holland Holdings (Overseas).

As a campaign against Leon and Bea, it had had no lasting or fatal affects. Each of the attempts had been thwarted, some by chance and some by the intended victim's quick reactions.

Still they kept coming. Bea hugged herself. What next?

'Shall I take a cuppa up to Anna?' said Dilys, shoving one in Bea's direction, too.

Bea shook her head. 'Leave it an hour. She's just dropped off to sleep.'

'I've phoned Keith, asked him to come back to look after us.'

Bea nodded. Yes, that would be sensible. She needed to think. At that very moment, she ought to be down in the agency rooms, answering queries, dealing with clients. She suspected that the next distraction would be another attack on the agency.

She took her mug of tea down the stairs and asked Carrie to come into her office.

Carrie said, 'We're getting a lot of hate mail. It's upsetting. The girls are behaving like Trojans, but it is making them nervous.'

'Ah.' Bea put her mug down. 'I think I know where they're coming from. We'll get Keith to deal with them when he returns. Leon had a whole batch of them this morning and has taken his computer to the police, together with the tape we made of Jennifer's confession. Anything else?'

'A man came about the drains. He said a neighbour had been complaining that our drain was overflowing into his back garden. I asked which neighbour, and he didn't know. I sent him off with a flea in his ear.'

'Good for you. Carrie, I need time off. I need to think. Someone is bombarding us with false alarms.'

Carrie grinned. 'I wouldn't have missed your throwing water over that man for anything.'

'It was good, wasn't it? Look, unless the sky falls in on us, I'm going to shut myself up and try to work out who is doing this, and why.'

'Isn't it Mr Leon's brother?'

'Leon said not, at first. Now he's wondering if his brother has succumbed to Alzheimer's and doesn't know what he's doing. And yes, I think the staff at the big house are involved.' Bea rubbed her temples. 'All these distractions . . . it's as if they're meant to stop us from . . . from what, that is the question.'

It was clear enough that big brother was trying to destroy little brother. Wasn't it? Big brother had even gone on record as saying so. He'd stirred up the bankers. He'd encouraged sacked managers to fight for reinstatement or compensation. He'd got his men to attack the college buildings.

Discount the near murder of Anna. That had probably not been planned.

Anna's car had been vandalized. Hari had said that looked like an amateur's attempt to inconvenience Anna, and Bea was inclined to agree with him. Yes, that was probably down to one of the men Anna had had to sack, getting his own back in petty fashion. Or one of the kitchen staff who had proved unsatisfactory. To be enquired about later.

On the other hand, Leon had said that there'd been no vandalism at any of his companies outside London, which indicated . . .

Well, it might not mean anything at all. Just that the men big brother was paying to annoy his little brother were London based and didn't travel outside the area.

But, Leon had said his brother had billions in the bank, and if you had billions in the bank then you could pay for hit men by the dozen. Hit men would go anywhere and do anything, to order, for money.

Which meant that . . .

She didn't know what it meant. She didn't turn on her own computer. She guessed it would be full of hate messages, even death threats.

Leon hadn't returned. She looked at her watch. Time to get some lunch? She couldn't be bothered.

He might still be at the police station. She hoped he'd had time to change. She grinned at the thought of his embarrassment at having to wear that outlandish rig-out. Still, it had got him safely away from the house. He'd be back this evening . . . if the house were still intact.

Think, Bea, think!

If these incidents were intended to distract, then what was it that needed to be kept hidden?

Big brother's motive was in plain view. So it probably – possibly – wasn't that.

She pulled the phone towards her and dialled. Asked for Inspector Durrell. 'Yes, it's me, and I know you're busy. How are you?'

'Mm. Actually, I have to thank you. We didn't go out last night, but after the kids went to bed my wife and I had a good long talk. I'm putting in for a spot of leave straight away.'

What a relief! Except that she desperately needed him to help her at the moment. She said, 'Before you depart, could you look up something for me? I know you keep lists of unidentified bodies found in the Thames, or on dump sites, or in derelict housing. Could you check to see if there's one which matches the description of Mr Adamsson, who is suppos-edly on holiday in France but probably isn't?'

Heavy breathing. 'What makes you think he isn't?'

'It's called sleight of hand. A conjuror's trick. The magician shows us a card. He lets us all have a good look at it, and then distracts us with a lot of jiggery-pokery, so that we don't see exactly what he does with it.'

'You want me to ask someone in the Magic Circle how they perform the three card trick?' He wasn't joking, exactly. There was an edge to his voice.

Bea refused to let herself be riled. 'No, I want you to check that Mr Adamsson isn't masquerading as a John Doe some-where. Don't say, "It's not my case." It won't take you five minutes.'

'What makes you think he's dead?'

'He was a conscientious little man who devoted his life to the Holland empire. If he'd really gone on holiday, he'd have left contact details. He's living with an elderly father, remember? He'd worry that his father might fall or have a stroke while his back was turned. He'd leave his mobile on all the time – but, it appears that his mobile is out of service. Why? Take it from me, the situation stinks!'

Should she remind him that he owed her one? No. That would not be right. She repeated, 'It won't take you five minutes. Ring me on my mobile.' And disconnected.

She crossed to the French windows, unlocked the grille that covered them, and threw them open . . . to be greeted by the penetrating chill of a spring day. A soft rain – more of a mist – was falling. At that moment she didn't care about the cold or the rain. She wanted to be a long way away. She wanted to be on a South Seas beach, lying on a hammock in the sun, with a soft drink to hand. She wanted to be in the Swiss Alps, sitting in a restaurant with a stupendous view, wearing appropriate skiing gear. She wanted to be in a bistro in the south of France, exploring an interesting menu.

Hadn't she worked hard all her life, and wasn't it time for her to relax and be cosseted, rather than have to look after the gaggle of geese currently occupying beds and settees in her house? She wished she could be rid of the lot of them.

Shoo! Get out! Find somewhere else to play! And don't come back.

Well, Leon could come back.

In fact – she looked at her watch – she was getting worried that he hadn't phoned her or contacted her since he left. Of course, he was a busy man. If he extricated himself from this particular situation, he'd still be jet-setting around the world, scrutinizing accounts here, talking to managers there . . . making deals and unmaking them. He'd probably be buying a private jet soon.

Did she want to be part of that life?

No, sirree. No way. Definitely not.

So why was she looking forward to his return?

She wiped the rain from her face. Or was she crying? Hard to tell.

Dear Lord, I hope you're listening because I'm fresh out of courage on this one. Reinforcements needed, definitely. Some idea about what's going on would be helpful. I'm feeling my way, blindfolded, through an obstacle course.

The wind was chilly.

What on earth was she doing on this bitter spring day, standing out in the open without even a coat! Enough of reality. Back to business. Her phone was ringing. She went back indoors, to answer it. Without thinking.

FOURTEEN

'**B**itch, you might have got away with it for a while, but . . .'

Bea dropped the phone. Stared at it. Gulped. Put it back on the hand-rest.

Oh. Nasty. Very.

She found the emergency make-up bag she kept in her top drawer and attended to her hair – dishevelled – and lips – though this lipstick was too pale and not the one she usually wore. Her eyes looked heavy. Well, tough. She zipped the bag up and slammed it back into the drawer.

Carrie put her head around the door. 'Keith's back. He came down to tell us not to worry if we'd heard the buzzer go under the mat upstairs, as he got Dilys to let him in. He, er, he's had his hair cut.'

Bea put on a bright smile. 'Excellent. Thank you, Carrie. Is there anything desperately important that I should deal with this afternoon?'

'The nasty messages keep coming but I told the girls to ignore them, and now they just giggle if one comes up on their screens. We understand they're coming from someone who hates Mr Leon, and we all like him, so they're coping.'

'Excellent. I think we ought to shut early, don't you? Who's on duty tomorrow morning?'

'I've swopped with one of the girls. I'll be in myself.'

'Thank you, Carrie. I don't know what I'd do without you.'

Carrie disappeared. Bea closed her eyes and did some deep breathing exercises. They were supposed to calm her down, though they didn't seem to be working today. She found her mobile and clipped it to her belt.

Up the stairs we go. Ah, was that the buzzer under the mat at the front door? Whatever next?

It was the police, responding to Keith's phone call about a

rogue camera in the porch. One small man and one large woman, both in uniform. Plods. Constables this and that.

Dilys was there, fluttering, rosy-cheeked and bright-eyed. Behind her was a bulky, dark-haired stranger . . . no, not a stranger, but Keith, who'd had his hair cut and his beard trimmed by an expert. He looked, surprisingly, rather cute. And authoritative.

'Do come in, officers,' he was saying to the police. And to Bea, 'Would you like me to deal with this? I'll show the police the camera in the porch and take it down for them so you won't have to be bothered about it any more.'

Dilys was radiant. 'Would everyone like a cup of tea in the kitchen? I think I can find some biscuits as well.'

'Oh, thank you so much, Keith.' Bea assumed, implausibly, a little old widow's plaintive tones. 'If you could deal with it for me, that would be wonderful. It's all been so upsetting.'

Keith winked at her, and she winked back. She was unsure whether to burst into tears, have hysterics or lie on the floor and have a toddler's tantrum. The day was not proceeding according to any recognizable plan, was it?

Dilys said, 'I took up some more tea and biscuits to Anna. She said she was going to try to get up in a bit. I said she should rest because she still feels a bit shaky. She did ask if you were around, and I said you'd be up to see her when you could.'

Thus directed, Bea climbed the stairs, saying she'd be back to give her statement to the police in a few minutes if they needed it. She found Anna standing at the window, looking down on the rainswept garden below. Her colour in general was better, but one eye was almost closed and the bruise on her face was a nice mix of red, green and yellow. Her hair was hanging loose. It could do with washing, but her hairdresser had chosen a good shade for the colour. There was no more than a touch of grey at the roots. She was wearing one of Bea's silk dressing-gowns and slippers. An empty mug and some crumbs on a plate showed she'd eaten the biscuits and drunk her tea. Phials and tubes of arnica and creams were also there. Dilys had been busy.

Bea said, 'You're feeling better?'

'I need a day at a spa hotel. Whirlpool, massage. Every

beauty treatment under the sun, including pedicure, manicure, waxing, and a face pack. Then I want to spend, spend, spend on a new outfit. From head to toe.'

'A girl after my own heart,' said Bea. 'We'll make it a double date, shall we?'

'With champagne cocktails before lunch at the Ritz—'

'I could do with another pair of boots,' said Bea. 'I have a "thing" about boots. I dream of them.'

'Retail therapy works, every time.'

'So it does. Are you strong enough for a debrief?'

Anna sank back on to the bed. 'Didn't I tell you everything before? Was it last night? What day is it? I seem to have lost my mobile phone. I was going to ring the college to see how they're getting on.'

'It's Friday afternoon. You can use my landline. There's an extension in my bedroom next door.'

'Just a quick call, then. I want to make sure they've switched to the new roster.'

Bea showed Anna where the phone was and decided to put on her diamond ring, which she must have left on the dressing table. Yes, there it was.

The phone rang, and before Bea could stop her, Anna picked it up and listened. 'Oh!' She crashed the phone down. 'What the . . .!'

Bea was annoyed that she hadn't thought to take the call herself. 'Was that another death threat? Sorry, I should have realized. We're under siege. Leave the phone off the hook.'

Anna had recovered enough to be angry. 'Who on earth would—?'

'That is the question. Are you well enough to hear what's been going on and to help me work out who's responsible?'

'The police—'

'They're downstairs now, dealing with another of the incidents from which we've been suffering. Leon has gone to the police station with evidence of hate mail on his laptop and the taped confession of a girl whom you may know . . . calling herself Jennifer? Worked at the big house?'

A shrug. 'There are a lot of them. Unless they've been trained by us, I don't suppose I'd know her.'

'Understood. Now as I said, nasty things have been happening here. Death threats are only the latest. It looks as if Briscoe Holland is trying to destroy Leon and, because I have supported him, he's also targeting the agency.'

A long, hard stare from one blue eye. 'You mean that it wasn't the woman in the kitchen who left the gas on at the college?'

'Possibly not.'

'And made sure my car wouldn't start?'

'Maybe. That was certainly someone you've upset.'

'Well, it wouldn't be Briscoe.' Anna was sure of that.

'Why not?'

'Well, he's . . .' Anna gestured widely. 'I only met him once. The postman had left some mail with us that was meant for the big house, and I thought it would be only civil to take it up there myself. Leon had told me that everything was fine between him and his brother, each having their own sphere of influence. And indeed it was. I mean, Briscoe wasn't in good health, you could see that. He was up and dressed and sitting in an armchair with a rug over his knees. He apologized because the room was very warm, and he feels the cold. He offered me tea, and we talked about my ideas for streamlining the timetable at the college. He said I knew what I was doing and that he'd have done the same himself, given the circumstances. Then he said he was tired and asked me to touch the bell for Angharad.'

'Who's Angharad?'

'His housekeeper. Mrs Evans. Angharad is Welsh for "best beloved" but I don't suppose anyone laughs when she says that's her name. She's a tough cookie, a real heavyweight and no great beauty, but she looks after him well. A couple of times she's come down to the college, to check that no further mail has been left with us, though I did say I'd send anything else back up to him. And she came to the "do" when Leon handed the college over to me. I thought she was there to report to Mr Briscoe. Mind you, she didn't look pleased at what we were doing.'

'Is she connected to Mr Denver, who runs the security team at the big house?'

'Dunno. But then, I wouldn't, would I?'

'You've met Denver?'

'Of course. Surly brute. Didn't like being told not to include the college buildings in his rounds when I took over. Said he would if he felt it necessary to do so. I asked him to let me have any keys he might have to the college. He said he'd send them over. He did. They're in a drawer in my desk.'

'He may have kept spares.'

Anna grimaced. 'Or the keys he gave me weren't for the college. Stupidly, I didn't check.'

Bea wandered over to the window, fingering her mobile. Why didn't the inspector ring?

Anna looked at the landline phone. 'Do you think I might try the college now?' She put the phone back on the hook, and it rang immediately. Anna put out her hand to touch it and withdrew. She tried to laugh. 'Look at me, frightened I might hear myself abused.'

Bea said, 'Lift the phone, break the connection, and dial out.'

'Why didn't I think of that?'

'Because you've been knocked for six. You're doing fine.'

Anna lifted the phone, tightened her lips as she heard words she did not care for, broke the connection and dialled out.

Bea's mobile rang. 'Yes?'

'I'm not sure if it's good news or bad.' The inspector. 'A John Doe who might match the description of your Mr Adamsson was found floating in the Thames. No one's claimed him. Stripped to underwear, Marks and Sparks. No wallet, watch or ID. Soft hands, not a labourer. Medium height, short-sighted but didn't wear contact lenses. Good teeth, expensively looked after. Brown hair, thinning. Presumed victim of robbery. You'd need more information to make a positive ID.'

'You've informed the DI who's in charge of the murders at the swimming pool?'

'She says the body is nothing to do with her.'

'She could get a positive ID through Adamsson's father. He'd know who his dentist was.'

'The inspector is about to have Margrete Walford's husband rearrested. You know, the woman who was found dead in the car park? Apparently, her unit has broken what passed for an alibi for him. She doesn't want to hear about anything else. And, I've just been rapped on the knuckles for trying to tell her how to do her job. I've got a couple of days in the office to clear my desk, and then I'm on leave.'

'I'm having death threats on the phone and via our computers.'

'Get your techie to find out where they come from, and put your solicitors on to it.'

Bea sighed. 'Point taken. Have a wonderful time away. Hey, wait a minute. Let me think . . . there's something . . . Ah yes, I know. Remember Al Capone? They couldn't prove he'd murdered all those men, way back, so they got him for fiddling his taxes. Right? Now I realize you can't interfere with what your colleague is doing, but you could take an interest in some of the other things that have been happening, couldn't you?'

'I told you, I'm going on leave. I can't help.' Pause. 'No doubt you'll invite me round for supper sometime. Perhaps tonight?'

He might have had his knuckles rapped, but he was risking that happening again in order to help her. Well done, Inspector. 'I haven't a clue what we're going to eat, but yes, come and take pot luck.'

Anna was still talking on the phone to someone at the college, so Bea left her to it and went downstairs to see how Keith and Dilys were getting on with the local constabulary. She really hadn't the time to waste to fill them in on what had been happening. She needed to get right away and THINK! Could she get away with being a dithery old lady when dealing with the police? Would they want to arrest her for throwing water over the man in the hoodie who'd been trying to refocus the camera in the porch?

The two PCs were in the kitchen, drinking tea, eating biscuits and taking notes. Keith was blinding them with science, giving them chapter and verse about the camera, who made it, what it did, etcetera. The PCs were valiantly trying to keep up. 'You mean, someone's got it in for you? Do you know who it is?'

Keith scratched the back of his neck. His beard had been closely trimmed and actually looked rather good, but the barber must have left some loose hairs around his collar, and so, he scratched. 'I don't know, exactly, no.'

Time for Bea to put in a word. 'We've had lots of hate mail coming through on our computers in the agency downstairs. If you took a look at them, Keith, you'd be able to work out who sent them?'

Keith lightened up. 'Let's go. I'll lead the way, shall I?'

Carrie was the only member of staff still downstairs. She was frowning at her computer. 'Mrs Abbot, how can we stop these emails? They don't count as spam. I've tried blocking all the ones coming from a particular source, but it's not working. It's giving me a headache!'

'Let's see,' said Keith, capably taking over her seat and reaching for the mouse. The two PCs hovered, interested, willing to learn.

Bea's mobile phone rang, and she went into her office to take the call. 'Leon?'

'I think I recognize your voice, but what date are we on?'

'Twenty-ninth of November. Where are you, and when are you coming home?'

'I'm on the steps of the bank, waiting for Hari to turn up with his bike.'

She relaxed into her chair. 'Dressed appropriately for the City, I trust? Did the meeting go well?'

'No bowler hat, but they didn't raise an eyebrow when I walked in wearing the motorcycle helmet Hari made me put on when we left the police station. The bankers have been mollified. The police said they'd pass the laptop on to someone . . . goodness knows when. The morning went well enough, I suppose, but now I'm short of another laptop.'

'We've got hate mail here too, in the office. Keith is looking at it at the moment, with two members of the police force breathing down his neck. I'm also getting abusive calls on my landline phone. Anna's OK. Dilys is more than OK. So far we've been able to repel all invaders. Inspector Durrell is trying to help us but he's about to take some leave. His colleague is going after Margrete Walford's husband and refuses to listen to anything Durrell says. Has even been rather unkind to him.'

A grunt. 'That won't stop Durrell if I read him aright.'

'He's worn out. I told you, he's put in for leave, but he's going to come for supper tonight. I haven't a clue what I'll be cooking . . .'

'Can't you and I go out somewhere?'

'And leave Anna, Orlando, Dilys and Keith to fend for themselves?'

'Understood. Leave it to me. I'll get something sent in. How is Anna, anyway?'

'Much better. Dilys is blossoming, becoming quite bossy. Keith has had a haircut.'

'And you?' His voice dropped an octave.

She felt herself become quite breathless. Oh, Mr Darcy! What an effect a deep voice could have on a woman!

'Me?' She cleared her throat. 'I'm fine. I've had an idea, though. If you've got Hari and his bike at your disposal, do you think you could zip out to Mr Adamsson's house before returning here? And yes, I know it's quite a way, right across town and along the Great West Road. But I think it would be worth it.'

'You've news? Has Adamsson been located in France? Is he on his way home?'

'I don't think so. There's a John Doe in the morgue who might answer his description. No ID. No clothes.'

Leon muttered something which she didn't ask him to repeat. He said, heavily, 'I liked the man.'

'It might not be him. The inspector can't be sure. I thought that if we could get the name of his dentist out of Mr Adamsson senior we might be able to prove it one way or the other. We know he doesn't answer his phone, but if you went out there in person . . .?'

A long sigh. 'Yes. I'll see what I can do. Here's Hari now.'

She could hear a powerful motorbike draw up and idle.

He said, 'I've got to put on this dratted helmet, so I'll ring off. Depending on traffic, I should be back with you about seven or half past.'

He clicked off. Bea breathed long and deeply, and went to admire Keith's work on the computers. Praise be for Keith. The police were happy bunnies, too, as he'd actually got them to understand what had been happening and . . . double praise be! . . . managed to stop it.

Statements all round. What a bore. But if it stopped the hate mail from coming . . .

Carrie was all perky. 'You learn something every day. Not, I sincerely hope, that I'll be called upon to deal with such a thing ever again.'

The police took themselves off. Ditto Carrie, though she hinted strongly enough that she'd like to join them for supper. Bea's face ached with smiling.

Dilys said she'd borrowed some clothing from Bea's wardrobe so that Anna could join them for supper and was that all right? Bea supposed so.

She dithered. Leon had said he'd get something sent in for supper, but what had he meant by that, and had he reckoned on . . . how many people? Bea was reduced to counting on her fingers, which showed her how much the day had taken it out of her. She counted up to seven and hoped that was all.

Keith picked up her moment of indecision. 'Shall I send out for some pizzas?'

The buzzer sounded. Dilys let Orlando in. He said, 'I'm weary to death, in case you'd like to know. I was going to go out somewhere for supper, but it all seemed too much trouble so I thought I might as well see what you've got on the menu.' He hadn't thought to bring anything in himself, of course.

The buzzer sounded again. A delivery boy on a bike.

'Careful!' cried Dilys. 'It might be a bomb.'

It wasn't a bomb, thankfully. Leon had organized and paid for a full Chinese meal with innumerable dishes accompanied by plain and special rice.

Anna appeared, wearing one of Bea's dresses, asking if she could help lay the table. Dilys decided they should eat at the big table in the sitting room and got Anna to help her. Keith said he didn't know about anyone else, but he'd enjoy a beer and would fetch some in. Where was the nearest off-licence?

Bea gave him directions, and he returned at the same time as Leon and Hari drove up.

Leon said, 'All right to bring Hari's bike indoors? He doesn't want to leave it in the street.' The men didn't wait for permission but manoeuvred a giant motorbike into her hallway, where it looked as alien as a helicopter and took up about as much room. Hari proved to be a dark-skinned – possibly Maltese? – youngish man who moved like oiled silk. He was wearing black leather. He brought with him an air of cold efficiency but managed to smile when Bea welcomed him into the house and thanked him for looking after Leon so well.

'It's my job,' said Hari. 'Where's the sleeping beauty? I want to talk to her about her car.'

Bea waved him into the living room. 'Anna. She's anxious to talk to you, too.' She'd miscounted. They were going to be eight for supper, not seven, because Hari would need feeding as well.

Leon put his arm around her and kissed her cheek. He was dressed in his city clothes.

'All right?' she said, checking that all his bits and pieces were in place.

He nodded. 'Not too bad. I have some news for the inspector. How are you doing?'

'I need time to think, and I'm not getting it.'

Another ring at the doorbell, and there was the inspector, brushing rain off his jacket. He, too, gave Bea a hug, his nose whiffling. 'Is that Chinese I can smell? I could eat a horse.'

Dilys sang out, 'Come and get it!'

Keith found glasses and poured beer. Bea placed bottles of water on the table for those who preferred it. Leon took his seat at the head of the table and Bea at the foot, which was the correct seating plan for the head of the household and his wife. Bea didn't object, as this gave her the inspector on her right and Orlando on her left. Leon had Dilys and Anna on either side of him. Bea was interested to note that Hari managed to get himself seated next to Anna. Bea made the introductions.

Hari and Anna looked at one another with reserve but interest. Anna hadn't washed her hair yet and had piled it up in a simple knot at the back of her head. She couldn't do anything about the livid bruise on her face, but Hari certainly didn't seem to be repelled by it. Bea reflected that they made a distinctive but mismatched couple: one so dark and the other so fair; she from the top of one profession and Hari, no doubt, at the top of his. But then, Bea told herself that she and Leon were also mismatched, for what had she to do with the affairs of multi-million corporations, and what had he to do with a small if thriving domestic agency?

'Cheers!' said Dilys. She took a gulp of beer and choked. 'Oh, Keith! This beer is strong. I'd better not drink too much.'

'I'll pour you some water, shall I?'

'I suggest we all eat first,' said Leon. 'Talk later.'

That was good sense. But even while dealing with the food, they couldn't keep off the adventures of the day.

Orlando started it: 'You'll never guess who rang me today. My darling ex-partner Charles. Wanting to know how I was holding up.'

'That's good, isn't it?' said Bea. 'Making up and all that?'

Orlando pulled a face. 'Jumping on to the bandwagon more like. If he'd shown any signs of sympathy when my father was killed I'd have appreciated it, but now that things are beginning to sort themselves out and I've come into a title he's all over me. I contacted my father's solicitor, who wants to see me tomorrow. He says that Father left detailed instructions for his funeral, which makes me wince, it really does, but they say it can't be yet because . . .'

Bea switched off. Anna and Hari were talking to one another. About her car? Yes, of course. But then Anna laughed and he smiled. Were they talking about the car still? Or about something else?

Anna announced, 'Hari says he'll help me find whoever it was who took the battery out of my car. Who dunnit, in fact.'

'You could do with me going over your security,' said Hari. 'As soon as I'm off this job, I'll ring you for a date.'

He didn't mean a date to see to her security systems, did he? Anna and Hari touched glasses.

Bea glanced across at Leon, and his eyes met hers, full of amusement. That was one of the joys of a good partnership, wasn't it, that you could communicate amusement or horror without words?

The inspector turned his attention to Keith, saying he'd

heard there'd been a lot going on at the agency that day. Keith and Dilys were happy to oblige with details.

Bea ate as much as she could, nodding and saying, 'Yes,' and, 'Well, I never,' to Orlando at the right moments. She allowed herself half a glass of beer, and then drank water. When all the cartons of Chinese food had been emptied and stacked away, coffee had been served and the fruit bowl had been placed on the table, Leon called for order by tapping his glass with a knife.

'Ladies and gentlemen, pray silence. I am about to give you an after-dinner speech on the subject of missing persons.'

'Sorry to interrupt,' said Bea, 'but I've asked the inspector here for a very particular reason. He is unable for professional reasons to investigate the murders of Lord Lethbury and Margrete Walford himself, but if we can report any other matter which would lead to police involvement, he may be able to take an interest in that. Is that right, Inspector?'

'Beautifully put. But remember that I'm going on leave next week, I don't know any of the background, and it may be that there is no way I can interfere. However . . .' He placed a small tape recorder on the table. 'Anyone object to my using this?'

No one did.

'For the record,' the inspector said, 'this is Inspector Durrell speaking at twenty hundred hours. Also present are . . .' He held the recorder out to each of them, to speak their names. And then nodded to Bea to continue.

'I understand,' said Bea, 'that each one of us has some knowledge of this tangled affair, so I'm going to suggest that we tell the inspector what we know, in chronological order. Much of this information has already been given to the police and therefore the inspector can't act upon it. But he does need some essential background. Leon, over to you.'

Leon said, 'Well, my older brother Briscoe built up and ran Holland Holdings (Worldwide) by himself for many years. It became unwieldy, and he began to feel his age. There was a nasty incidence of financial mismanagement which could have brought the whole edifice crashing down. Mr Adamsson was appointed chief accountant to clear the mess up, and the corporation was divided into two parts; I took over the British-based companies, while my brother kept control of the Overseas Division. This was all done by the book, and Briscoe gave the split his blessing.

'I moved into a flat in the big house and ran my side of the business from there. Relations with my brother were good, though he tired easily and could be crotchety on occasion. I visited him most evenings, but I kept a small flat in the Barbican for overnight use when I was travelling around. Also living in the big house were our sister Sybil, my niece Dilys, and her daughter Bernice. Dilys: would you like to say how you found your father at that time?'

Dilys was eager to tell what she knew. 'I saw Daddy some part of every day. I hadn't anything much else to do as Bernice was at school and Aunt Sybil was always out. I used to take him up some of my home-made lemonade, and we played backgammon, though I'm not very good at it. He played chess with Lord Lethbury, who visited him every weekend. They looked forward to that. Daddy suggested I went out with Orlando here—' she sent him an affectionate smile – 'and of course that was fun in a way, but he and I are not really, we don't exactly click . . .'

Bea suppressed a smile. She noted that everyone except Orlando was also suppressing a smile.

Dilys said, 'Then Daddy got a really bad cold and wouldn't let me near him for a while. After that I seemed to irritate him, and he sent me away as soon as I tapped on his door. I asked Uncle Leon what to do when he got back from one of his business trips, and . . .' She looked at Leon.

He grimaced. 'What Dilys doesn't know was that I'd been after my brother to make some financial provision for her, while he'd said she should marry Orlando and be done with it.'

Orlando said, 'We did try, didn't we, Dilys? But it was never going to work.' He explained to the inspector, 'My father was an old friend of Mr Holland's, and they'd hatched this plan together for us to marry.'

Leon picked up the tale. 'When Dilys said my brother wasn't letting her in to see him, I tried, too. And got the same treatment. Mrs Evans – that's his housekeeper – said he didn't want to see me any more. My sister Sybil tried. Same thing. Sybil was due to return to the States, which is where she lives most of the year, and had planned to take Dilys and Bernice with her for a holiday. Dilys refused to go, hoping Briscoe would soon change his mind and send for her, so Sybil asked Mrs Abbot if Dilys could come here for a bit and went off with Bernice. I, too, thought he was sure to relent. But, far from it, he sent messages saying he'd finished with me, that I'd betrayed him of all things! He ordered me out of the house.'

Bea said, 'Let's stop a moment and look at the timescale. Briscoe was ill, and Leon was away. After that, Briscoe sent messages saying he didn't wish to see his family any more. Now; Leon, tell the inspector about the attempt on your life.'

FIFTEEN

Leon grimaced. 'I still find it hard to believe that Briscoe would send someone to kill me. But, when he forbade me to visit him, I realized I had to make alternative arrangements. I continued to sleep at the big house when I wasn't travelling around, but I began to move my stuff out to the flat in the Barbican. I found and staffed new offices in the city. Dilys was safely out of the frame with Mrs Abbot, but she and I were not the only ones to be worried by my brother's behaviour.

'Mr Adamsson, my brother's chief accountant, used to see my brother every morning at eleven. If Briscoe felt too frail for a visit, he'd ring Adamsson and they'd go through what needed to be done by phone. Suddenly, Mr Adamsson was informed by Mrs Evans that my brother no longer felt it necessary to speak to him every day. Adamsson was concerned. There was a lot of outstanding business and no one making decisions. Adamsson asked Mrs Evans whether Briscoe needed to see a doctor and got short shrift. He knew Briscoe and I had had a good relationship recently, so he rang me to ask for an appointment. We met at my new offices in the City last Thursday, just over a week ago.

'Adamsson was a conscientious man. He said he'd been put in an impossible position, that he couldn't go on working for my brother if he was refused contact. When he discovered that I, too, had been denied access, he saw no alternative but to resign. He was a valuable man. Perhaps rashly, I said that if he did resign I'd be happy to give him a job. He said nothing about going away on holiday. In fact, we agreed to meet this week when I returned from a business trip.

'At that point I was still going back to the big house at night. My chauffeur had walked out on me, and I was driving the Rolls which Briscoe had set aside for my use. It developed a fault. I asked Denver to put the car in for repair and service and—'

'Who's Denver?' said the inspector.

'Head of security for Holland Holdings at the big house. He found me a courtesy car, but on Sunday afternoon it refused to start. I was due in Birmingham for meetings early on Monday morning so I decided to walk to the station. On the way I was nearly run over by a van. No, I didn't get the licence number. It had gone by the time I'd picked myself out of the ditch. A van, dark blue or black. No obvious lettering on the side. The road was clear in either direction. It looked – felt like – a deliberate attempt to run me down.'

'Did you report it?' said the inspector.

'I was in shock, and what proof did I have? A ruined over-coat and a twisted ankle? A dent in my briefcase? On the train to Birmingham I received a recorded phone message from Briscoe, alleging I was a traitor. He said I was not to return to the big house, that he was having my things packed up and so on and so forth. I couldn't understand what was happening. Had he heard that Adamsson was proposing to resign and that I'd offered him a job? Did that amount to treachery? I contacted Adamsson to confirm our meeting—'

'How did you contact him?'

'By phone. He was on his way out somewhere so we didn't have time to chat. He just said he was still on board for our meeting and rang off. I finished my business in Birmingham, and returning on the train on Tuesday morning I received a text message on my phone purporting to be from Adamsson, arranging to meet at his place. Arrived in London, I took a taxi out there, only to get another message rearranging the venue to the car park of the swimming pool. I took the taxi on and spotted his car in the car park. Unoccupied. I left in a hurry. The rest you know.'

'Orlando?' said Bea. 'Your turn next.'

'Well, I knew Adamsson, of course. My father was always praising him, saying Holland Holdings would have gone under without his expertise. He kept the books tickety-boo, stainless steel, pure as Simon.'

Anna nodded. 'I had some dealings with him when we took over the college, changing bank accounts, that sort of thing. Straight as a die.'

Dilys said, 'He was always kind to me. Lots of people used to look right through me, but he always had time for a word. He used to test my little Bernice on her multiplication times tables. I don't think they bother with them so much in schools nowadays, but he encouraged her to learn them off by heart. He's away on holiday, isn't he?'

Bea shook her head. 'I don't think so. Orlando? The car park.'

'Oh. Yes. My father and Mr Holland thought that Dilys and I would be well suited, and we were to try to make a go of it. If it didn't work after six months they offered to set me up in my own business. So when I had a text from my father to meet him and Mr Adamsson I thought it was about that and I went along, a lamb to the slaughter, and . . .' He told the rest, growing paler and paler as he did. He finished up by saying, 'And no, I didn't ring the police then, but I did make a report later.'

'Now,' said Bea, 'we were led to believe that there were two people killed in the car park, but I think there were three, and that the third was Adamsson, because—' She turned to the inspector.

He picked up the tale. 'Mrs Abbot asked me to check if a body had turned up which matched that of Mr Adamsson. And yes, there is. Fished out of the Thames, no ID. It may or not be the missing accountant. Mr Holland, why didn't you use your phone to ring Adamsson in the car park and ask where he'd got to?'

'I did. His phone was out of service. Also, the back offside window of his car was starred as if someone had tried to break it.' He grimaced. 'I've just realized. If Adamsson's mobile was in his car or in his pocket at the car park, I'd have heard it ring and gone to investigate. Where was he? Hidden in the bushes?'

'No, I think he'd been dumped in the boot of his car with a blanket or a sheet of plastic, perhaps, thrown over him before you got there. His phone must have been put out of action when he was killed . . . which means he was dead by the time you arrived.'

Dilys said, in a tiny voice, 'Was it all my fault? Were they killed because Daddy didn't want to provide for me?'

Bea said, 'No, Dilys. Don't beat yourself up. It had very little to do with you. This was a very careful and elaborate plot for money. Let's deal with one of the red herrings, shall we? Margrete Walford. She went there for a tryst with her lover who worked at the pool. She chose to drive into that end bay because she didn't want to be seen meeting him. Perhaps she drove in just as the killer was dealing with Lord Lethbury. She was killed because she was in the wrong place at the wrong time.'

Leon was frowning. 'Our phones were tampered with. What about Lord Lethbury's? Have the police checked?'

Bea said, 'I hope they have, but I think they're diving down the wrong rabbit hole. Orlando, I know you've been through this before, but what else did you see when you were in the car park?'

Orlando ruffled his hair. 'I've already told you. I didn't see anyone apart from Leon, until the woman arrived with her kiddies.'

'There must have been some other vehicles there. Think!'

He closed his eyes and leaned back in his chair. 'I drove off the main road into the grounds of the swimming pool, which is set well back from the road in its own grounds. Straight ahead there were a couple of cars parked close to the steps leading up to the building. That's the parking for people with disabled stickers. Over to the left was the coach park: kids were piling into a school bus as I arrived. I turned right, into the visitors' car park. One way system. You drive along one lot of parking bays looking for a space. The bays are lined with hedges so you can't see ahead or to either side. Just before the last bay you can turn left and left again – like the top of an inverted "U" – and motor back down through another set of bays till you're back at the start. Each bay contains six cars, three on either side of the central traffic "lane". I parked in the first bay nearest the road, got out and walked along looking for my father's car. Mine was the only car there in that bay or the next . . . except for a dark-coloured SUV. No one in it.'

Leon nodded. 'Adamsson's.'

'Well, I wouldn't have known it from Adam, would I?' He

squeezed his eyes shut. 'I'm walking through the next bay now. An abandoned car, stickers on it, pigeon poo. Two more cars: nobody in them. One was a red sports car, the other an estate, I think. Next bay: empty? There was an old, rusty bicycle and a cart from a supermarket thrown into the hedge. Nothing else. Fourth bay: also empty. Then came the turning off to the left, but ahead of me I saw two cars in the end bay: my father's and one other.' His voice cracked.

Bea prompted him. 'What about the bays on the other side of the hedge?'

He pulled at his lower lip, frowning. 'Dunno. I have the impression there were a couple of other cars, perhaps. A flash of sunlight on metal? That sort of thing. Oh, and a cyclist. At least, I think it was a cyclist. I caught a glimpse of his helmet.'

Bea sighed. 'Ah, now I understand.'

Orlando said, 'I suppose it must have been a cyclist, because nobody else wears helmets like that, do they? He was in the parallel bay to the one in which I'd parked my car, but further away from the road.'

'Age? Height? Dressed?'

A shrug. 'I don't know, do I? Lycra, I suppose. I didn't peer through the hedge to ask if he'd seen any murders lately. I was panicking, wanting to get away as fast as I could. I spotted Leon and hid till he'd gone. Then a family car drove in and parked near mine. Some kiddies got out with their mother and went up into the swimming pool. I waited till they'd gone, scrambled into my car and got out of there in a hurry.'

The inspector pointed to Leon. 'Close your eyes. Concentrate. Think back to when you were standing in the car park, seeing Adamsson's car, noting that the back window had been damaged. Did you see the cyclist? Were there footsteps running away?'

'No, no. Nothing like that.' A shake of the head. A frown. 'It was extraordinarily silent. It spooked me.'

'You were being watched.' Bea exchanged glances with the inspector. She thought that he'd probably come to the same conclusion as her, that if either Orlando or Leon had gone to investigate the cyclist, they'd have ended up dead, too.

Hari thought it, too. 'The murderer would have killed

Orlando if that woman hadn't driven into the car park with her children just then.'

'A cyclist,' said Bea. 'It's a good disguise. How can you tell what a man looks like when he's dressed up in Lycra with a helmet and goggles on? Gloves, too. Which means no finger-prints on the car.'

The inspector threw out his hands. 'Motive? You said it was money?'

'Billions,' said Bea. 'Briscoe is a multi-billionaire. But, if he had changed his will or died unexpectedly, several people would have kicked up a fuss; Adamsson, Lethbury and Leon. Sybil, too, but she had gone off to the States – her heart is really there, isn't it? – and Dilys has been through such a rough time recently that they probably felt both women might be discounted. I think the original idea was to kill all three men and make Orlando the scapegoat.'

'Slaughter at the swimming pool?' said the inspector with a flash of his old style.

'Carnage in the car park?' said Bea.

Orlando stared. 'But why should I want to kill Leon and Adamsson? At a stretch I can see why someone might think I'd want to kill my father . . . but Leon? And Adamsson?'

'No reason. That's why Leon and Adamsson's bodies were supposed to disappear. I don't know what they planned to do with Leon's body – possibly dump it somewhere and make it look like a mugging? – but Adamsson was to be disposed of in such a way as to make us think he'd gone to France.'

Bea took a deep breath. 'What I think happened was this: the killer arrived early, on his bike. Dressed in biker's gear, he was anonymous. I don't know who was killed first, but he murdered two out of his three targets straight away – Adamsson and Lethbury. Margrete must have been killed because she had seen something she shouldn't. The killer left Lethbury and Margrete sitting in their driving seats. Adamsson's body was transferred to the boot of his car, during which process some part of his body – maybe a ring on his finger? – struck the back window and starred the glass. The murderer took Adamsson's keys and smashed his mobile. So far, so good.

'The murderer then waited for Leon to arrive, but Orlando

turned up first and discovered his father dead. That upset the killer's timetable. He didn't want to kill Orlando, who was supposed to carry the can for the murders. As he hesitated, Leon arrived. Good. Extra good because he'd arrived in a taxi which wasn't going to hang around waiting for him, was it? But Leon didn't go far enough into the car park for the killer to catch him. The killer could only watch in frustration as Orlando spotted Leon and dived into the bushes on the opposite side to where the killer was lurking! And Leon turned round and left before he could be killed! Orlando was saved by a family parking nearby. He fled, but that didn't matter as he could still take the blame for his father's death.

'Now the original plan was that, after the killings, the murderer would add Leon's body to Adamsson's at the back of his SUV, shed his biker's gear, put the cycle on top of the bodies and drive away, thus removing the two bodies from the scene. That way there would be only two victims left – Lethbury and Margrete – and no one would be able to tell which had been the original target.

'But the timing went awry. The killer watched Orlando flee. He must have thought Orlando was going to the swimming pool to raise the alarm. He hadn't time to manoeuvre the bike into the back of Adamsson's car – always a difficult business – change his clothes and drive the car away. He couldn't abandon the bike because he hadn't had time to clean off any fingerprints, and he couldn't drive Adamsson's car away dressed in biker gear – far too noticeable. So he decided to cycle away, leaving Adamsson's body in his car, hoping it wouldn't be discovered. Which it wasn't. Either he or his accomplice then sent a Trojan message to Leon and to Orlando's mobiles. When they opened it, it would release a virus that would eventually destroy all the earlier messages and texts, leaving them without proof that they'd been lured to the car park. Orlando fell victim to that, but Leon didn't.'

The inspector asked, 'Have you two still got those mobiles?'

Both men shook their heads. 'Handed in to the police,' said Leon.

'Going back to the day of the murder,' said Bea, 'the killer returned to the swimming pool a few hours later. He came on foot or arrived by bus. Why not? Lots of people do. He'd changed out of his Lycra, looked like any other man visiting the swimming pool. There were police all over the place, and they'd cordoned off some of the bays in the car park but not the first one. As would be natural on seeing the police presence, the killer probably asked around, "What's happened, is it an accident? How shocking." He unlocked Adamsson's car with the keys he'd lifted early. No one was going to challenge him if he had the keys, were they? He got into the car and drove it away with Adamsson's body in the back.'

The inspector said, 'What a nerve! You're thinking of a contract killer?' in tones of doubt.

'Yes, I am. You see, there's one interested party who might well have a motive for doing away with those close to Briscoe. It occurred to me to wonder where Angharad Evans, Briscoe's formidable housekeeper, might fit into this scenario, and I think she fits rather well. Does anyone know if she has a connection to Denver, the head of the security team?'

Leon said, 'Aren't they related? Half brother and sister?'

Dilys lifted her hand. 'She told me once. They were brought up together. I think one of them was fostered with the other's family, but I can't remember which way it was.'

Leon snapped his fingers. 'Briscoe said Mrs Evans had recommended Denver to the post when his previous head of security retired. Bea, are you trying to say that Mrs Evans turned my brother against us, and then set out to murder his old friend and his accountant?'

'You gave me the clue yourself. You were semi-joking, but you said he'd probably got married years ago because his then housekeeper had given him notice and he'd felt he couldn't do without her. And she gave him Dilys.'

Bea touched Dilys's hand. 'Your mother died when you were still quite young, didn't she? I'm wondering if the pattern might have repeated itself. Angharad had become essential to Briscoe. He was failing. Look at it from her point of view: when he died, she'd be out of job . . . and he's worth so many billions! If she could only get him to marry her, or to change his will in her favour . . .! But he'd been on such good terms with his family recently that she felt she must first drive a wedge between them. Remember that she had had access to him at all hours and could drip what poison she chose into his ear. He'd had a bad cold. Leon had gone away. For perhaps a week she had him to herself, and after that he said he didn't want to know any member of his family. Leon, you thought it was because both you and Adamsson had tried to get him to provide for Dilys and been rebuffed.'

Dilys perked up. 'I don't need money, I really don't. That is, of course I—'

Keith patted her hand. 'We know what you mean. You are your own person. You can make your own way in life.'

Dilys was grateful that he understood. 'Yes, as a housekeeper and cook for you. You said.'

Bea avoided looking at Leon to see how he'd taken this. She said, 'Keep thinking how it looks from Mrs Evans's point of view. I don't know what background Mr Denver has. He's the head of the security team at Holland Holdings, and according to Jennifer he asked her to infiltrate the agency and arrange for my phone to be bugged. If it was him, he certainly had a nerve. Would he have taken Adamsson's car back to the big house?'

She answered her own question. 'No, I don't think so. He probably used a lock-up garage somewhere for the next bit. He took Adamsson's body out of the boot of the car and stripped him to his underwear to delay identification. The clothes and personal effects were probably discarded in the nearest rubbish bin. He dropped the body into the Thames at a time and place when he wouldn't be noticed. He left the car somewhere it was likely to be vandalized before morning. And that's how Adamsson disappeared.'

The inspector was not happy. 'I suppose I can pass your ideas along, but—'

'I know,' said Bea. 'Let us bring you up to date on what else has been happening. Leon . . .?'

'I've certainly been kept busy.' He explained how he'd taken refuge with Bea, who'd found a taxi driver to take him around and give him a bed for the night. Bea then asked Orlando to pick up the tale. He said he'd been convinced he was going to be framed for his father's murder and asked

Dilys to hide him . . . only for Mrs Abbot to find him the following day.

'Meanwhile,' said Bea, 'he'd given his dicey phone to Dilys to be charged up, which resulted in all the computers in the agency being infected with a virus—'

'Which brought me in,' said Keith. 'Unfortunately, I didn't know anything about the murders, so I cleaned up everything in sight, which had the side effect of removing the incriminating messages on Orlando's phone.'

'But,' said Leon, 'later that day both Orlando and I went to the police with what we'd seen and done, and handed over our phones for inspection. We were told we might be asked more questions later but allowed to leave. At that time the police seemed convinced that Margrete had been the real target.'

'Which,' said Bea, 'is when I first phoned you, Inspector, and you said you couldn't interfere. So, moving swiftly on, we leave the murders behind and start looking at what happened next, which was a deliberate and sustained policy of harassment aimed at Leon and, because he'd come to me for help, at me and the agency. I noticed that there were phone calls for him the moment he stepped through the door here. How did they know? Fortunately, Keith was still with us and discovered that my phone downstairs had been bugged. We traced that to one of our agency workers, a woman called Jennifer, who'd arranged for someone to visit the agency to "clean" the phones but had planted a bug instead. Keith removed the bug. Jennifer went AWOL before we could question her. But still someone at the Holland organization seemed to know exactly when our visitors arrived. I couldn't work out how.'

Bea continued, 'Moving swiftly on . . .' She outlined recent happenings, ending with the tale of the toy cat, 'which resembled my cat Winston – who I observe is currently sitting on Keith's knee. I was upset, which was probably the intention. No, I didn't report it. We have the box it came in, still, but . . . so much else was happening, and it knocked me off balance. Meanwhile, Leon was dealing with major trouble on several fronts: some of his personnel decided to sue when they were sacked, and the banks were pressed to look at his finances.

The pressure was intense. One of the precautions Leon had taken was to give the training college, lock, stock and barrel, over to . . .' Bea gestured, and Anna took up the tale.

'To me. I was working late last night when . . .'

She told the tale well, holding herself together as she recounted the horror of finding herself locked into a gas-filled building. Then came her rescue by a couple of security guards from the big house, who'd put her on a train back to London.

'They didn't suggest calling the police?' said the inspector.

'No. And I was too shaken to think straight. Sorry.'

'Has this been reported?'

'Not yet,' said Bea. 'Anna wasn't well enough. She's slept most of today, and there was so much else going on that we didn't get round to it.'

'So I can take it,' said the inspector, 'that you are now asking me to investigate something that has not previously been reported? Well, that makes a change. What do you think happened?'

'My turn,' said Hari. 'I run a protection agency. Leon had been using me. I have a powerful bike. I got out there to find the college in darkness, with padlock and chain on back and front doors. No sign of anything untoward except for the broken window . . .' He told the tale well.

When he'd finished, the inspector said, 'You're thinking that someone from the security staff organized what might have been set down as an accident to the building, but that a couple of them didn't realize Anna had been locked in by mistake and so got her out in time?'

Hari nodded. He laid a tape recorder similar to the inspector's on the table and shot it across to him. 'I made a full report to Leon. There's a copy for you. It's enough to let you go in and investigate, isn't it? I dossed down in the college last night to make sure there weren't any other accidents to the gas, but there weren't. When the first lot of cleaners arrived at the college this morning, I attended to the lady's car and made my way back here to collect Leon.'

'By which time,' said Bea, 'the situation here had deteriorated once more.'

Leon said, 'Death threats on my computer. So like a good

boy I take it into the local police here, together with some evidence which Bea had collected.'

Bea said, 'You remember one of the girls in the agency had arranged for someone to come in and bug my office? Well, she returned this morning, trying to sell us information. We think she'd been promised a bonus by her boss . . . Oh, yes, there's a definite tie-up there with Holland Holdings, as she had previously worked for them in the maintenance office. We got a confession of sorts from her, and yes, that is also now with the local police. To be fair, they did send a couple of constables around to take notes on what's been happening. I suppose they'll report back and we'll be visited by a more senior officer eventually.'

The inspector winced. 'Look, you must understand the way the police work. You take a complaint to one of the local offices. They assess it, and if they think it needs attention they send someone round, which they have done, to see if it checks out. In this case they'd need to find an expert to assess your reports before they can link them to the murders. And that takes time.'

Bea said, 'We understand that. But unless and until they do something about it, we remain open to attack. This morning Keith discovered that a camera has been fitted in our porch, allowing someone in a van – a florist's van, we think – to monitor who was coming and going in this house. So now we know how the enemy became aware of who entered or left the house. Keith turned it so that it only got pictures of the steps down to the agency. Leon had to get out of the house to take various bits and pieces of evidence to the police and go on to a series of important meetings. We didn't want him being run down in the street on his way to the police station so we dressed him up as Orlando, and he was about to leave when we found a man trying to turn the camera back on to the front door . . . but we got rid of him all right.'

'How?'

Bea blushed. 'I pretended I thought he was a homeless man looking for a place to sleep and threw a bowl of water at him. So he ran away.'

'And,' said Orlando, holding up his mobile, 'I got some

photos of him and the subsequent traffic jam when the florist's van tried to get out to follow Leon at just the wrong moment.'

The inspector's face was a picture. 'Who do I charge on that one? Bea or the intruder? Is the camera still there?'

Keith shook his head. 'I showed it to the police constables who came round this afternoon, and they removed it.'

Bea said, 'The thing is that the distractions keep on coming. Hate mail on the agency computers. Death threats on my landline phones. I couldn't think straight . . . until I took time out and realized that they were nothing but that. Distractions. That's when I asked you, Inspector, to see if there was a John Doe body somewhere which might match Adamsson's description . . . and you found that there was.'

'Not yet proven,' said the inspector. 'We'll need to visit his father and—'

'You can't,' said Leon, heavily. 'As soon as Bea realized everything stems from the fact that Adamsson had gone missing, she sent me out to check on what was happening at his house. Hari took me there late this afternoon. We found the house deserted and up for sale.'

'What!' Consternation.

Leon said, 'Inspector, I am asking you formally to file a report for Mr Adamsson junior as a missing person.' He produced a packet wrapped in a plastic bag from his pocket and spun it down the table till it ended up in front of the inspector. 'Hari and I looked through the front window of Adamsson's house. No furniture. No curtains. We looked through the letterbox. There's a few letters, some daily papers and some junk mail on the hall floor. We knocked on neighbours' doors. Elderly couple, retired professionals, on one side. A young family with a baby on the other. Both were mystified by what has happened. Father and son had been living there in relative harmony. The old man was a bit of a moaner, walked with a stick, always complaining about something. The son kept himself to himself but was always civil. When he went on holiday – which was infrequently – he'd go round to the neighbours, leave them a key and ask them to look out for the old man.'

'And this time he didn't?'

'No, he didn't. One minute the car was there, and the next it had gone. The neighbours weren't sure when it went but they think it was on Tuesday morning, which would tie up with my seeing it in the car park at the swimming pool on Tuesday afternoon. Incidentally, the swimming pool is only a hop, skip and a jump from his house. Parking is difficult around there, and if the neighbours failed to see Adamsson's car in front of his own house, they'd assume he'd had to leave it up the road somewhere.

'The elderly neighbours are at home most of the day. They say the old man had a visitor in a flash car late Tuesday afternoon. They couldn't remember the make or number, but it was large and black. Possibly a Jaguar. They didn't see who the visitor was, but they were expecting Tesco to deliver their weekly shopping order so were on the lookout when they heard his front door open and the old man inviting someone in. They always get their shopping delivered on a Tuesday afternoon, so they know exactly which day it was. The next morning Mr Adamsson senior called on them to say his son had decided to move abroad and that he couldn't manage on his own, so he was going to move into a posh home where he'd be looked after better than his son had ever done and he wouldn't be left alone all day. He said he was fed up with people trying to contact his son who was a grown adult and should be able to answer the phone for himself. He gave the neighbours a twenty-pound note to pay off the milkman and the paper boy and asked them to return the keys to his house, as he'd been told they'd got a vacancy in the home for him straight away and he was going to pack up and move the very next day.

'The neighbours were surprised but supposed it was all for the best. They asked for a forwarding address. He said he'd leave one with them, but didn't do so. They offered to help him pack, but he refused. Sure enough he went off next morning, Wednesday, in a car that had come for him. That afternoon the "For Sale" sign went up, and yesterday the house removal people took out everything, including the carpets. It's a prime position, overlooking the park at the back, and the neighbours say there's been someone round to view it already.'

The inspector fingered the packet Leon had passed to him. 'Are those his keys?'

'The old people had given Mr Adamsson senior back the keys that they had, but the young mother on the other side still had hers. She'd been out for the day when he left so was shocked when she met the older couple in the street and they told her he'd packed up and gone. She says the son left the keys with her some time ago. I'm hoping he licked the flap before sticking it down, which would give you his DNA for comparison purposes, but in any case, it should have his fingerprints on it.'

Hari held up an expensive camera. 'Give me your email address and I'll send you pictures of the house with the "For Sale" up, and the view through front and back windows.'

No one asked how he'd got to the back windows.

The inspector nodded. 'I'll let you have it when we've finished. I may have been warned off the murders, but I can ask someone to investigate the disappearance of a man who was supposed to have met people in the car park and didn't. And of his father, too, come to think of it.'

Orlando's voice was sharp. 'That's all very well, but I want to know who killed my father.'

SIXTEEN

'Yes,' said the inspector. 'I'd like to know that, too.'

Leon put his hand over his eyes.

'Leon, it wasn't Briscoe, if that's what you're thinking,' said Bea, quickly. 'Why? Because no one who knew him thinks he was capable of it. You said he wouldn't. Dilys said the same thing. Anna agreed. He wouldn't. So, he didn't.'

The inspector said, 'Come on, now. Everything you've all said seems to indicate that Briscoe's security men are behind the attacks on you, and that he ordered his men to destroy the college.'

Leon said, 'I think he's dead. I can't think of any other explanation. He was not well. He was becoming very frail. He was so much older than me. I ought to be able to accept it.'

'He may not be dead,' said Bea. 'If he'd died of natural causes in hospital or with a doctor attending we'd have heard. So he's not officially dead. Angharad Evans ran his household. Briscoe married his housekeeper first time round because he'd become dependent upon her. I think that's what Angharad has been working for. I don't know if he has actually gone through a form of marriage with her yet, but I suspect that's what she wants. Failing that, she would like him to make a will leaving everything to her. It might not be necessary for his solicitor actually to attend. She could write out a letter of intent and get him to sign it.

'The courts would honour it if no one else objected, but if he had died with his loving family around him, there'd be endless fuss and bother with lawyers, because Leon, Lethbury and Adamsson would have challenged a will which left everything to her. The affair would have rumbled on through the courts, probably for years. The only winners would be the legal eagles. So, to make a will that will stick, she has to arrange that Briscoe quarrel with his immediate family and friends by drip-feeding him with false information and cutting off his contact with them.'

Dilys mopped up tears. 'Don't say that! It was my dream to look after him in his old age . . . until Angharad said that I irritated him so much that he didn't want to see me any more.'

'A clever woman,' said Bea. 'You see how she got rid of everyone around him? Leon and Dilys were driven away. His sister went to the States. There remained Adamsson – with whom he communicated daily – and his old friend Lethbury, whom he saw every week. She isolated Adamsson from Briscoe till he talked about resigning. Well and good. But even if he left the organization, he'd still be pretty vocal if Mrs Evans produced a will in her favour, because he'd never agree to her trying to run an international corporation such as Holland Holdings. But, he could vanish to the Continent on permanent holiday, couldn't he? Lethbury was a different matter.' Bea took a deep breath. 'Orlando, what did your father have that Briscoe didn't?'

Orlando blinked. 'Well, they were much of a muchness, I suppose. Been pals for ever.'

'You've missed the point,' said Bea. 'Briscoe had his millions. Lord Lethbury was a wealthy man, too. I'm speculating here, but I think I'm right. He also had . . . a title. Dilys, did your father ever say he'd like to crown his achievements with a peerage?'

Dilys perked up. 'Why, yes; he did. He even showed me a list of possible titles which he was thinking about. I suggested Lord Holland of Holland Park, but he said that was silly, and I suppose that it was. I really am not very clever, am I?'

Keith patted her hand, and she turned eagerly to him. 'It was all terribly hush hush. He told me that if you're offered one, you have to keep quiet about it for ages. That would be, oh, just before Sybil and Bernice went to America.'

'Leon; did you know about this?'

Leon lowered his eyelids and shrugged. Which meant that yes, he did know?

'And how,' asked Bea, 'was he going to get this longed-for title?'

Orlando slapped the table. 'Through my father, who was on committees for this and that, and knew exactly who to have a word with.'

'I think we can take it that Briscoe's old friend did have a word with someone, and Briscoe did get a letter asking him if he'd care to receive an honour. A warning was attached: he'd have to keep quiet about it till the next Queen's birthday honours list. Now either he told Angharad or she was monitoring his post, because at that moment she could see the future in terms not only of money but also a title. From being simple Mrs Angharad Holland, she'd become Lady Holland. And that's why I think, I hope, that she's keeping Briscoe alive. He won't get the title until the next list is published and that only happens twice a year: on the Queen's official birthday and at New Year.'

'Or,' said Leon, washing his face with his hands, 'he may have died but she has to keep it quiet until then. I can't think how she'd do that. Or yes, I can. Put him in the freezer?' His voice cracked, and he stared down at the table.

Leon saw things too clearly, didn't he? Bea had hoped he wouldn't think of that, but he had. Yes, it was more than likely that Briscoe was dead. But maybe not. It's best to keep hoping. 'No, he's got to be alive to accept the title, which means it's not in her interests to let him die yet. I think he's being kept alive but sedated.'

Orlando was so pale, he looked transparent. 'You mean, my father was killed because he might have made a nuisance of himself, visiting his old friend? Or because he'd recommended Briscoe for a title? That's monstrous!'

The inspector got to his feet with an effort. And stretched. 'You've given me more than enough to make a start. I'll have to get a warrant . . . First things first. I need Anna and Hari to make and sign statements. The incidents which concern the plan to blow up the college are the easiest lines of enquiry to follow, leading as they do to the involvement of the Holland security guards. We'll start there.'

Anna said, 'And how many days is it going to be before you actually make a move?'

'And where will the next attacks be made?' said Bea.

'And how long can Briscoe last?' said Leon. 'I can't bear to think of him alone in that great house, being looked after by people who wish him ill. I must try to get in there tomorrow. Or even tonight.'

The inspector shook his head. 'How would you get through the security guards? Even if not all of them think you are the enemy, they have their orders and will deny you entrance.'

'Which reminds me,' said Bea. 'How many people are involved in this conspiracy, do you think? That wretched girl Jennifer – the one who let the woman in who bugged our phones – said that the people in the maintenance department thought that Leon had taken over part of Holland Holdings in an underhand fashion and that they were going to lose their jobs because of him. They are convinced that Leon is a Bad Thing. I suspect that Angharad and Denver are playing on the fears of lots of different people to target Leon and the agency. Hence the hate mail we've been receiving and the horrible phone calls. Let me test it again now.' She put the phone back on its rest and waited for the inevitable nasty phone call . . . which didn't come. 'Hurray. The enemy has closed down for the night. Hopefully.'

Hari was restless, prowling around the room. 'Can Anna give you her statement first, Inspector? I want to go round the house, check that all the windows and doors are locked.'

'Must I?' said Anna. There were dark shadows under her eyes, one of which was still almost shut.

'We'll take it gently,' said the inspector. 'I really need your statements before I can take any action.'

'More coffee, everyone?' Dilys started to clear the table, assisted by Keith.

Most people shook their head, but the inspector said, 'Yes, please: it will help to keep me awake.'

Leon took his laptop to the table at the far end by the windows down to the garden. Bea followed him. She put her arms around him from behind and rested her head against his. 'Another new laptop?'

'Mm. May I stay the night again?'

'If you can manage with the settee.'

He nodded, concentrating on what he was doing.

Hari had followed her. He drew back the curtains and unlocked the grille which protected them from burglars. 'There's an iron staircase down into the garden? May I explore?'

She nodded. It would take an exceptional burglar to climb over the high walls surrounding the gardens in this terrace of houses, but Hari was being thorough.

Orlando said, 'Well, I might as well go to bed,' and went off up the stairs, making more noise than was necessary, taking out his mobile phone, starting a conversation . . . with his ex-partner?

Bea made and took another cup of coffee in to the inspector, who was sitting at the table with Anna, taking her statement. Without surprise, Bea noticed that when Hari returned from the garden, he propped himself against a wall to watch Anna. Anna was very aware of Hari's interest in her and was not objecting to it. In fact, she was playing with her hair, trying to coax it into a prettier shape. Hm. Well, the admiration on Hari's face was doing Anna more good than aspirin.

Hari felt Bea looking at him and made a business of looking over the front windows, opening and shutting the curtains, checking the locks. He said, 'Nothing suspicious in the street. Do I go home, or stay on guard?' He answered his own question. 'I stay. Too much has been going on here to risk it.'

'You want to check the bedrooms?' She led the way upstairs. 'I agree it's a respite and not the end of the war. When we're done up here, I'll show you the alarm system.' Did he think there might be further alarms and excursions that evening? Heaven forfend. She was too old for SAS-style manoeuvres. Leave it to the police. Now the inspector was on board, they could relax. Couldn't they?

Yes, there was a constant worry about Briscoe but nothing they could do that night. Leon must curb his impatience. They could all do with a good night's sleep.

Hari checked every room, knocking on each door and asking permission to enter. Keith and Dilys were sitting side by side in the living room at the top of the house. Orlando was pacing up and down, talking on his mobile next door. As they descended, Anna came up the stairs, slowly, holding on to the banister. 'I told the inspector everything I know. Leon's with him now. He's quite bright, isn't he?'

Bea wasn't sure whether Anna was referring to Leon or to Hari, who went into her room with her to check the window and look under the bed. But, it was Hari whom Anna was looking at when she spoke, and she smiled at him as they left.

Hari checked Bea's own bedroom, saying, 'Anna. Spoken for?'

'Forty-two. Married once, divorced. Two teenagers, now at university. Owns her own house. An excellent administrator. Ran a charity for a long time till Leon recruited her, first to run and then to own the college.'

He nodded, testing the lock on the window at the back. 'Forty-five last month. Married once, divorced. One son living in the States. Own my own block of flats, live in the penthouse. Worked since leaving school, own and run my own protection agency.'

So that was his CV? Was he checking to see if she'd object to his going after Anna? Well, Bea wouldn't object, but it would be as great a mismatch as her and Leon, wouldn't it? She showed him how the alarm system worked in the hall and took him down to the agency rooms.

He tested every lock, on every door and window. 'They've been quiet for some hours. If they attack anywhere, it'll be through the basement.'

She nodded. 'There's a separate alarm system for the basement.'

He frowned at it, opened his mouth to make a comment. Shrugged. 'I could disable that in seconds. You could do with something better. I'll see about it tomorrow.'

Oh. Yet another thing to worry about. She showed him where they kept the spare key to the door which closed off the basement from the rest of the house.

He said, 'If you like, I'll sleep down here tonight.'

She nodded. She hoped he was mistaken in fearing another attack, but she had a feeling he wasn't often wrong.

He said, 'You're keyed up, waiting for something else to happen. What?'

She shrugged. 'Another distraction, I suppose. To keep us off balance. It seems to me that the killer has a cold brain. Possibly, it's Denver. I don't know him so can't say if he's capable of such efficiency. Possibly, it's a man they've brought in from outside to do the deed. Someone murdered three people, disposed of Adamsson and then, job done, disappeared from the scene. He's left it to others to do the rest: to whip Adamsson's father away, to bug my office, put in a camera, send me a toy cat, organize hate mail. If he'd still been around then the nasty distractions we've faced recently wouldn't have been so amateurish and reasonably easy to thwart. They wouldn't have ended with a sigh of relief on our part. No, there would have been drastic consequences. It seems to me this is a good reason to think he's an outsider and not Denver, who presumably is still at work at the big house. Mind you, if it hadn't been for Keith, we'd be up the creek without a paddle. What terrifies me is that if we go on batting off the distractions more or less successfully, the killer will be commissioned to act again, and this time he'll go after Leon with a vengeance.'

She led the way back up the stairs.

Hari said, 'I agree. Leon, now . . . he thinks the world of you.'

A buzzer sounded. Bea and Hari froze. Bea said, 'Keith installed a buzzer under the doormat in the porch.' They both looked at their watches. Half past ten. An ordinary caller? Not at this time of night.

The buzzer continued to sound. The inspector appeared in the doorway of the living room with Leon behind him.

Bea said, 'It's another distraction.' And, to Hari, 'Can you warn the others?'

He floated up the stairs without making any sound.

The front doorbell rang. Insistently. Leon put his arm round Bea. 'What do you want to do? Shall I answer it?'

Bea snapped, 'Be your age!' Which sharp rejoinder made him blink and had the inspector covering his mouth to hide a smile.

Down the stairs came the others; Orlando looking cross, Dilys looking anxious and Keith looking lively. Thank God for Keith. No Anna? She'd probably gone to bed already. Hari leaned against the wall with his arms folded. Waiting to spring into action.

Bea said, 'I've always meant to have a spyhole put in the door. I really must do something about it.'

'Shall I look through the curtains at the front?' Dilys darted into the sitting room. She called back, 'It's that Jennifer woman, the one who used to work for us and got us bugged.'

Everyone but Bea relaxed.

'Shall I let her in?' said Leon.

The inspector looked at his watch. 'It's late. Why has she come now?'

'Distraction technique.' Bea was still wound up. 'She's come here to offer us something, probably not much, to distract us from . . . whatever it is they're planning next. I can feel it! We mustn't let our guard drop.'

Jennifer pressed the bell again.

Bea said, 'Everything that has happened since the murders has been by way of a distraction to stop us trying to find Adamsson. Nothing recently was meant to kill. Anna was locked into the college by mistake. Yes, there were near misses. Some were closer than others. Yes, Denver does seem to be running the show. Or Angharad. Oh, I don't know!'

'Mrs Abbot!' Dilys, calling from the front room. Panicking. Urgent. Danger! 'I think someone's on the pavement on the other side of the road, looking this way. I think he's waiting to see if we're going to let her in. I can hardly make him out, he's all in black and wearing a balaclava. It might be a man walking a dog—' doubtfully – 'but I don't think so.'

'I could do with having a word with this Jennifer woman,' said the inspector. 'The rest of you can disappear for the moment.'

Leon said, 'Into the kitchen, everybody, and push the door to. Bea, will you let her in?'

Hari disappeared down the stairs to the agency rooms.

Bea negotiated her way round Hari's giant bike, shut off the alarm system and opened the door.

'You took your time!' Jennifer pushed past Bea into the hall. 'What's that bike doing there?'

Bea ignored that. 'It's late. I don't usually let anyone in at this time of night.'

'I came to warn you. It can't wait. Where can we talk?'

Bea gestured that Jennifer follow her into the sitting room, where the inspector was seated waiting for them. Jennifer hesitated. 'Who's he?'

'Inspector Durrell. An old friend. He's very interested in what's been happening. Have a seat. Now, what did you come to say?'

Jennifer was uneasy. She sat, holding on to her handbag, fiddling with the clasp. 'I came to warn you. This is so difficult. If they knew I'd come, they wouldn't be pleased.'

Meaning that if she'd known Bea had a policemen in the house, she wouldn't have come?

The inspector produced his notebook and pressed the button on his recorder. 'Shall we start at the beginning? What's your name, and where do you live?'

Out of the corner of her eye, Bea saw a shadow pause in the doorway, beckoning to her. Hari.

She excused herself and went out into the hall, pulling the door to behind her.

Hari was smiling. 'Another amateur. I went out by the agency door and stood in the shadows at the bottom of the stairs to have a look. Jennifer is only the starter. The main course has now arrived. A man with a long ladder, which he's set up against the house. He's all in black, carrying a tool bag. He's up the ladder now, trying to fit something on to the window frame of your bedroom.'

Bea was incensed. 'How dare he! Right! Shall we have some fun with him?'

She eased past the bike and opened the front door. Closely followed by Hari, she negotiated her way round the ladder to reach the forecourt between the house and the pavement. All they could see from where they stood was a man's boots, a capacious bottom and his arms as he fiddled with something . . . wiring?

What wiring? There shouldn't be any exposed wiring there.

Setting explosives?

Bea shuddered. No, no. Surely not. Not in a terrace house. The damage could not possibly be contained but would affect houses on either side. There would be fatalities.

Was the enemy prepared to go that far? No, not if previous incidents were anything to go by. They were not murderers, or they would have left Anna to die.

On the other hand, it might be an entirely different man, with a different errand to run. It might be the killer, who didn't object to taking human life.

Could he be fixing up bugs which could relay what was said inside the house to the florist's van? No, the van had gone, hadn't it? Had they some other base in the vicinity?

Perhaps he was fiddling with the old leaden drainpipes to cause a flood which would flush out the inhabitants . . .

Well, whatever it was, it was about time it was stopped.

She grinned. 'Let's shake the fruit from the tree, shall we?'

She laid hands on one side of the ladder, and Hari took the other.

'One, two, three!' said Bea, and together they shook the ladder. It was heavy, but they managed it all right.

'Oi!' A voice from above. 'What you think you're doing?'

Bea floated her voice up to him. 'I will not put up with another burglary. Come down at once, you horrible man, do you hear?'

'Wha . . . t?' The man had a coil of wire in one hand and pliers in the other. He was a hefty bloke, dressed in black jogging trousers and sweater. And a balaclava. Eyes like currants in a suet pudding stared down at them in alarm. Eyes that were sending unwelcome messages to his brain. 'You stop that, you hear?'

Not the killer. Not enough brains to come out of the rain. 'Let's shake again,' said Bea. 'One, two, three and shake!'

They shook.

The man dropped his pliers and wire and clung to the ladder. 'Help!'

'What you doing, missus?' said a passer-by.

'This man is trying to burgle my house!'

'You should call the police, missus.' A concerned man,

elderly, walking a small dog. That was the beauty of living in a built-up area. There were always people passing the street, going out for the evening, coming home from work, walking the dog.

'I would, but my hands are full,' said Bea. 'Shake again, Hari. Let's get him down before he can break the window!'

The man yelled, 'You can't do this to me!'

'One, two, three and shake!'

They shook. The 'burglar' yelled some more. Perhaps he wasn't all that good at heights? He hugged the ladder with both arms. His tool bag slid down the ladder and thudded to the ground. A fine collection of coils of wire and bits and pieces of black plastic spilled out. They didn't mean anything to Bea, but she assumed they'd been supposed to be placed against her window with malice aforethought.

'Alright! I'm a-coming down!' screamed the man. 'Don't you dare stop me!'

Another couple of passers-by had gathered to watch. One was taking photographs on his camera. At night? Daft creature! But the flash was disorienting the 'burglar' nicely. The man with the dog was using his mobile phone for a different purpose. 'Police, please!'

Bea shouted up, 'It would serve you right if I put you in hospital! Your sort is scum of the earth, terrifying a poor widow woman in her own home!'

The man yelled again as, missing his step, he slid backwards down the ladder and ended in a heap on the ground. Cameras clicked.

The dog walker said, 'Yes, officer. A burglar. The house-holder has been most resourceful, but—'

'Let me out of here!' The man blundered to his feet and shook his fist at Bea. He turned to run away and was brought down by Hari in a flying tackle.

Bea risked a look along the street. Her own car was parked . . . where? Heaven forbid that it had been tampered with. She hadn't used it for a couple of days. Suppose it had been sabotaged? What must she do to find out?

The dog walker was an ex-army type. 'Want me to do a citizen's arrest, madam?' Hari had the man in an arm lock, but the elderly man wanted to join in the fun. He must have been eighty in the shade and looked hardly capable of running, never mind apprehending a fleeing man.

The man who'd been using his camera was still at it. 'I've got five, no, six pictures of him. How long are the police going to be?'

'They take their time, don't they?' said a woman in a fake-fur coat.

'Thus perish all traitors.' Bea clung to the ladder herself, feeling the need for support.

The inspector appeared in the doorway, setting off the buzzer under the mat. Leon and Keith were close behind him. Dilys was dancing up and down between them. Dilys was enjoying herself. Well, she could give Bea thirty years. Or was it the other way round? Could Bea give Dilys thirty years? Whichever.

Bea said, 'He's all yours, Inspector.'

Hari pulled the man to his feet and stripped off his balaclava.

Dilys stopped dancing. 'Johnny? Johnny Allister? No, it can't be. Can it?'

'One of your father's security force?'

'One of the maintenance men. Yes. I mean, I suppose he is. He was when I was living there, but . . . Johnny? How could you!'

'My name's not Johnny whatever.'

Hari held him with one hand and delved into the man's pockets with the other, producing a wallet, which he opened, one handed. 'John Allister. Bank cards.'

Spellbound, the gaggle of bystanders was growing by the minute. The inspector took charge. 'Bring him up into the house, Hari. I'll ring for reinforcements.'

Hari propelled the man up the steps and into the house, keeping a tight hold on him. The man kept his head down, not meeting anyone's eyes. Ashamed of himself?

Bea was about to follow Hari in, when the woman in the fake-fur coat said, 'You're not going to leave the ladder there all night, are you? It's an open invitation to burglars.'

Yes, it was. The inspector said, 'I'll get my men to take it away as soon as they arrive.' He pulled his mobile out and started talking into it.

Bea thanked the bystanders. 'Ladies, gentlemen: your presence of mind has saved us from a really nasty experience. May I ask you to send the photos on your camera to my office inside? I'll give you the number. That way you won't have to wait till the police reinforcements get here.'

This caused the group to melt away. No one wants to wait around for the police, who would delay them from going about their business with questions and requests for statements and goodness knows what. The man who'd been taking shots showed his phone to Bea, who gave him the email address to forward the photos to her computer. Night time shots never came out well, but you never knew and these might be helpful.

Dilys reappeared, wearing rubber gloves. 'Is this the right thing to do, do you think?' She picked up the bits and pieces which the burglar had left strewn around and popped them into his tool bag. Bea squinted at the ladder. 'Inspector, that ladder has some sort of label on it. Does it say "Holland Holdings Maintenance"? It's hard to see at this distance, but I think it does.'

Amateur night again.

Bea relaxed, muscle by muscle. Smiling, she waved off the last of the bystanders. The elderly man with the dog was the most reluctant to leave as the animal nosed at something on the pavement. Bea picked it up. Another piece of black plastic. An awkward shape, with wires attached. She told herself she oughtn't to have touched it without gloves on, and didn't care.

She returned to the house, slammed the front door shut and set her back to the door, breathing deeply. Was that going to be 'it' for the night? No more distractions? She set the house alarm, then remembered that the inspector was summoning police reinforcements who would need to be let in. She hesitated. Then decided to leave the alarm on. There was no point in taking chances.

She put her spoils of war down on the hall chest to negotiate her way round the bike – when would Hari be taking it away, and where did he keep it normally? Well, never mind that for now.

Keith was hovering. He picked up the piece she'd removed from the pavement and looked worried. 'What's this?'

'It's something that man dropped when he fell off the ladder.'

He took a deep breath. 'This is a timing device. It's like a clock. See, here's a tiny dial. It's set for . . . midnight. Where's the rest of it?'

'Dilys picked all the other bits up and put them in the man's tool bag.'

Did Keith go pale? In a strangled voice he said, 'The sooner these things are out of the house, the better.' He barged into the sitting room. 'Sorry to interrupt, but I think that man was trying to plant a bomb on Bea's window sill. Ought we to get the flying squad or something?'

'What!'

Keith held the odd-looking bit of plastic out for them to see. 'You see this, looks like watch dial? This is meant to set something off at midnight tonight. Where's the rest of it?'

'I never,' said the 'burglar', who had been sat on an upright chair. Hari was feeding his arms through the slats at the back of the chair and tying his thumbs together.

'It's all in here.' Dilys held up the 'burglar's' tool bag.

'Give it me. Carefully,' said Keith. 'Don't drop it, whatever you do.'

The inspector got out his mobile phone again. 'I'm afraid I don't know anything about bombs.'

''Snot a bomb,' said the 'burglar'. 'I wouldn't. Honest. And you've no right to tie me up and keep me here. I'm going to complain to my member of parliament about you, I am.'

'Then what is it?' Keith stood over him.

'Dunno. A firecracker. To give her a fright.' He nodded in Bea's direction. 'She's giving us gyp, so we thought we'd do likewise, right? Something left over from the fireworks, that's all.'

Hari said, 'I'll check there's nothing left on the window sill, shall I?' And slid out of the room.

Leon sighed audibly. 'Have you seen my brother recently, Allister?'

Allister tried to swivel round in his chair, but couldn't quite make it. 'What? Your brother? Briscoe? Chance would be a fine thing. You've got a nerve, upsetting him the way you have. It's no wonder he's taken to his bed.'

Leon insisted, 'Then you haven't seen him recently?'

'No. Nor likely to. I'm maintenance, see.'

The inspector clicked off his phone. 'Someone's on their way to deal with the firecracker, or whatever it is.'

The buzzer sounded.

Bea said, 'That'll be Hari trying to get back in. I told him about the alarm system.' She went out, preparing some sharp words, to see that the front door was firmly closed . . . and smelled petrol.

Petrol. You pour it through the letterbox and 'post' a flaming rag after it, which starts a . . .!

She screamed, 'Fire!'

She ran for the fire extinguisher which, thank God, was up to date and in the kitchen, just where it ought to be . . . and Leon was at her side . . . taking it off her as someone thrust a burning rag through the letterbox. Whoosh! Flames started up the inside of the door, but Leon was there, taking charge, dowsing the flames. If they'd reached Hari's motor-bike, the whole lot would have exploded and . . . best not to think of it.

Bea collapsed on to the hall chest. She was not going to cry. Or have hysterics. Or scream. Definitely not!

Leon dropped the extinguisher and took her in his arms. 'It's all over. You are a brave girl.'

She turned into his shoulder and screamed. Softly. And bit hard on his jacket. She pulled back. 'I am not going to cry. I'm not. Honest.' She closed her eyes, took a deep breath. 'But I am just the tiniest bit worried about Hari. He went out to see if our burglar had left anything on our window sill, and he hasn't returned.'

'I'll look, shall I?' said Keith, wrestling the door open and setting off the alarm. 'Ouch! It's still hot!' He got it open. 'The ladder's gone!'

With the last of her strength, Bea killed the house alarm.

A fire engine powered its way down the road towards them,

followed by a police car. The inspector had come out to see the fire. He got tangled up in Hari's motorbike. The others followed, anxious to see what was happening. Cars in the street hooted, because the fire engine and the police car were blocking the traffic.

Bea stayed where she was in the hall. She started to laugh. She put both hands over her mouth and tried to contain hysterics. She despised people who had hysterics.

'Where's the fire, sir?' A fireman appeared in the doorway, in full fig, setting off the buzzer under the mat. Large, eager and willing.

'Up the non-existent ladder,' said Keith, who was outside on the pavement, staring up at the front of the house. 'There's a man perched up there. Can you see? How about getting him down before he loses his grip?'

Hari, who was indeed perched on the window sill, called down, 'I considered jumping, but thought it might be hard on the legs.'

The police car screeched to a halt and disgorged more men who also wanted to know what the problem was.

The inspector flashed his shield and pointed to Hari, who was clinging to the facade of the building like Spiderman.

'Ah. A burglar? We'll have him down in two shakes.'

'No,' said the inspector, 'we've got one of those inside, but that man up there is one of ours. Get him down, will you?'

The firemen ran a ladder up the front of the house, and Hari came down it, one-handed, holding something in his free hand. Once on the ground he said, 'I'd just picked this little beauty from the sill when the ladder vanished from beneath me.' He handed it over to the fireman. 'Gelignite, do you think? We've got the timer inside.'

The fireman nearly dropped what he was holding. 'What's going on here, World War Three?'

The inspector peered at what the fireman was holding. 'Looks fairly lethal. By the way, someone has also tried to start a fire by pushing a burning rag through the letterbox. You might like to inspect the damage, though I think it's safe now. Best come inside. Yes, the police, too. We've got the man who tried to blow the house up, but I'm afraid his accomplice must have got away with the ladder. You didn't see a van careering off with a ladder on top of it, did you?'

No, they hadn't. They trooped inside. Two, three? More and more. Large men, content in their skins. Knowing exactly how to deal with burglars and arsonists.

Bea tried to explain, found herself crying. Flapped her hands and retreated to the kitchen, letting Leon put the newcomers into the picture . . . which he was perfectly capable of doing. She set about making cups of tea and coffee and locating the biscuit tin, which was almost empty. She must order some more food in tomorrow.

As she took the refreshments into the sitting room, Dilys, quivering, indicated where the bag of lethal bits and pieces was lying on the table.

'We'll take charge of that,' said the chief fireman, removing it with care.

'And we'll take charge of him,' said the police, laughing as Allister, with his thumbs tied together through the slats at the back of his chair, tried to walk himself out of the room. He didn't even get as far as the hall before he was cautioned, charged, and led away.

The firemen confirmed that the damage to the door was minimal – 'It's OK missus. Just needs a good clean and a nice coat of paint.' Forms were filled in. Cups of tea and coffee were drunk. The biscuit tin was emptied. The experts departed with a flourish, allowing the stalled traffic to pass along the street once more.

The inspector said he'd be off in a minute but just wanted to check through something on his notebook.

Bea sank on to the settee, thinking she needed a brandy. Large. Neat. She hadn't any in the house. What a pity.

Dilys hovered, anxious and pale. 'Can I do anything?'

'No, my dear. Thank you.' And that was the first time Bea had used an endearment to Dilys.

Dilys, pale but still mistress of herself, smiled at Bea. Who smiled back.

Keith put his arm around Dilys. 'Surely we're done for the night?'

Bea looked around. Leon was checking something over

with the inspector. Orlando and Anna would be in bed by now.

Somebody was missing.

'Where's Jennifer?' said Bea.

SEVENTEEN

Indeed, where was Jennifer?

Recap. Jennifer had arrived just before the 'burglar' who'd tried to plant an explosive on Bea's window sill. Bea had shown her into the sitting room. Jennifer had sat down. The inspector had started to interview her. Bea had been called out of the room by Hari, saying someone on a ladder was working on her bedroom window. Leon had followed, and so had Keith and Dilys. The inspector, too.

They'd shaken the man off the ladder, and Hari had brought him inside. Hari had tied the man's thumbs together through the slats of the chair and then . . .

'Hold on!' said Bea. 'Can anyone remember whether Jennifer was still in the room when Hari brought Allister in?'

Heads were shaken all round.

'She can't have got out by the front door,' said Leon. 'Not with all of us in the hall.'

'Has she gone upstairs?'

Hari was on his way. 'Anna!'

There was a scrabbling sound from the kitchen followed by an enraged squall. A bundle of black fur streaked into the sitting room and dived for safety under the settee.

Bea started up. 'That's Winston! Something's upset him. Jennifer must have tried to escape through the kitchen door and got down into the garden. But the walls are so high, she can't get out!'

Leon and Keith started for the kitchen. 'Yes, the door's unlocked and . . . Yes!' Leon began to laugh. 'It looks as if she tried to climb the wall and fell off it on to a flower bed.'

Bea screamed, 'She's smashed my beautiful planter! The bulbs were just coming into flower, and now look at them. All over the place!'

'I'll bring her in.' Hari pushed past them to run down the stairs. More squalling and squealing. Jennifer had a good squeal on her, but Hari knew what he was doing. He brought her up through the kitchen and pushed her before him into the sitting room. Jennifer's foray into the garden had not improved her appearance. She was a sorry-looking sight, streaked with mud. She'd lost a shoe and was weeping copiously. 'You'll be sorry, you'll be ever so sorry. I came to warn you, and look what you've done to me!'

'What you've done to yourself,' said the inspector. 'Now, where were we when we were so rudely interrupted? Your name is Jennifer—'

The woman spat . . . directly at Leon. 'He's going to get you! You can be sure of that! I came to warn you but you wouldn't listen and now . . .' She drew herself up. 'You can't charge me with anything because I haven't done anything, and you've got to let me go. You can call a taxi for me, now!'

'Not so fast,' said the inspector. 'I can have you for wilful damage to Mrs Abbot's garden, as well as conspiracy to place a bomb in this house.'

Jennifer tossed her head. 'I know my rights. I'm not saying a word more until my solicitor gets here.'

Silence.

Jennifer looked triumphant. 'That's what's called a stalemate, isn't it? You can't prove I'm involved in anything.'

'Then why did you try to escape through the garden?'

'I came here with the very best of intentions, to warn you.'

Bea said, 'Warn us about what?'

'That he's on to you. All of you. You'll be sorry you were ever born. And that's all I'm going to say.'

The inspector said, 'In that case, the sooner we can get you down to the station and your solicitor is contacted, the better.'

Leon brought across his laptop. 'I know who's behind this now. When Bea explained so clearly what had been going on, when she gave us a profile of the killer, I began to suspect who he might be. Dilys, do you remember that when the old head of Briscoe's security unit retired, Mrs Evans persuaded my brother to appoint Denver because he was a member of her family? Yes? Now, what you may not know is that the man who was second in command at the time had expected to be made up to head and, when he wasn't, he made such a stink that Briscoe set him up as manager of a garage business nearby.'

Jennifer went rigid.

Aha! Was Leon on the right track?

Dilys shook her head. 'It must have been some time ago.'

'Yes, it was. Now, the garage was one of the companies I took over from Briscoe. I made a point of visiting each one, often unannounced. I spent time getting to know the managers. I looked at their books and talked through their plans for the future. I watched to see how they related to their staff. The name of the manager at the garage is Valentine. Denis Valentine.'

Jennifer closed her eyes and clenched her fists. 'You might offer me a seat. It's the least you can do, after pushing me down the stairs into the garden and making me lose my shoe.'

Hari took a newspaper from the side table and placed it on a chair, before handing Jennifer into it.

Leon continued, 'I didn't care for Valentine on our first meeting. He seemed too cocksure for my liking and, when I walked around the workshop with him, I noticed that his staff didn't look at him, or at me. He was too jolly, and they were too quiet. In my book, that meant they feared him. I wondered why. I let him talk. He gave me his life history. He'd been a sergeant in the SAS, and when he left the army he went to work for Briscoe in the security team. He'd expected to get moved up to head of security when his boss left and was annoyed that he hadn't got the promotion. But, he said he liked the garage business and found it a "doddle" to run. He said that in the old days cars needed an engineer to understand them – which he did – and nowadays it was a case of knowing what software was needed. All of which was true.

'His books seemed in order, but I had an uneasy feeling I wasn't getting the whole picture. I asked my chauffeur about Valentine, because he had far more contact with the man than I. He shrugged, said he supposed he was all right. Which made me more and not less anxious about him. So a couple of weeks ago I walked down to the garage by myself, to find Valentine beating six bells out of one of his workmen for losing a tyre lever. The rest of the staff were standing around, watching but not daring to interfere. Fortunately, I had my mobile with me and took a couple of pictures before Valentine realized I was there. He tried to bluster it out. I took him into the office and asked what his plans were for early retirement. He said he hadn't any. I suggested that he consider it seriously as, if he weren't gone within the month, I'd have to sack him and he'd lose his company pension.

'The following day my chauffeur didn't turn up for work, and the rest you know . . . except . . .' Here he turned his computer around. 'Facebook. Our Jennifer delights in Facebook. There's pictures here of her with her partner. Like to see?'

Bea gasped. 'Why, her partner's name is Denis. Do you mean . . .?'

They all turned to look at Jennifer. Who looked up at the ceiling.

'Here's Jennifer again, on holiday with her partner. At work in the garden of their brand new house. He's working on the barbecue in the background, see? Here she is, at home with her little dog. On holiday again . . . and again . . . always with her partner. And here she is with her partner – or maybe he's her husband? – at the garage. Point taken?'

'Let me see,' said the inspector, and took the laptop into his own hands.

Keith looked at Dilys. 'Did you know about this?'

'No, I hardly ever went into maintenance. If something about the house needed attention, light bulbs blown or a window broken, say, I used to ring them and report it. Or Mrs Evans did. Then a man would come round and fix it. That's how I knew John Allister. Let me see . . .' She peered into the computer. 'Oh. Yes, I remember this man. I tried to make a pet of a stray cat that used to hang around the college, until he killed it. I was ever so upset.'

Bea said, 'Leon, this is all circumstantial. I can see that you'd like the killer to be Denis Valentine. He's got the background and the training to commit the murders, and I can see he'd have it in for you if you were forcing him into retirement, but what proof have you?'

'None.' He clicked the laptop shut.

'None,' echoed the inspector. 'But I already have Allister in custody, and I'm about to take Jennifer in as well. There will be consternation in the enemy's camp when their fellow conspirator returns with the ladder but without them.'

Leon said, 'And tomorrow you'll be able to get a warrant to move against the security team at the big house on account of the gas leak, right?'

Inspector Durrell nodded. 'I dare say I'll be taking a ride out there to ask some questions, yes.'

'I'm coming, too,' said Leon. 'I won't rest until I've seen how Briscoe is for myself.'

'Me, too,' said Dilys, sticking out her chin, and then, turning to Keith, she added: 'You don't mind, do you?'

Jennifer said, 'You can't hold me. You can't prove anything. And if I don't get home tonight, my husband will come here looking for me.'

'Indeed.' The inspector narrowed his eyes at her. 'How will he know where you are?'

'Of course he knows!' She realized what she'd said and gasped. 'What I mean is that I left him a note to say I was visiting a friend at this address.'

'At this time of night?' said the inspector. 'I don't think so. Jennifer Valentine, I must caution you that—'

'Hold on a minute,' said Bea. 'Her visit here is another distraction. She says she came to warn us about her husband and that he knows where she is. All well and good, but is that really what she came for? She's acted as a Trojan horse for him before now. I don't know if he's acting for Mrs Evans or Denver, but Jennifer is the link between them. Denis Valentine is the killer. He had the training for it. His job was on the line. I think that he was hired through Jennifer to commit the murders, but he left it to the others to tie up the loose ends. They fumbled around with dead cats and hate messages and cameras, but that wasn't his remit. He's SAS, remember. Specialized forces. Killing to order. Silence. Speed. Knives. Jennifer says she came here to warn us but tried to escape as soon as she realized her distraction technique had failed her . . . which shows she knew exactly what was planned. So what did she really come for?'

All eyes were on Jennifer, who shook her head and laughed.

Keith clicked his fingers. 'She brought another bug, so that he could tell what we were up to. He's listening to our conversation as we speak.'

'Where's her handbag?'

Dilys looked under chairs. 'Dunno.'

'She dropped it in the garden, I expect,' said Leon. 'Shall I fetch it?'

Jennifer laughed again.

'No,' said Bea. 'She was alone in this room for a few minutes while we were attending to the man on the ladder. It's in here, I'm sure of it. Or possibly she's hidden her mobile somewhere, leaving it on so that her partner can hear what's happening. Now, where is it?' She upended the chairs round the dining table, and then, struck by a thought, looked across at Hari. And then at the door.

Hari nodded and melted out of sight.

Hari had said that the killer would come via the agency in spite of the alarm system down there. The outer doors were shut and locked. There was a grille over the windows which gave on to the garden. But Bea knew Hari was right. That was the way the killer would come. And she couldn't remember whether or not she'd turned the alarm back on the front door when the police and the firemen left.

'Not here,' said Leon, checking the chair and table by the end window.

Dilys looked under the rug in front of the fireplace. Silly girl. It wouldn't be there.

'Got it!' The inspector was under the dining table, flourishing Jennifer's handbag.

Bea headed for the door. 'The alarm system! I must turn it back on.' Only to be brought up short by a large man in black holding a revolver. And smiling. Not nicely.

'Sit,' he said, motioning her to a chair with the revolver, which had a large bulge at the end. A silencer?

Jennifer screamed with laughter. 'Oh, your faces!'

Bea risked a glance over Valentine's shoulder.

He grinned. 'Hoping our tame watchdog will come to the rescue? I dealt with him on my way up. You!' He waved his gun in an arc covering the whole room. 'All of you. Sit where I can see you.'

Jennifer got to her feet. 'What you going to do with them, lover boy?'

'There's going to be a break-in. Nice house, nice pickings. A genteel dinner party. Everyone had too much to drink and made the mistake of challenging the burglar, who shot the lot of them before escaping with their jewels . . . such as that rock you're wearing, missus.' And he gestured to Bea's ring. 'You can give that to me for a start.'

Bea slid her diamond ring off her finger and shoved it down her cleavage. 'Over my dead body.'

'That can be arranged.'

Keith said, 'That type of revolver holds six bullets. Just saying. One for each of us. I doubt if he has brought spares. I suppose he knows how to use it?'

'Be sure I do. Jenny, tie their hands behind their backs.' He threw a bunch of leather straps at her. 'Tightly. Start with him.' The revolver in his hand twitched towards Leon.

Jennifer laughed. She'd slipped off her one remaining shoe. In her stockinged feet, she made her way over to Leon, who was standing by the far window and who didn't move when she approached him. 'Turn round, you stupid, silly man,' she said.

'Not on yours!' said Leon, not moving.

'Don't be absurd,' said Jennifer. 'He's an ace with a pistol.'

'Do as the lady says,' said Valentine.

'Just a minute,' said Leon, meeting Bea's eye.

'Do as you're told or your lady gets it.'

'We need to talk—'

'You asked for it,' said Valentine, and raised his gun . . .

Pfft! He fired the gun in the direction of Bea's feet . . .

. . . as she dived to her right, ending up on the floor, but still in one piece . . .

. . . as Keith dropped behind the settee, dragging Dilys with him.

Leon leaped on Jennifer . . .

Who screamed.

Leon twisted her round so that she hung from his arms.

She screamed again, feet off the floor. 'Let me go!'

Pfft!

The bullet went high. Glass smashed, showering down from over the mantelpiece.

My mirror! My mother's mirror! How dare he!

Bea could hear someone murmuring nearby. The inspector, under the table? On his mobile?

Summoning reinforcements? Pray God they come quickly.

A hand grasped her wrist, and she was lifted to her feet, willy-nilly. Valentine grinned down at her.

She kicked at his legs. She might as well have tried kicking an oak tree.

She felt the barrel of the gun laid to her forehead. Oh, typical! Typical! Stalemate. Villain seizes heroine and threatens to kill her if her friends don't do exactly as he asks. Friends oblige and are killed one after the other. Over my dead body!

Well, yes. Probably.

Distraction!

She filled her lungs – and she had good lungs. And screamed. She had a good scream.

He yelled in her ear, 'Shut up!' and ground the barrel of the gun into her skin.

She filled her lungs again, ready for another go . . . and got walloped.

Dizzy.

Limp.

She must not pass out. No.

How many bullets did he have left? Four?

And there were five of them.

He shook her, hard. And let her drop to the floor.

She stayed where she had fallen, arms and legs all over the place.

She tried to raise her head. He kicked her on the jaw. Ouch.

There was a ringing in her ears. Due to the blow she'd had to her head?

No. It was the landline. The telephone.

Everyone looked at it. Even Valentine.

'Well, aren't you going to answer it?' said Leon, still hanging on to Jennifer.

No one moved. Well, they wouldn't, would they?

Footsteps. Light footsteps coming down the stairs. 'Bea, are you there? I think I've blown a fuse on your hairdryer.'

Bea groaned. She'd hoped Anna was well out of it.

A radiant vision appeared in the doorway. Anna's hair hung in a golden bell about her shoulders. She was wearing one of Bea's most revealing nightdresses and swinging a hairdryer by its cord, round and round and . . .

Valentine gaped. The gun in his hand wavered.

Bea chose that moment to claw at Valentine's leg. He glanced down, furious, signalling his intention of kicking her into next week and beyond, shifting from one foot to the other.

'Aaargh!'

The hairdryer flew through the air with malice aforethought and a good swing from an angry, healthy woman. It knocked the gun right out of the warrior's hand . . .

He jerked, eyes rounded in surprise . . .

. . . and folded over at the knees . . .

. . . as a hand chopped into the back of his neck.

His eyes rolled up in his head . . .

. . . he dropped like a stone . . .

. . . and lost all interest in the proceedings.

Jennifer screamed, 'You've killed him! Murderer!'

There's altogether too much screaming going on. We'll have the neighbours complaining.

Anna was smiling. 'I love you, Hari. Have you killed him, or will you let me have a go?'

'I love you, too, Anna,' said Hari, deftly securing the man's hands behind his back. 'No, I haven't killed him, but he won't be making any more trouble for a while. You all right?'

'I always had a good aim. We must go tenpin bowling some time.'

'Tomorrow do you?'

Leon hoisted the struggling Jennifer high. 'Take this one as well, will you? Bea, are you all right?'

'Someone do something about that gun,' said Bea, through her teeth. She struggled to her feet, hanging on to the nearest chair. 'Because if you don't, I won't be answerable for the consequences. I shall put it to that man's head and pull the trigger, and you will all swear on your mother's graves that it went off by accident, understand?' She stood over Valentine, arms akimbo. 'That mirror was my mother's that survived two world wars and look what you've done to it, you nasty piece of—'

'Three bullets left,' said Keith, grinning, as he rose up from behind the settee with Dilys in his arms. 'I'll deal with it. The bullets should match those from the bodies in the car park.'

'Inspector?' said Bea, bending down to look under the table.

He groaned. 'My back's gone. Help me out, will you?'

Hari took Jennifer off Leon, dumped her in a chair, and repeated his trick of tying her thumbs together through the slats at the back. She tried to kick him, at which he just laughed.

Leon eased his neck and came to check Bea over. 'Are you really all right?'

'Apart from my diamond ring digging into my bra, yes.'

He picked her up in his arms and held her tightly. She didn't object, though her feet were off the ground. But after a moment she did ask to be put down. 'Please?'

Leon put her down but kept an arm round her. 'Hari, I thought he'd dealt with you on the stairs.'

'He tried. That alarm system for the agency is not worth the wiring. He was good. I didn't hear him coming, but a shadow moved on the wall and I ducked, though not quite fast enough. I lay still, pretended he'd knocked me out. He kicked me a couple of times, and I played dead. Foolish of him not to make sure. I kept remembering Mrs Abbot talking about distraction and I wanted to see if Anna was all right, so popped upstairs to see if His Lordship would phone for the police and then ring down here—'

'Which I did.' Orlando appeared, in his outlandish, paw-printed silk pyjamas, grinning and holding up his mobile phone. 'I say, Anna! You look . . . wow! I could almost fancy you!'

Anna blushed, holding her hands over her breasts in mock embarrassment. 'Hari thought I might divert his attention if I wore one of Bea's revealing nightdresses . . .'

Bea felt every man look at the nightdress and then at her.
Their thoughts might have been written across their foreheads.

Bea wears that sort of nightdress?

She was *not* going to look to see if they'd all got an erec-
tion. Well, probably not Orlando, but the others . . .

'That's enough of that! Someone get the inspector out from
under the table and, yes, I think I can hear the buzzer on the
mat outside the front door going which means the cavalry has
arrived, and they'll need to be let in and fed and watered and
if anyone thinks I've got the energy for that after everything
that's happened, they've got another think coming. And, there's
no more biscuits. And for heaven's sake, don't let Jennifer walk
around without any shoes on or she'll get glass in her feet and
sue us for damages, which I fully intend to do to you, you
horrible mutt, Mr Valentine, as I see you are conscious again
and you'll wish you weren't any minute now, because I'm going
to . . . I'm going to . . . I don't know what I'm going to do,
but whatever it is, you're going to wish you'd never been born!'

'There, there,' said Leon, putting both arms around her, and
holding her tight. 'You are a brave girl.'

Dilys said, 'There, there. I'll get you a nice hot drink in a
minute. You'll be fine in the morning. Just a mo while I let
the police in and tell them what to do.'

Bea met Anna's eye, and they both began to laugh. Dilys
playing 'mother'?

Anna had Hari's jacket over her shoulders and was holding
it close around her. Shivering. She could do with a hot drink
and an early night, too. Not that any of them were likely to
get to bed before dawn.

Keith helped the inspector to his feet, inch by inch.

The inspector sneezed. 'It's the dust under that table.'

'Oh, let me get the vacuum cleaner out, and I'll deal with
it straight away!' Bea was overwrought. She let herself down
into a chair and closed her eyes. 'Wake me when it's all over,
will you?'

Dilys ushered a couple of policemen into the room, saying,
'I keep wanting to say, "You rang, My Lord?" Because that's
what Orlando did, you know? Oh dear, I think I'm going to
be sick.'

'No, you're not,' said Keith, putting his arm around her. He held out the gun to the inspector. 'Dilys and I will get some tea and biscuits going. Tea, anyway. And perhaps I should pop out for some more biscuits at the all-night place. Everybody take sugar?'

Saturday morning

Bea and Anna went to bed just before dawn and were still asleep when the inspector led the raid on the Holland head-quarters. Orlando woke them at eleven with tea and biscuits, saying that everything was under control and they should go back to sleep. So they did.

When the sun was high in the sky – and how pleasant it was to see the sun after so many cloudy, rain days – Bea got herself out of bed with an effort, groped her way into the shower, dressed in whatever came to hand, gave a little scream when she saw herself in the mirror, and sat down to see what art and a steady hand might do to improve matters.

There was a nasty bruise coming up on her jaw. Drat that man! And who was going to have to clear up the mess? Not the police, oh no! That mirror . . .! Her mother must be turning in her grave. And if there were shards of glass in the hearth-rug, that would probably have to be dumped, too. And then the front door would need stripping and repainting, and the planter in the garden would need to be replaced and all the bulbs replanted. She could have screamed with frustration.

Anna knocked on the bedroom door and came in. She was dressed and made-up. Her hair hung loose about her shoulders. Both eyes were now open. Sort of. She said, 'Are you awake? I feel like death. How about you? And before you say it, I know I shouldn't have borrowed your nightdress.'

Bea grinned. 'Keep it,' she said. 'It looked better on you than on me, and I suspect your need of it is more urgent than mine.'

Anna blushed. 'I don't think Hari needs much stimulation.'

'Nor Leon, come to think of it. Although we haven't got that far yet.'

'No? You could have fooled me.'

Bea sighed. 'Conflicting lifestyles. I don't see how we can work it out.'

Anna also sighed. 'I know what you mean. But that doesn't mean we can't look for a way round it. I must go back home today. Pick up the pieces. I'll take the clothes I've borrowed and have them cleaned, right?'

'Thanks. I'd be grateful. And we must make a date to go shopping.'

'And to devise a working relationship between the college and your agency.'

They smiled at one another. Friends.

Down they went to find Orlando in an apron. He was cooking breakfast for Keith, who was looking heavy-eyed but pleased with himself.

'Behold the wanderer returns,' said Orlando. 'Seat your-selves, my dears, and let me revive the flagging spirits with orange juice, eggs Benedict – which is a speciality of mine – and toast with honey. Coffee or tea?'

'Coffee.'

'Twice.'

Languidly, they took seats at the table and waited for Orlando to provide. 'What news?'

Keith said, 'All good. I took Dilys and Leon in my car. She refused to be left behind. Quite right, too. I envy Leon his unflappability. The inspector told us we were not to try to storm the castle until he'd got his warrant. Hari said he'd pop along to see if the college was all right and the rest of us went to an all-night service station on the motorway to wait. Leon got us some breakfast and the newspapers. He suggested Dilys might like a nap, but she refused. The way he went about things, it might have been any ordinary day at the office. He worked on his laptop, took some phone calls. At half past ten the inspector rang to say the warrant was through and he was about to go in, but we were to wait outside the college till he'd got the security team mopped up. We met up with Hari . . . Oh, Anna: he says everything's all right there, in case you were worrying.'

'I'm not worrying with him on the case,' said Anna, trying not to sound smug.

Keith went on: 'It took Durrell about half an hour, then he rang Leon to say they'd arrested Denver, and we arrived in time to see him being removed. Durrell had the rest of the security team lined up, with one of his sergeants and a couple of constables taking statements, so we rolled through the gates and into the courtyard. You remember that there are offices for Holland Holdings all leading off the courtyard? We had to go through them to get into the main house. Durrell went ahead into the maintenance department and showed them his warrant. Talk about setting the fox in the henhouse. You never heard so much hysteria in your life. All guilty, the lot of them.'

'For the hate mails and death threats?'

'Oh yes. They all knew about them, even if they didn't all take part. Durrell left a couple more of his men – I tell a lie: one of them was a woman – to start taking more statements while he, Leon, myself and Dilys, with Hari spreading menace around him, moved up into the big house. All quiet down below; a secretary person at a desk, who dropped the phone when she saw us coming and ran away. Mrs Evans tried to stop us at the top of the stairs. Leon picked her up and dumped her to one side. You should have heard her squawk. Shouted she'd have the law on us. Durrell showed his badge and said he *was* the law. Leon pushed past her and tried the door to his brother's rooms. Locked. He demanded Mrs Evans hand the key over. She said she didn't know what he was talking about, but Durrell informed her that he had a warrant to search the premises and that Valentine, Jennifer and Allister were already under arrest. She handed over her keys. So we got in all right.'

Bea said, 'Briscoe?'

A heavy sigh. 'Mm. Alive, as of an hour and a half ago.' He stopped eating, had a sip of coffee. 'What we saw, it upset me and Durrell, never mind Dilys. Her father was in a hospital bed with the sides up, his wrists taped to the sides. No bell within reach. Lying in his own filth. He wasn't conscious, which I think was a blessing. Dilys called his name, but he didn't respond. I think, I hope, he's merely been sedated. Leon, cool as you please, took a couple of photographs and rang for an ambulance. Leon's a tiger when he gets going, isn't he? Not a sign of emotion. "Do this, do that!" and it is done. Dilys, Leon and I followed the ambulance into hospital. Not just a private room, but a suite so that Dilys and Leon can stay with him. Briscoe's got tubes coming out all over him now. The doctors are not sure if he's going to live or is too far gone. If his kidneys have packed up . . .' He shrugged.

Anna said, 'What about Hari?'

'He vanished when we located Briscoe. He asked me to tell you tenpin bowling was on for tonight, and he'd ring you to fix the time. I told him you might not be up to it, after the rough treatment you've been having, and he grinned and said it was up to you to set the pace.' Keith sighed. 'At least you know you can see him tonight. I'm afraid Dilys won't be so—'

'Resilient?' said Bea, pushing her cup towards Orlando for a refill. 'Never fear, as soon as she's got a minute, she'll be on the phone to you. She knows a good thing when she sees it.'

Two phones rang. Everyone groped for their mobiles. Keith and Orlando found theirs. Anna and Bea looked at one another and exchanged smiles.

Anna said, 'No phone call for us this time. Actually, I have no idea where my phone is.'

'I suspect Hari always means what he says,' said Bea. They watched as Keith murmured into his phone. No prizes for guessing who'd rung him. She sighed. 'I'd better go down to the agency and see what's up. It's Saturday. We work half a day then. Carrie said she'd be in.'

Orlando snapped off his phone. 'Who does he think he is? Oh, he comes running now he thinks I'm in the clear, but it was a different matter earlier, wasn't it?'

'Your friend Charles?' said Bea. 'A murder enquiry does tend to skew things.'

Orlando snorted. 'More like he wants to be able to introduce "my friend, Lord Lethbury!" I've got his measure now, and I'm not going back to him. You'll let me stay on for a bit, won't you, Mrs Abbot? I'm fully house-trained and can cook a bit when I'm not working.'

Bea didn't know what she felt about that. 'But Orlando, you'll be getting something from your father's estate, won't you?'

'That's what Charles was saying, which didn't endear him to me, my dears, not one whit. My father always threatened to leave everything to the Tory Party or the National Trust. If I'm left enough to cover the funeral, that'll be as much as I can hope for. Just as well. I'm not cut out to be landed gentry. Too, too boring. I like what I do for a living, and I'd hate to live in the family house.'

Anna had his measure, too. 'You might want to buy yourself a penthouse sometime?'

He smiled and flicked his dishcloth at her. 'Now you're talking. Oh, and Mrs Abbot, that Carrie did come up earlier when I was cleaning up in the drawing room and asked if I could wake you, and I said no, and she said she could manage by herself, and to tell the truth, I didn't altogether like her tone. But there, we have to make allowances, don't we, because I don't suppose she liked mine, either.'

'Thank you, Orlando,' said Bea. 'Have you really cleaned up in the drawing, er, sitting room? That's brilliant.'

'I fear the rug is past it. Shredded by shrapnel. Well, glass, anyway.'

Bea nodded. She'd thought as much.

Flump! Squawk!

Keith had put his head down on his arms and had fallen asleep, which had caused Winston – who'd been sitting on his lap – to tumble down on to the floor as Keith relaxed.

'We'll put him on the settee next door,' said Bea. 'He's earned a few hours' sleep.'

'I must go,' sighed Anna. 'My car's at the station in the country. I'll get a cab home and start getting back to normal.' Bea suppressed the thought that with Hari in her life, Anna was not going to fall back into her usual routine.

The landline phone rang, and this time it was for her. Carrie, putting through a phone call from an old client who needed attention.

EIGHTEEN

Bea went back to work. She gave Carrie a raise and took on another girl to replace the defaulting Jennifer. She looked for but failed to find another mirror and hearth rug as good as those she'd had to throw out, but she did get a contract gardener in to repair the ravages Jennifer had wrought in the garden.

Orlando stayed and, once he'd understood Bea was not prepared to wash and iron his clothes, proved to be a thoughtful house guest and a reasonably good cook. He introduced her to sushi – which Bea didn't care for – and a special lamb curry, which she did. He failed to ask her before he repainted his bedroom, but she had to agree the colour he'd chosen was an agreeable one. It turned out his father had made a will when Orlando had first gone to boarding school and had failed to amend it. So in due course he would inherit the old house and the companies his father had owned. He didn't give up work and said he'd rather not use his title either. They both agreed there was plenty of time to decide what he wanted to do in the future but that for the moment he could rent the upstairs flat from Bea during the week and go down to the family place at weekends. He said that his distant cousin was still in situ and refused to move and that she drove him mad . . . but on the other hand he did realize it was in his best interests to let her stay and housekeep for him. For the time being.

Anna returned to work, wearing her hair up during the day and down at night. She bought some new boots for Bea as a gift and several new outfits for herself, choosing lower necklines and shorter skirts than before. She also had her eyelashes dyed. She kept to herself what she did in her evenings. In the daytime Anna and Bea had a series of meetings to consider how best to synchronize the two businesses, and they booked themselves into a spa for a weekend of pampering.

Keith cut back his working hours so that he could pick Dilys up from the hospital every evening and take her out for a meal. He dropped in to see Bea most days, telling her that he was only looking after Dilys until she found her feet. It was, he said, a difficult time for her and he was being there, like an elder brother, to help her through it. Bea told him it didn't matter much what he said or thought, as Dilys knew exactly what she wanted and would no doubt get it.

Leon rang every day at five o'clock, which was, he said, his changeover time from tycoon to hospital visitor. He was always at Briscoe's side in the evenings, when Dilys went out with Keith. Bea longed for his presence and found these conversations unsatisfactory. He could barely hold back his anxiety for his brother and was distracted by the necessity of having to take over so much more of the business affairs of Holland Holdings. He mourned the loss of Adamsson, whose body had been formally indentified from dental records. He said how much he missed seeing Bea, but she knew that if he'd been given the choice, he'd still sit with his brother every evening. Sometimes he asked after the cat Winston, or how Orlando was doing. But she could tell his mind was centred on Briscoe's fight for life.

Briscoe woke up on his second day in hospital. He was confused. His first words were, 'Don't hit me!' And then, wonderingly, 'Where am I?' When he saw and recognized Dilys, he said, 'Now don't fuss, there's a good girl.'

To Leon, he said, 'What took you so long?'

When told that Angharad was under arrest, he wept with relief. The police found evidence that he'd been given many different drugs to break his spirit and make him malleable to her demands. He'd held out, more or less, sometimes able to reason that Leon was not trying to undermine him, sometimes floating in a sea of doubt and confusion . . . and eventually drifting away into unconsciousness.

Now, safe at last, and understanding how he'd been taken to the brink of death, tides of fear still swept over him, when he would weep and cling to Dilys and Leon, begging them not to leave him alone.

He wept more when he heard that his old friends Lethbury

and Adamsson had died, but he had no more interest in business, saying that it was up to Leon to take over now. When interviewed by the police he said that he'd been ill and could hardly remember what had happened. There'd been nightmares, in which a menacing figure had warned him that Leon and Dilys were plotting his death but that Angharad would save him, if he did what he was told. He remembered little more of that time. He said some days he couldn't even remember what his name was and on others Angharad had been furious with him because he'd been too weak to sign his name to some paper or other.

The doctors warned the family that the prognosis for Briscoe was poor. His kidneys were failing, and even if a transplant kidney could be found, he was unlikely to survive the operation. He couldn't return home as he needed to be nursed round the clock.

He lived for ten days. His sister Sibyl returned from the States with little Bernice, in time to see him before he died.

After a while, news trickled back to Bea that the police discovered Mr Adamsson senior had been found wandering along a country road in a disorientated state. He'd told the police a confused story about having been abandoned in a lane by some people who'd promised to give him a better place to live, and he was now safely lodged in a nursing home, paid for by the sale of his house. Alzheimer's had set in with a vengeance, but he enjoyed having good food served to him at regular intervals. His belongings were found in a shed at the back of Valentine's garage and restored to him in due course.

And, yes, it transpired that Valentine had been involved in Angharad's schemes from the start. It was Angharad and Denver who had told Leon's chauffeur to leave his job, and it was Valentine who had tampered with the brakes on Leon's Rolls and subsequently arranged for his courtesy car not to start. It was Denver who had tried and failed to run Leon down in the road: just as well, said Leon, as Valentine would have made a better job of it.

It was Valentine who had killed Adamsson, Lethbury and Margrete Walford, and then disposed of Adamsson's body and his car. It was he who had opened the gas taps at the college, but it was the security men who had padlocked Anna into the building by mistake. And it was the kitchen helper at the college who had put Anna's car out of action.

It was Angharad and Denver who lured Lord Lethbury and Adamsson to the car park . . . and later sent identical messages for Orlando and Leon to join them. It was Angharad who sent Bea the toy cat and organized the maintenance department's office to make the hate phone calls and emails. How much or how little Jennifer knew was open to conjecture. Certainly, she had known about most of what had been going on and had enthusiastically sought a job with the agency in order to learn what she could and to do as much damage as she was able. But she told so many different stories about her guilt or innocence that it was hard to know exactly how culpable she had been. As Valentine's wife – yes, indeed, they were married – she probably knew more than anyone else, but the difficulty was going to be to prove it.

Valentine, Denver and Angharad Evans were held without bail for trial. Against Inspector Durrell's advice Jennifer was eventually granted bail and, predictably, disappeared. Two members of the security squad were also charged, bailed and lost their jobs. Leon asked Hari to find him replacements.

At first the media went to town on the arrests. And then they went quiet. Too quiet, thought Bea, scanning the financial pages every day.

She guessed Leon was up to something. If only he would take her into his confidence! But there, he'd always been the same, hadn't he? He was a loner. He couldn't change his ways now.

It was one of the most infuriating things about him.

Eight days. Nine. Ten. Absence does not make the heart grow fonder, but drives it into whiny mode. She wondered why she'd ever been weak enough to allow him into her life when he could cut her out of it like this. All right, she knew he was busy, but he could spare time to keep the home fires burning, couldn't he? Yes, he was a single-minded so-and-so, incapable – unlike women – of doing more than one thing at once. But, she felt neglected. If this was what the future held, then she wanted none of it.

Of course she missed him but told herself she'd get over it.

He phoned, yes. But their conversations were not lover-like. He seemed distant, distracted. Impersonal.

She tried to match his manner. Twice she arranged to be out at the time he rang.

She met her ex-husband for an evening at the theatre and managed to converse in semi-sensible fashion. She visited Max and his growing family and sympathized with their current problem of having to find a nanny or au pair for the children. Except for this domestic problem, Max was in charity with the world. He'd forgotten his previous scare about Holland Holdings being due to collapse and was full of the joys of spring as he'd been offered a good price for his shares in the Holland Training College. Max was cock-a-hoop, full of his financial expertise. Hmph! said Bea to herself, thinking he'd have done better to hang on to the shares which would no doubt appreciate in value.

She had her front door repainted, didn't like the new colour. Had it redone.

Leon sent her gifts. One was a superb diamond pendant on a platinum chain. As promised. She'd been thinking about how she'd feel when he put the chain around her neck and admired the pendant, but delivery by courier was . . . well, it was as if she'd been paid off for helping him. She dropped the pendant into the bottom of her jewel box, thinking she'd return it to him sometime.

A superb rococo mirror arrived, a genuine antique. And a sheepskin rug. Ordered online, delivered by courier. She told herself it was no use refusing his gifts as she'd earned them. She thanked Leon by email. Orlando installed the mirror and spread out the rug, chattering the while. She thought she much preferred silence.

Normal life resumed. Her ex-lodger Maggie confirmed that she was indeed pregnant. Sybil Holland took little Bernice over to see Maggie in her new flat and pronounced it 'a dolls' house'. Bernice also visited her mother and Keith and announced with a sigh of relief that that was one less thing to worry about and didn't Bea think Uncle Leon had managed things beautifully? And Sybil actually agreed.

Another of Bea's worries was laid to rest when her other old-time lodger, Oliver, returned from university for a long weekend to inspect Orlando. 'Wary' on both sides. But at least they didn't come to blows, and Oliver did say as he left that it was good for Bea to have someone else living in the house for the time being.

On the tenth day Leon rang at lunchtime to signal that the waiting was over. Yes, Briscoe had died, peacefully, with Dilys on one side of him and Sibyl on the other. Leon regretted he'd been out at the time, but he'd seen his brother the night before and they'd talked of this and that and the future before Briscoe had fallen asleep. The doctors had done their best, but it had been Briscoe's time to go. Funeral arrangements, etcetera, would now be occupying his mind, but was she free for supper the following evening?

First she thought she wouldn't go, and then thought she might as well. It would save her cooking, and the new dress could do with an airing.

As Bea descended the stairs there was a ring at the front door.

Keith, looking harassed. 'Bea, for heaven's sake, tell me what to do. Dilys rang me this afternoon and said Briscoe had died and could I collect her, which I did. Then she asked to see my house, and she . . . she's moved in! She said I'd offered her a job as my housekeeper, and of course I did say that, but now she wants me to collect all her belongings from you . . . not that there is much, she says. She wants to know if I'll take her in the clothes she stands up in, and of course I said "yes", but I'm sure she doesn't really mean it. Tell me what to do!'

Orlando appeared from the kitchen, oven gloves on his hands. 'I packed up all her stuff ages ago. I'll bring it down for you, shall I?'

Keith tugged at his hair, which was much shorter than it had been. His beard was still closely cut and well shaped, too. He was also, Bea noted, wearing a fine leather jacket and new jeans. He looked good, almost sexy.

She said, 'I suppose she's putting clean sheets on the spare room bed as we speak?'

'Well, yes. But—'

'You're having wedding nerves, Keith. The sooner you get hitched the better. Think of the delicious supper she'll have waiting for you when you return.'

Bea thought, but did not say, that by the end of the week, Dilys would have reorganized his kitchen, moved the furniture around in the sitting room and thrown out all his oldest clothes.

What she did say was, 'You'd better get a marriage licence tomorrow. You can have the wedding reception here, if you like.'

'I thought you'd tell me it's a preposterous idea to think of her and me.'

'You thought you needed my blessing. And Leon's. Well, you have it.' She glanced at her watch and checked she had her keys in her evening bag. Leon said he'd send his car for her at eight, and it was one minute to. She was unaccountably nervous. She hadn't seen him for so long. Well, it wasn't really so very long, but it certainly felt like it.

Keith muttered, 'I don't deserve it.'

'Who does?' A car horn tooted. 'And there's my lift. Orlando—' calling out – 'don't forget to put the alarm on after Keith leaves!'

An old-fashioned restaurant, spacious and quiet. A reputation for simple English food, perfectly cooked. No frills. No flambés. No temperaments flying around.

Leon was waiting for her. She was glad she'd dressed up in the new midnight-blue silk and had worn her diamond pendant, for he was in black tie and looked fabulous. Sleek. Pleased with himself? Mm. Yes. So, what had he been up to?

He kissed her cheek. They were shown to their table. A good table, discreetly lit. He said, 'Are you very angry with me for neglecting you?'

Yes, she was. She excused him. 'You've been busy.'

Menus were laid in front of them. He said, 'I thought you'd better hear the news from me, before it hits the papers.'

Aha. Now, let's guess. 'You never really wanted to be an international tycoon, did you? It was forced upon you, and you had to do what you could. Successfully, the papers say.'

'Some good luck. Some good advice. I miss Adamsson more than I can say.'

'But you've appointed someone else. You must have done, or the value of your shares in the market would have plummeted.'

'You've been keeping track?' He was pleased.

She frowned. 'You have to wait till probate is granted to get rid of the international side of the company, don't you?'

'Negotiations are under way.' The waiter hovered. 'Bea, what would you like to eat?'

They ordered. The menus disappeared.

She said, 'You're tired of your toys and want to throw them out of the pram?'

'It will take time, but yes, that's just what I'm doing. I shan't be the loser by it. Sybil will get some shares and so will Bernice, who refuses to go to live with her mother. She's devoted to Sybil, and Sybil to her. A good result, don't you agree? They are talking about boarding schools at the moment. Bernice is keen to go where they give students a good grounding in maths. She plans to live with Sybil between times.'

Bea didn't raise the subject of Keith's pre-wedding nerves. He'd get over them. She hoped. 'What will happen to the big house and offices?'

'For the time being Sybil and Bernice will live there. I've moved back into my old quarters at the big house, and the Barbican flat is usable once more. Neither is satisfactory. Hotel life doesn't suit me.'

Was he angling to move in with her? Ten days ago she'd have said 'yes'. Now she was not so sure. 'What about the UK division of Holland?'

'I am having talks with various people about selling the lot. Fortunately, I had made myself aware of the strengths and weaknesses of each of my companies before recent events overtook us. We are now discussing how many of the old managers should be kept, how many made redundant and so on.'

'Redundancies? That's what Jennifer and her fellow conspirators in maintenance were so worried about. That's what drove them to join in the conspiracy against you.'

'There are bound to be redundancies, but we're arranging for good pay-offs. Sybil will manage the conversion of the big house into flats to be sold off, retaining the largest one for herself and Bernice. That's her next project. The training college is being fenced off from the estate and given a new entrance. It's safe in Anna's hands, don't you think?'

'Are you ready to retire? No, of course you aren't.'

'Are you?'

'Of course not.' No, she certainly was not!

They accepted their starters. Duck pate. Delicious.

She ought to be able to work it out. He had money. He would have no responsibilities, work-wise. His family was provided for. Ah, she had it. 'A charity. You're going to work for a charity. Now, don't tell me. It won't be one of the big, well-established, well-run organizations. They don't need you. It won't be one of the little ones that raises a few thousands every year and has limited effect. No, you'll choose one which has the potential to do a lot of good but which is struggling for various reasons. I know!' She mentioned a name. 'Their chairman and secretary have recently been caught up in nasty scandals. That's where you'll go.'

'Well done. Of course, you're right. The downside is that I'll still need a woman on my arm for social purposes. Would you object to becoming Mrs Holland?'

'Strenuously,' said Bea, paying him out for her neglect of her. 'I have no intention of marrying again. Tell me, did I guess correctly? Was Briscoe offered a knighthood?'

'A life peerage. He did consider it but decided he couldn't be bothered. Angharad found out by reading his mail, and that's when she started to put the pressure on him. I'm sad that the end of his life was so difficult.'

'You rescued him in the end. That must be some consolation.'

'I was too slow. When he lashed out at me, I was hurt. I didn't stop to think. I reacted just as Angharad intended I should and left him to her tender mercies. It was only when you spelled it all out to me that I saw how much I'd let him down.'

She put her hand over his on the table. 'If you hadn't had

the strength to overcome that barrier, if you hadn't loved him, deeply and truly, he'd have died in despair, without seeing you or Sybil or Dilys again. You must forgive yourself, because he has forgiven you.'

The waiter removed their plates and poured wine. A good red.

He kept his eyes on his glass. 'So, mind-reader mine, tell me where I'm going to settle?'

She frowned. Sipped wine. Admired the diamond in her engagement ring. 'You don't like hotel life, and you won't need to go flitting around the world when things calm down. You sold your house in the country, didn't you? And you don't want to be stuck out at the old Holland place. You'll buy a house in town. A good one. With room for offices. And, perhaps, a dog? I see you walking the dog in the park every day to keep your weight down.' Which was a nasty crack, as he had perhaps put on a couple of pounds recently.

He looked self-conscious. 'Too many business breakfasts, lunches and dinners. I've put in an offer for a house in the next street to you. Back to back with you. My garden wall is also yours. I thought we might cut a door through some time.'

Bea said, 'You can't do that without my consent.'

'Of course not.' He didn't seem fazed by her rejection of his idea. He said, 'The house has been used for business purposes before, and they don't object to some rooms being used for a charity. I think I draw the line at a dog. What would your cat Winston say if I dropped in every day with a dog in tow?'

'Miaow,' said Bea, accepting her rare fillet of steak and frites. 'This looks good.'

'Salad on the side, madam?'

'Certainly. I have to watch my weight.' And, when the waiter had withdrawn, 'All right, I withdraw my suggestion about a dog.'

'To the future.' He lifted his glass to her in a toast.

'Agreed.'

'But,' he said, attending to his steak, 'I can't sit on the secret any longer. I, too, was offered something in the next Honours List. Not by Lethbury, but through someone else. It's only a knighthood and not a life peerage, but it would still make you Lady Holland.'

Bea's fork clattered on to the floor, to be retrieved by a pained-looking waiter, who provided her with a clean one.

Leon hid amusement. 'Take your time. I'm in no hurry.'

'You are, without doubt, the most irritating man I have ever met!'

'I'll take that as a "yes", then, shall I?'